SO-AZD-926

Books by Tom Hoffman

The Eleventh Ring

The Thirteenth Monk

The Seventh Medallion

Orville Mouse and the Puzzle
of the Clockwork Glowbirds

Orville Mouse and the Puzzle
of the Shattered Abacus

Orville Mouse and the Puzzle
of the Capricious Shadows

Orville Mouse and the Puzzle
of the Last Metaphonium

Orville Mouse and the Puzzle
of the Sagacious Sapling

The Translucent Boy and
The Girl Who Saw Him

*Available online at Amazon and Barnes & Noble*

JUN 2 2 2021

# THE TRANSLUCENT BOY

## and the girl who saw him

by Tom Hoffman

393 5352

Copyright © 2019 by Tom Hoffman

All rights reserved.

Cover design by Tom Hoffman Graphic Design
Anchorage, Alaska

No part of this book may be reproduced in any form or by any
electronic or mechanical means including information storage and
retrieval systems, without permission in writing from the author.
The only exception is by a reviewer, who may quote short excerpts
in a review.

This book is a work of fiction. Names, characters, places, and
incidents either are products of the author's imagination or are
used fictitiously. Any resemblance to actual persons, living or
dead, events, or locales is entirely coincidental.

Tom Hoffman
Visit my website at thoffmanak.wordpress.com
Email: OrvilleMouse@gmail.com

Printed in the United States of America

First Printing: 2019
ISBN 978-0-9994634-6-8

With lots of love for
Molly, Alex, Sophie, and Oliver

# Table of Contents

For all the amazing
translucent kids out there
who spend their days
listening, reading,
and thinking.

"Could a greater miracle take place than for us to look through each other's eye for an instant?"

– *Henry David Thoreau*

**"We strangers know each other now as part of the whole design."**

*– Suzanne Vega*
*"Gypsy"*

# THE TRANSLUCENT BOY

### and the girl who saw him

# Chapter 1

# Little Dove
# Peach Blossom Bouquet

The old man tapped the simmering flask with a long bony finger, adjusting the hissing blue flame, watching the swirling vapors cool and condense in a gleaming spiral glass tube. Droplets of the iridescent pink fluid trickled through a complex array of piping and filters, their circuitous journey ending at the bottom of an exquisitely carved crystal phial.

The hurried footsteps were muffled by plush maroon carpeting, but still startled him. He turned quickly, one arm extended, palm facing outward.

"Relax, it's just me."

"It went well? They accepted my proposal?"

"It was far from unanimous. They have concerns over the timespan and the lack of hard scientific data to support your initial premise. The Counselor reminded me more than once how capricious the events of life

3

can be. In the end they agreed to let you move forward. You do have a certain reputation."

The old man shook his head. "Sleepwalking fools, seeing only chaos where there is order, blind to the hidden threads that connect all things. The events of our world are anything but capricious."

The woman smiled sympathetically. "They are afraid, doing the best they can. Few of us are able to see through the veil, speak with our deeper selves."

"I suppose you're right. Calling them names will not further a satisfactory outcome to the issue at hand."

The woman closed her eyes, sniffing the air.

"Peach blossom scent?"

"Your olfactory acuity is unsurpassed."

"You scanned her data stream?"

"She has bought perfume no less than nineteen times in the last twelve years, invariably choosing peach blossom scent. Her routine is remarkably consistent, spraying it once on her left wrist prior to each purchase."

He shut off the burner and picked up the crystal phial, turning it to reveal a delicately embossed silver label.

The woman studied it with a quizzical smile.

"*Little Dove Peach Blossom Bouquet*? Why Little Dove?"

"Her father called her his Little Dove."

"Excellent. Well done."

"You brought the final ingredient?"

"Of course. It took some engineering, but the technicians assured me it will perform as requested."

The woman removed a four inch long black metallic case from her coat pocket, setting it on the marble countertop.

The old man pressed a tab and the lid whirred open. Nestled in black velvet was a narrow glass vial holding a green glowing liquid.

"One thousand nanobots per drop."

"Percutaneous absorption?"

"Of course, it only requires contact with her skin."

"I don't wish to ruffle your feathers, but you're quite certain it will only modify the boy's genome and not affect anyone else?"

The woman stared silently at the old man, a dark look on her face.

"I will take that as a yes. All right then, it's time to set our little friends free."

He twisted the top of the vial, gingerly releasing ten drops of the viscous green fluid into the perfume bottle. After attaching its delicate pink atomizer, he placed the phial in a velvet lined glossy white box. Written on the lid in flowery gold script were the words, '*A special gift for a valued customer*'.

"We have the bait, now we set the trap."

The woman was silent.

The old man's face softened. "Something is bothering you. Tell me."

"I feel such sadness for the child, and much guilt. We are condemning him to a life of unbearable heartache."

"I am well aware of this. My deeper self has spoken of it. The boy's life will be achingly lonely. He will experience rejection, anger, despondency, and despair. That being said, from these scorching flames of adversity a hero will arise, the boy who will save our world."

"At what cost to the boy?"

The old man had no answer.

The woman touched his arm. "Perhaps one day he will forgive us. You have the mother's address?"

"Mrs. Petunia Whitley of 11949 Asper Street."

"I will deliver it tomorrow. When shall I return?"

The old man pulled an oversized gold watch from his vest pocket, studying it closely.

"Sixteen years from today."

# Chapter 2

# Heavenly

Mrs. Petunia Whitley of 11949 Asper Street flipped open her mailbox, pulling out the usual assortment of bills, advertisements, flyers, and husband Albert's beloved train magazines.

She sniffed. "Albert and his magazines. I'd rather get a root canal than read about model trains."

She giggled at her joke, imagining the look on his face if she said that in front of him. She peered inside the mailbox to make certain she hadn't missed anything.

It has been said that fateful events are seldom recognized as such by the participants, and this was no exception, Petunia Whitley blissfully unaware that peeking into her mailbox would alter the course of history for a thousand worlds. Her eyes glimmered when she saw the white box sitting in the shadows.

"Oh, my. How very lovely. Maybe it's a gift from Albert. It's not our anniversary though. Or my birthday."

She removed the mysterious package, turning it slowly.

*A special gift for a valued customer.*

"A valued customer. It looks very expensive, elegant. Who would send us such a thing?"

Her eyes widened when she raised the lid and saw the exquisitely carved crystal perfume bottle with its lovely delicate pink atomizer.

"Oh dear, this must be a mistake. Surely it was sent to the wrong address. It can't be meant for me."

She gingerly removed the perfume bottle from the box, tears filling her eyes when she read the silver embossed label.

*Little Dove*
*Peach Blossom Bouquet*

She pressed one hand to her chest, her heart racing.

"Little Dove! That's what Daddy called me. And it's my peach blossom scent. This is a sign from above. Daddy did this, I know he did. He's sending me a message from the other side, from the great beyond."

She turned away from the mailbox, her face darkening.

"Albert won't believe Daddy sent it. He'll think I'm daft. I can just hear it, I ordered it without asking him, we can't afford frivolous luxuries, it's a plot, a crazy neighbor is trying to poison us."

She slipped the perfume bottle into her coat pocket

and stepped back into the house, calling out, "Albert, your model train magazines came today! I'll put them on the kitchen table."

"Bring them here. I'm busy."

Petunia rolled her eyes, murmuring to herself, "Busy eating crackers and reading the newspaper."

Albert didn't look up when she set the magazines on the table next to him.

"We're almost out of crackers. They arrested the mayor. I told you he was a crook. I could tell just by looking at him. Shifty eyes, too close together. Didn't I say that when he got elected?"

"You did say that, I remember. I'll get crackers next time I'm at the store."

Petunia turned and hurried back to the kitchen, pulling the perfume bottle from her apron pocket.

"It's a miracle, that's what this is. A true miracle from above."

She set the white box on the kitchen counter, eyeing a slip of folded paper tucked inside it.

"What's this?"

She removed the note, reading it carefully.

*Use of this product during*
*pregnancy may result in the birth*
*of translucent children.*
*Refer to Paragraph 1.e.2411f.4:*
*of Dr. Griffin's treatise*
*'Translucent Child Syndrome'.*

Her heart was pounding.

"Daddy knows I'm going to have a baby! He's watching over me."

She read the note again, frowning.

"What's a translucent child? It can't be bad, Daddy wouldn't send me something bad."

"Albert! What does translucent mean? Is that good or bad?"

One of Albert Whitley's more unfortunate traits was his unwavering inability to admit he didn't know something. In this case, although it sounded vaguely familiar, he had no idea at all what translucent meant. He scrunched his face, trying to remember where he had heard the word. Was it something about monks or holy people? They were translucent, above the ordinary, above all things. That was it.

"It means wise, like a monk or something! I can't believe you don't know that. Everyone knows that."

Petunia rolled her eyes. How many times had she heard those words? *I can't believe you don't know that. Everyone knows that.*

She held the perfume bottle in the palm of her hand.

"Who wouldn't want a wise child?"

Mrs. Petunia Whitley of 11949 Asper Street spritzed the Little Dove Peach Blossom Bouquet onto her left wrist, its delicate aroma filling her nostrils.

"Mmm, a heavenly gift from the great beyond. Thank you, Daddy."

# Chapter 3

# Another Day

Sixteen years later Odo Whitley lay in his bed gazing up at the ceiling, the soft early morning light filtering into his room through gauzy blue curtains.

"Another day…"

He gave a deep sigh, putting one hand over his eyes. He could see the bedroom window through his palm.

"…and I'm still translucent."

He pulled the covers over his head, closing his eyes, wishing he could sleep away the rest of his life. No one would notice, no one would care.

"ODO!! You're going to miss the bus!"

With a groan he threw off the covers and climbed out of bed, pulling on his school clothes. He eyed the pair of mismatched wooden bookshelves crammed with hundreds of volumes.

"Good morning, books." Closing his eyes, he ran a finger across the bindings, stopping at a heavy volume titled *Principles of Neurophysiology*.

11

"I guess today is science day."

Odo slipped the book into his backpack and ran downstairs, setting his pack by the front door. He stepped into the kitchen and slid into a chair, eyeing the bowl of steaming oatmeal in front of him. His mom was sitting across the table, a look of growing frustration on her face.

"ODO! YOU'RE GOING TO BE LATE!"

"I'm right here, mom."

She blinked.

"Sorry sweetie, I didn't see you. Eat your oatmeal before it gets cold. Warm oatmeal is good for you."

"Right. Warm oatmeal good. Where's dad?"

"He had to leave early. They're testing the new line of Silver Chocko CrunchCakes today and he's in charge. If it goes well they'll make him a permanent Silver CrunchCake Supervisor, and that means a big raise."

"That's great."

The first time Odo tried a Chocko CrunchCake he'd spit it out in front of his mom. She had whispered, "Tell your dad they're nice and crunchy, that you like them."

"I hear the bus."

"Okay, bye mom."

Odo dashed to the front door and grabbed his backpack, running down the front walk just as the orange school bus screeched to a halt. He could see the driver peering through the grimy glass window. Odo pounded on the door.

"I'm here!"

The door squealed open.

"Sorry, kid, didn't see you."

The driver said the same thing every day. Sorry, kid, didn't see you. Every. Day.

There were plenty of empty seats, but Odo walked to the rear of the bus and grabbed an overhead rail. When he was seven, a burly high school football player named Bruno Lesky had boarded the bus, spotting what he thought to be an empty seat. That particular seat was occupied by a very translucent Odo Whitley, engrossed in a book about the fall of the Roman Empire. All two hundred and twelve pounds of Bruno's massive frame descended onto little Odo. That was the day he decided it would be best to stand at the rear of the bus.

Odo was well aware that most people didn't have the slightest idea what it was like to be translucent. He had tried to explain it to his mom once, telling her it felt like life was a play, and he was in the audience, an observer, not a participant. No one ever said, "Hey, Odo, see you at lunch!" or "See you tomorrow, Odo!" or "Hey, Odo, wanna play ball after school?"

His mom had nodded sympathetically, but there had been no light of understanding in her eyes. She told him his dad had said translucent meant wise, like a monk. His dad always said it was his mom's fault, that she shouldn't have used the perfume. He would have told her to throw it out if he'd known about it, that some crazy neighbor was probably trying to poison them.

Odo had turned fifteen four months ago, a great many of those years being spent trying to understand why it was that people didn't notice him. Clearly there was a vast difference between being invisible and being translucent. He remembered looking up 'translucent' in the dictionary, expecting it to be something extraordinary, a definition overflowing with roiling emotions and power and passion, something to justify his overwhelming feelings of despair and loneliness. It wasn't and it didn't.

**Translucent** *Permitting light to pass through, but diffusing it so that persons, objects, etc., on the opposite side are not clearly visible. "Frosted window glass is translucent, but not transparent."*

Odo was frosted window glass. Eyes peered through him, not at him. It took an immense amount of concentration to notice him, even for his parents. This idea came into sharp focus one sunny day when Odo was walking down the sidewalk reading a book. He realized that a small part of him was aware he was walking past houses and trees and gardens, but he didn't really see them, couldn't remember them, couldn't describe them. He was a tree that people walked past while reading a book.

The bus screeched to a halt, the students pouring out, hollering and laughing, savoring the last few minutes of freedom before the first bell rang.

Odo waited until the bus was empty, then stepped off, his tried and true method of avoiding painful collisions with unseeing schoolmates.

"Sorry, didn't see you." Even as they apologized they were peering through him at their laughing friends. Frosted glass.

He trudged toward the main door, his thoughts drifting to another time. Odo was remembering a singular moment in his life when someone had seen him. Really seen him.

He was remembering the man in the gray hat.

# Chapter 4

# The Man in the Gray Hat

On Odo's sixth birthday a package had arrived for him, the return address being that of a distant uncle his parents had never met.

Albert was immediately suspicious.

"My great uncle twice removed? Don't open it. It could be anthrax. Or worse."

It was too late. Odo had torn off the colorful wrapping paper.

Albert looked at the toy as though it might sprout claws and attack him, snapping and snarling.

"I don't like it. It's weird, definitely not from the Toy Farm. What is it? Some kind of truck boat thing?"

Petunia gave the disarming smile she reserved for those times when Albert suspected a nefarious plot to be in play.

"I think it's sweet, a lovely six-wheeled truck with a

bright blue sail. It's probably from another country. They have lorries in England instead of trucks, you know. Lots of countries have different kinds of trucks. Some probably have sails in case their engines don't work, or they run out of gas. Very clever. In England they call gas petrol. I read that in one of my magazines."

"I know what a lorry is, and they don't have six wheels or a sail. Everyone knows that. Why is a yellow octopus driving it?"

"It's probably something from a whimsical children's book. Children like whimsical toys. Look how much fun he's having."

"I won't allow it. He's strange enough as it is. He doesn't need to be playing with weird toys from who knows where."

Petunia had nodded agreeably, but always let Odo play with the six wheeled sailing truck when Albert was at work.

Not long after his birthday, Odo had been sitting in the front yard busily helping the yellow octopus load crunchy autumn leaves onto the six-wheeled truck. His ears perked up at the sound of footsteps. He jumped up and ran to the picket fence.

At six years old, Odo was well aware he was different from other children, but he was not yet aware of how much this particular difference would affect his life. He knew by this time that people said hello to other children, but not to him. They never seemed to notice he was there, even when he waved at them. It was because of this that he felt quite comfortable standing next to the white picket fence and studying closely the faces of the people walking past.

It had not taken him long to realize that a face could be a mask, that someone could smile when they were feeling sad, or look friendly when they were angry. He was also quite aware there were no masks on the faces of people who walked alone. They were lost in their thoughts, some happy, some sad, some angry, some with faraway dreamy looks in their eyes.

On this particular day, a distinguished elderly gentleman wearing an old fashioned gray tweed suit and matching gray hat was walking briskly down the sidewalk. Odo thought the man looked like a nice old grandpa, someone who would never get angry, never say mean things about someone else. Never hurt anyone's feelings. Always notice them and say hello.

As the elderly man was walking past, a very unexpected thing happened. The man in the gray hat stopped, turned, and looked directly into Odo's eyes.

Odo could not speak. The yellow octopus fell from his hand, landing with a soft thump on the grass.

"Hello, young man, I do hope you're having a marvelous day. Such lovely weather we've been having lately. I always enjoy a nice brisk walk on a sunny day like today. Very good for the constitution, especially for an old fellow like me."

Odo had no idea what a constitution was. He managed to croak out a single word.

"Hello."

"What a marvelous toy truck you have there. You must have lots of fun playing with it. I do like the yellow Plindorian."

Odo's initial shock was fading.

"Octopus."

"Of course, my mistake, a lovely yellow octopus from the deepest depths of a vast and mysterious sea."

"I got it for my birthday. Daddy says it's weird."

The man in the gray hat gave a cheery laugh.

"I suppose it is a little weird, but that's what makes it special and fun. Sometimes weird things turn out to be the most precious things in our lives, things we cherish above all others. I'm a little bit weird myself, wearing this old fashioned suit and my funny gray hat, but people don't even mind a bit once they get to know me. Is there anything weird about you that makes you special?"

"I can see through my arm."

"So you can. I didn't even notice. You know, I have a funny feeling that you will grow up to be someone very, very special. And I suspect you will make some dear friends along the way, people who will love you very much."

Odo's eyes were wide. He would remember these kind words as long as he lived.

"The truck tickles my fingers. I didn't tell Daddy."

The old man's faced softened.

"Ahh, that means you are a very special young man indeed."

"I'm Odo."

"It was my great and profound pleasure to meet you, Odo. Perhaps one day we shall meet again. I'd best be moving along now, as I have a very busy day ahead of me, a very busy day indeed."

He tipped his hat with a cheery smile and strode off down the sidewalk.

Odo watched the man in the gray hat grow smaller and smaller until he turned left on Expergo Street and disappeared from view.

# Chapter 5

# **The Note**

Odo strolled down the empty hallway to Room 2B, his homeroom. The other students were already seated, doing the things students have done since the beginning of time; whispering secrets, searching for lost homework, passing notes, throwing spitballs, frantically studying for a forgotten quiz. None of them saw Odo walk into the room. The teacher barely glanced up at the sound of his footsteps. Odo slid into his seat, pulling *Principles of Neurophysiology* from his pack, opening it to chapter one, soon immersed in a fascinating discourse on synaptic signal transmission and large scale network synchronization.

The homeroom teacher, Mrs. Penuria, was taking daily attendance, checking the little box next to each student's name. When she came to Odo, she was vaguely aware there was someone there, but he was a tree she walked past while reading a book.

When the bell rang, Odo waited until the other students had left, then grabbed his pack and headed for the next class. This was his daily routine, one providing him all the time he needed to read as many books as he wished. In all his years at school he had never once been called on by a teacher. When he was small he would raise his arm to answer questions, but to his great dismay no matter how hard he waved he was never picked.

His fourth period of the day was science class, with Mr. Gnaritas. Odo slipped into his chair and opened his neurophysiology book, the teacher's voice fading to a dull drone.

Peripheral vision is the ability to see things that are beside you while you are looking straight ahead. As fate would have it, this was something Odo excelled at. While he was reading his book he could watch the students on either side of him.

He was poring over a diagram of synaptic neurofibrils and vesicles when he noticed something in his peripheral vision. The new girl was staring at him.

Odo froze, his eyes focused like white hot burning lasers on his book. There was no doubt about it, she was staring at him. Not at his face, but at his head, studying it like she was examining a coconut in the grocery store.

"What is she doing? Why is she looking at me?"

He remembered the teacher introducing her to the class. She was Sephie Crumb, had bright flaming orange hair, and was very smart. A few people had snickered, calling her Creepy Crumb.

"Maybe she's looking at my hair. It might be sticking up and looking all weird. Wait, she can't see my hair."

Nevertheless, Odo nervously brushed his hair with one hand, his eyes still riveted to his book.

Sephie Crumb, aka Creepy Crumb, was still staring at him.

Odo's heart was thumping like a bass drum. This had never happened before and he had no idea what to do. He desperately fought the urge to turn and look at her. Bad idea, it would definitely make things worse. Who knows what someone called Creepy Crumb might do or say.

The girl turned away.

"Whoa, that was weird. Scary. Maybe I was wrong, maybe she wasn't looking at me, maybe she was looking through me at someone else. That makes more sense." He relaxed and went back to his reading.

When the bell rang he stuffed the book into his pack. He sat at his desk, waiting for the other students to leave.

What happened next would change Odo Whitley's life forever. The orange haired girl named Sephie Crumb leaned toward him and tossed a folded note onto his desk.

Then she was gone, the classroom empty.

Odo's frozen stare was locked on the white square of paper sitting silently in front of him. He tried to calm himself. One breath in, one breath out. Relax. Calm. Just a note. Someone passed him a note. Notes get passed a thousand times a day. His hands were clammy, sweating. He poked at the note with one finger.

"Probably nothing. Just... something silly about... something."

He gingerly picked it up, unfolding it, trying to act casual in case Sephie Crumb was watching him.

He read the note. Then he read it again. And again.

*It's not your hair, it's what's under it.*

Odo spent the next fifteen minutes in the lavatory, examining his scalp in the mirror.

"There's nothing weird under my hair. My scalp looks fine. What is she talking about? Why would she write this? What's wrong with her? Why does my first note have to be so weird?"

# Chapter 6

# Looking for Adventure?

"If he wants a bicycle he has to earn the money himself. I'm not paying for some fancy bike while he lounges around reading his smarty brain books. Waste of time. He needs to get a job, get a taste of the real world."

"I'm right here, Dad."

Albert blinked. "Don't sneak up on people like that. It's rude. Everyone knows that."

"I didn't sneak up, I walked into the room to ask you if—"

"The answer is no. If you want a bike, you pay for it. Find a job. Something where you don't have to be around people. You can't work at Burger Heaven if no one can see you."

Petunia put her hand on Albert's arm.

"He'll find something. There are plenty of jobs out there for a hard worker like Odo. Maybe in a big warehouse or something."

"Fine, I'll get an after school job." Odo grabbed the newspaper and headed up to his room. He could hear his dad's voice echoing up the stairway.

"How is he going to get a job when no one can see him? You can't show up for an interview if you're invisible. Everyone knows that."

Odo flopped down on his bed and closed his eyes. His dad was right. Who would hire someone they couldn't see?

"I hate it. It's not fair, everyone else's life is so easy. They just walk around all day saying hello to each other and looking at each other, laughing and talking and passing notes in class, waving to each other in the hall."

He pulled Sephie Crumb's note from his pocket, reading it again, hoping he'd missed something. He hadn't, and it still didn't make sense.

"I wonder what she's like, besides being smart and creepy. I kind of like her orange hair. It's sort of cute, different. She didn't actually say anything mean to me, just something I don't understand. She seems nice enough. Maybe I should try talking to her."

A dreadful chill shot through him, his insides twisting into painful knots. He'd never talked to a girl before. He had no idea what to say. Maybe she liked neurophysiology or deep physics. Ungh...how dumb was that? He slumped down, closing his eyes. This was the worst day of his life. The worst. Well, maybe not *the* worst. *The* worst day was when he was in the seventh grade, a terrifying day that would burn forever in his memory.

He had been in his room rummaging through old toys when he pulled out the six-wheeled sailing truck, grinning at the sight of it. He had loved playing with it when he was little. He pulled the yellow octopus from the cab, remembering the man in the gray hat and the kind words he had said. He'd called the octopus a Plindorian. Maybe that was the Latin biological classification for an octopus. Maybe the man in the gray hat was a scientist.

The truck still made his hand tingle, almost like a tiny electric shock. What was that about? When he looked down at his tingling hand he let out a piercing scream that would have terrified his parents, had they been home.

His right hand was no longer translucent, it was solid, opaque. That in itself would have been good news, but unfortunately, besides being solid, his hand was also very large, covered with iridescent spiky green scales, and had four enormous black curved claws. He skittered backwards, trying to escape from his own hand. His left foot landed on the six-wheeled sailing truck, which proceeded to shoot out from under him. The last thing he remembered was his head hitting the floor.

When he woke up his hand was normal, translucent. That was definitely the worst day of his life. He had been terrified for months that it might happen again. Terrified that it might happen in school. He imagined the other students screaming at the sight of his horrible scaly monster hand.

As time passed, he managed to convince himself he'd slipped on the truck, hit his head, and then dreamed he had a big scaly green hand. It was all a bad dream, nothing more.

Odo shrugged. "Over and done with. I have to find a job. I'm smart, and I'm a hard worker. I should be able to find something. He tried to visualize himself in various occupational scenarios, but each time his translucency brought the vision to a screeching halt. He picked up the newspaper and opened it to the classified ads.

"Okay, lots of jobs. Here we go. Time to find a job."

Fifteen minutes later he threw the paper on the floor next to his bed.

"There's no way I'm getting a bike."

He leaned over the edge of the bed, glaring at the paper.

"How can there be so many jobs I'm not qualified for?"

Then, like a brilliant shooting star on a pitch black summer night, a single word caught his eye, a word he had not expected to see in the classified ads.

The word was *translucent.*

He grabbed the paper, scanning the ad.

*Tired of flipping burgers?*
*Looking for adventure?*
*Make your own schedule, set your own hours!*
*121577 Expergo Street, Saturday 9:30 a.m.*
*You must be translucent to apply for this job.*

Odo gaped at the ad. This was almost too good to be true. Who else would apply? He was the only translucent person he knew.

"Whoa, suppose there are lots of translucent people, but I don't see them, just like no one sees me?"

His heart sank.

He read the ad again.

"It doesn't matter. Saturday morning I'm going to be at 121577 Expergo Street and I'm getting that job."

Odo ran downstairs and showed the ad to his parents.

His dad snorted, "It's a scam. Real jobs don't have adventure. Real jobs are hard, boring work, day after day after day. It's probably one of those phony 'make a fortune working out of your home' scams."

Odo gritted his teeth. "It might be real, it might not be a scam. Why would they only want translucent people?"

"If you want to waste your time, go ahead and go. Probably a good learning experience. There's no such thing as a free lunch. Everyone knows that."

Petunia smiled brightly. "Maybe it's a nice job in a big warehouse."

# Chapter 7

# Number 317

Bright and early on Saturday morning Odo was standing in front of the ramshackle gray house at 121577 Expergo Street. He was an hour early and there were already four people lined up at the front door.

"It doesn't look much like a business, it's just an old house."

Odo stepped down the walkway, taking his place at the end of the line. No one noticed him, but he noticed instantly that none of the other applicants were translucent.

"That's weird. Why would they be here if they're not translucent?"

Three more people arrived and got in line behind Odo. None of them were translucent either. Odo's ears perked up.

"What do you think the job is?"

"I dunno. Adventure sounds fun though. And working when I feel like it."

"What's the translucent thing?"

"Not sure. I'll just fake it, tell them I'm translucent."

"I don't even know what it means. Is that the thing where you can speak a bunch of different languages?"

"I don't think so. It doesn't matter. Just say you know how to do it and then learn how after you get the job. How hard can it be?"

"That's how I got my last job."

Odo grinned. He scrutinized the line of applicants, focusing, making certain there weren't any other translucent people. There weren't.

"This is great, I'm the only translucent person here. I'm sure to get the job. Unless I'm not qualified and they decide to hire someone who's not translucent." His grin faded.

When the front door opened there were twenty-six people in line. A middle aged woman wearing a remarkably ill fitting gray dress stepped onto the front porch.

"Good morning, everyone. Please take a number as you come in. Find a seat, and when your number is called go into the interview room. Good luck to you all!"

Odo frowned. She must have noticed none of these people were translucent. Why hadn't she said anything? Why didn't she send them home? Maybe his dad was right, maybe it was some kind of scam.

He stepped into the foyer of the old building, tearing a number off the dispenser, glancing around the room. A crooked sign taped to the green door at the rear of the room read 'Interview Room'.

"Smells musty. Someone should clean the windows. Kind of grimy looking. Okay, it won't be long, I was fifth in line."

Odo sat in one of the rickety wooden folding chairs that ran along the wall, studying the other applicants.

"That guy looks really strong. He'd probably be good at adventure stuff. I should start lifting weights. Whoa, look at that guy wearing the brown leather jacket and fedora. He looks rugged, like he's spent half his life exploring wild jungles. This is bad. They're not going to hire a high school kid. Maybe I should go."

A voice echoed across the room.

"Number one? Number one?"

The man in the brown leather jacket stood up and strode toward the green door. He swung it open and entered, closing it behind him.

Six minutes later the voice called out again.

"Number two? Number two?"

A woman wearing khaki pants and knee high brown leather boots stood up.

Odo looked down at his number and froze.

## Number 317

"That can't be right, I was fifth in line, I should have number 5. I should tell that lady. Wait, maybe everyone has a weird random number."

Odo peered at the woman sitting next to him. Her ticket was number 17. The man on the other side of him had number 9.

"I can't believe this. It has to be a mistake."

He folded his arms and glared at the ticket dispenser by the front door, remembering his dad's words, "It will probably be a good learning experience."

"I don't care how long I have to wait. I'm getting this job and I'm getting a bike."

Odo sat patiently for one hundred and forty-two extraordinarily long minutes. Finally the last number was called and Odo was alone in the silent room.

"I am not leaving until I get my interview." He leaned back in his chair, eyes on the green interview door.

Nineteen minutes passed before the voice rang out.

"Number three hundred and seventeen? Number three hundred and seventeen?"

Odo leaped out of his chair, bolting across the room.

Much to Odo's surprise, when he swung the door open, instead of entering the small cluttered office of a weary interviewer, he entered a large room, empty except for a single green folding chair. Sitting on the chair was a thin blue notebook and a yellow pencil.

"What is this?" Odo studied the room. There were no windows, just a door opening to the alley outside. He walked over to the chair and picked up the notebook, flipping it open. The pages were blank.

"Hello? Anyone here? Am I supposed to write something?"

There was no reply.

"Maybe they want me to write down why I'd be

good for the job, why I want it."

He sat down in the chair, his mind spinning. Something was definitely off.

"Okay, twenty-five other people entered this room and none of them came out. That means they all left through the alley door. There's something else going on here. It's some weird kind of test."

He stood up, turning slowly, studying the room. Something caught his eye.

"There's something odd about that section of wall. It looks different."

Odo strode to the rear of the room. There was definitely something off about the wall. It was barely perceptible, but it felt like it was... rippling.

"It's the same shape as a door. That can't be a coincidence."

He poked the wall.

"Whoa!"

The wall was not solid, his hand had gone right through it.

"It feels like water, but it's not wet. This is getting seriously weird. I have to think. Okay, I have two choices, leave through the side door, or walk through this crazy wall and see what's behind it."

Odo grinned. He really only had one choice.

He stepped through the rippling wall.

# Chapter 8

# The Interview

Walking through the wall felt like walking through a soft breeze on a spring day. Except for the curious tingling sensation that ran through Odo's body.

His thoughts were cut short when he saw the woman seated behind a large wooden desk covered with stacks of papers. It was the middle aged woman in the ill fitting gray dress, absently sipping a fizzy pink drink through a bendy straw. She set the drink down, looking up at Odo with a pleasant smile.

"Number three hundred and seventeen?"

Odo nodded. "Yes."

She motioned for him to take a seat in the cushioned chair in front of her desk.

When Odo reached for the chair two things happened. First, his hand stopped in mid air, and second, he stifled a scream. His hand was solid. Both his hands were solid. He was no longer translucent.

"What? What happened?" He looked at the woman

in the gray dress, his eyes wide.

"If you would take a seat, we will begin the interview."

The woman slipped a form into her clipboard and picked up a yellow pencil.

Odo sat in the chair, unable to take his eyes off his solid fleshy hands. He wiggled his fingers, mesmerized.

"Name please?"

"Um… Odo Whitley."

"Address?"

"11949 Asper Street."

"Age?"

"Fifteen. I turned fifteen four months ago though, so I'm actually a bit older than…"

Odo noticed the nameplate on the woman's desk.

### Mrs. Myrtle Preke
### Administrative Asistant

He cleared his throat.

"Yes?"

"Um, I don't mean to be rude, but assistant is spelled wrong on your nameplate. It's missing an s."

"Mm hmm." Mrs. Myrtle Preke checked a box on her form.

"Odo, would you say you had a happy childhood?"

"What?"

"Your childhood, was it a happy one? Lots of fun, birthday parties, that sort of thing?"

Odo stared blankly at Mrs. Preke.

36

"Your childhood, Odo?"

"I'm translucent. I mean, I *was* translucent. I didn't have what you'd call a happy childhood because no one ever saw me. I don't have any friends and I think my parents are embarrassed to have a translucent kid, especially my dad. They blame each other for it. Mostly I read books. I read a lot."

Mrs. Preke's face softened. She studied Odo carefully.

"You must be angry about that."

"I was for a while. It didn't seem fair. I'm not too angry now though. Just sometimes. I guess I'm used to it. It's just the way things are. Everyone has stuff they wish was different."

"I see." She checked three boxes on her form.

"Allergies?"

Odo had realized by now this was not a normal interview. He also realized he was immensely curious.

"No, not really."

"Anything that makes your fingers tingle?"

Odo's mouth opened and closed like a fish out of water.

"I had a toy truck with six wheels and a sail. When my hand got near it my fingers would tingle."

Mrs. Preke checked a box.

"Any temporary physical deformities? Feet? Hands?"

Odo shook his head. There was no way he was going to tell her his green scaly clawed hand story.

"I see." Mrs. Preke did not check a box.

"If you were approached by a tall, thin creature with dark violet skin, burning yellow eyes, no nose or ears, long white hair that moved when there was no breeze, and pointy blue teeth, what would you do?"

Odo burst out laughing.

Mrs. Preke did not.

"Sorry, I thought you were being… um… well, to be honest, I'd probably hide under my bed."

Mrs. Preke nodded, checking a box.

"As was mentioned in the ad, there is a certain amount of adventuring required for the position. Would you say you are a novice adventurer or an experienced one?"

"I haven't really had any adventures exactly, but being translucent is kind of an adventure, I guess."

"I see. Very good."

Mrs. Preke checked a box.

"Last question. Would you say life is capricious, or do you think there is a hidden, deeper purpose to events?"

Odo grinned to himself. He knew what capricious meant.

"Sometimes it seems capricious, but things usually work out the way they're supposed to, even if we don't like it that way." He thought about how Sephie Crumb just happened to be sitting next to him in science class and happened to be the one who passed him his first note. Maybe he was supposed to be friends with her. Maybe it was destiny.

Mrs. Preke leaned back in her chair, setting the

notepad down on the table, studying Odo's face.

"This concludes your interview, Odo Whitley. The job is yours if you want it. You are exactly the sort of person we are looking for. You are patient, you are inquisitive, determined, knowledgeable, and not afraid to speak your mind or admit your fears and limitations."

"Really? I have the job? Wait, what is the job? What do I do?"

"That will get sorted out as time goes by."

Mrs. Preke reached into a drawer and pulled out a bright yellow envelope and a small black box, setting them down in front of Odo.

"You may open them."

Odo flipped open the box, a puzzled look on his face.

"It's a ring?"

"It's your work ring. When you are ready to work, put the ring on. When you are done, take the ring off. You'll be paid by the hour, at a rate yet to be determined."

Odo opened the envelope.

"Whoa! What's this for?"

The envelope contained five crisp one hundred dollar bills.

"It is your monthly retainer. You will receive the same amount on the first of every month in addition to your hourly wages, if you decide to take the job."

"I'll take it." Odo was almost bouncing out of his chair. There was enough money in the envelope to buy two bicycles.

Mrs. Preke set a sheath of papers in front of Odo.

"You'll need to sign and initial each page. It's just a formality to keep the corporate office happy."

Odo grinned, signing the papers one after another. When he was done he set the pen down.

Mrs. Preke stood up and took Odo's hand, shaking it firmly.

Odo's eyes were on his solid fingers.

"Congratulations, Odo. It was my great and profound pleasure to meet you."

Odo blinked. Those were the same words the man in the gray hat had used.

Mrs. Preke smiled. "We'll see you soon, I'm sure. You may leave through this doorway." She pointed to a rectangular section of wall.

Odo picked up the ring and the envelope. As he turned to leave he had a sudden thought.

"Umm...you wouldn't happen to have a mirror, would you?"

Mrs. Preke shook her head. "I'm sorry, Odo, I don't have one. Maybe next time."

Odo nodded and stepped through the wall.

# Chapter 9

# Serendipity Salvage Co.

Odo stepped into a small sunlit kitchen. A woman stood at the sink, her back to him, humming as she washed the dishes. She turned at the sound of Odo's footsteps. It was Mrs. Preke. She pointed to the door at the end of the hallway.

"Right through that door. Pick up your envelope here on the first of every month. The address is on the front door. Have a lovely day, and congratulations on your new job, Odo Whitley."

Odo gaped at Mrs. Preke. "Weren't you... just... um..."

"We'll see you soon, Odo."

"Okay, bye."

When he reached for the door he noticed he was translucent again. With a sigh he stepped outside. He was on Nox Avenue, four miles from the gray house on Expergo Street.

"I don't think they buy their doors at the Home

Emporium."

He checked his pocket to make sure the yellow envelope was still there. It was. He counted the money three times. As he turned to leave he noticed a small brass plaque on the door.

## SERENDIPITY SALVAGE CO.
### 41483 Nox Avenue

"Serendipity Salvage Company? That must be who I'm working for. Whoa, maybe they salvage old shipwrecks and sunken treasure. How amazing would that be? I'd better get home before Mom and Dad start worrying. I've been gone a long time."

He headed west on Nox Avenue until he reached Asper Street, then turned left. Forty-five minutes later he was home.

Flinging open the front door he called out, "Sorry I'm late, I had to wait over two hours to be interviewed. I got the job!"

Albert poked his head out from the kitchen.

"What kind of job? It's not selling magazines door to door, is it? That's a scam, half the time they never pay you."

"No, it's for a salvage company. They seemed pretty nice."

"A salvage company? That might work for you. They tear down old buildings and sell whatever they find. It's good hard work and you won't have to talk to people, just demolish old buildings. You won't make much money, but it will be good experience. Maybe in a few months you'll have enough to buy that bike you want."

Odo nodded. "I hope so." He had already decided not to tell his parents about the envelope full of money and the mysterious work ring. He would wait until he understood exactly what it was the Serendipity Salvage Company did. He was pretty sure they didn't tear down old buildings.

Odo spent the rest of the afternoon at the public library, searching for information on the Serendipity Salvage Company. When he left, he knew exactly what he had known on his arrival. There was not a single mention of the company anywhere, even on the library's computer.

That evening Odo lay on his bed, turning the gleaming work ring slowly in his hand.

"It's heavy, maybe solid silver. Whoa, there are words inside it."

He squinted, trying to read the tiny letters.

*aperi oculos tuos et vide*

"It's definitely Latin, but I have no idea what it means. Maybe the ring is really old. Suppose it has weird powers and changes me, turns me into a scaly monster. Mrs. Preke seemed nice enough, but there was a lot she wasn't telling me, like what the job is. I need to find out what these words mean."

The next morning Odo woke early, eyeing the silver

ring on his bedside table. Maybe he was overthinking this, maybe it wasn't so mysterious. Maybe the ring had a little computer in it that tracked his hours. It was obvious that Mrs. Preke and the Serendipity Salvage Company had access to some pretty advanced technology, like those weird rippling doors.

He picked up the ring.

"It's just a ring, nothing creepy. Just an old work ring that tracks my hours. Some kind of computer or something."

He positioned the ring over the end of his finger.

"Okay, I'll test it… just a little."

He poked the end of his finger through the ring.

"Whoa, the ring turned translucent! That's kind of weird, but not exactly scary."

He waited to see if anything was changing.

"So far so good. No big green scaly hands with black claws. Here goes."

He slid the ring onto his finger.

"Nothing. I don't feel any different. I'm still translucent."

His mom hollered up the stairs.

"ODO! You need to get up!"

Odo groaned. It was Sunday morning. They were supposed to let him sleep late on Sundays. He pulled his clothes on, brushed his teeth, and headed downstairs.

His mom was standing at the stove. "After breakfast you need to run an errand."

"What kind of errand?"

She held up a small brown package tied with green twine.

"This came to our house by mistake. You need to take it to the right address. It could be valuable."

Odo sighed. He was supposed to be working, not delivering packages. A curious thought popped into his head. Mrs. Preke had asked him if he thought life was capricious, or if everything happened for a reason. She had checked a box when he said things turned out the way they were supposed to. Maybe it was no accident that the package had been delivered to their house. Maybe he was supposed to deliver it. Maybe that was his work. He decided to test his theory. He pulled the ring off his finger.

His mom set a plate of toast and eggs in front of him.

"It is Sunday. You can wait until tomorrow if you want. Take it there after school. It's probably nothing."

He slipped the ring back on.

"It could be valuable though, or have something in it they need, like medicine. You should take it today. They might give you a nice reward."

Odo grinned. "A new bike?"

Petunia laughed. "Finish your breakfast before you go."

With breakfast done, Odo headed for the front door, package in hand. He read the address.

**Wikerus Praevian**
**92075 Expergo Street**

45

"That's not too far. I wonder who he is? That's a weird name."

Odo stepped out the front door and turned left, the package clutched in his hand. He had walked a half mile when he spotted a black dog fifty feet ahead of him.

"That's a scary looking dog."

He slowed down, eyeing it cautiously.

A low threatening growl rolled out of the dog's throat, its teeth bared.

"Okay, doggie, you win."

Odo crossed to the other side of the street. The dog lay down on the sidewalk, resting his head on its paws.

Odo was approaching Expergo Street when he heard the voice.

"Odo Whitley!"

Odo froze. The voice was coming from above him. He looked up.

Sephie Crumb was sitting on the roof of a bright blue house next to an open window, the morning sunlight reflecting off her brilliant orange hair.

Odo stared at her, his mouth open.

"Where are you going, Odo Whitley?"

"You can see me?"

"Of course I can. Where are you going?"

"I have to deliver this package. It came to our house by mistake."

"I'll go with you."

Odo felt his chest tighten. "I... um... well..."

46

Sephie stood up and walked to the edge of the roof, sliding down a drain pipe, dropping to the grass with a thump. She stepped over next to Odo.

"Let's go, Odo Whitley. Time is money."

Odo started walking. His legs felt like sacks of wet cement. His throat was dry, his hands clammy. He tried desperately to think of something to say.

"That's your house?"

"Why would I be sitting on someone else's roof? Do I look like a cat burglar?"

"No, I was just… um…"

"That was a joke. Did your parents think you looked like an extinct bird?"

"Did what?" Odo was in full panic mode. There was something very wrong with this girl.

"Odo sounds like Dodo, the bird that lived on the island of Mauritius, east of Madagascar. Dutch sailors ate them all because they were so easy to catch. They're extinct now."

Odo looked at Sephie in surprise. "You know about the Dodo birds? Their biological classification is Raphus Cucullatus. They went extinct in 1681."

"You're a big bright smarty brain." Sephie burst out laughing.

"What?"

"My parents found me in a snow drift."

"Uhh… they found you in a snow drift?"

Odo decided he liked Sephie's green eyes. They weren't scary at all, kind of mysterious.

"When I was a baby they found me in a snow drift in

47

their backyard. I was crying. There were no footprints. I was just there. They adopted me."

Odo tried to process this information.

"Oh, I didn't know you were adopted. Did they ever find out who... um... left you there?"

"No, I was just there. I don't know where I'm from."

"That must be hard for you. Really hard."

Sephie studied Odo's head like she was examining a coconut at the produce market.

"Are you going to call me Creepy Crumb?"

"No, I wouldn't do that. What did your note mean?"

"It's not your hair, it's what's under it."

"Right, that's the one."

"What's in the package?"

"I don't know. My mom thinks it might be valuable and maybe they'll give me a reward."

"What kind of reward? A Roman solidus?"

"You know about Roman history? The solidus was a gold coin, worth a lot. I wish they would give me one."

Sephie grinned.

Odo realized it was the first time he'd seen her smile. He also realized he was talking to a girl, and it was a lot easier than he thought it would be.

# Chapter 10

# Wikerus Praevian

Odo strolled along next to Sephie, trying to hide the smile that kept creeping onto his face. He'd never walked anywhere with a friend before. It was nice.

Sephie was studying his head like a coconut.

"Sephie, do you know any Latin? I'm trying to figure out what a certain Latin phrase means."

"*Audaces fortuna iuvat*?"

"You know Latin? Really?"

"What are the words?"

Odo didn't want to take his work ring off. He suspected it had caused the growling black dog to appear, forcing him to walk past Sephie's house, and she might go home if he took it off. He didn't want her to go home. He furrowed his brow, trying to remember.

"I think it was *aperi oculos tuos et vide*."

Sephie turned and gaped at Odo, her eyes extraordinarily wide.

"What's wrong, what does it mean? Is it something bad?"

She opened her eyes even wider.

"What? It's worse than bad? What is it??"

*"Open your eyes and see."*

"That's what it means? Open your eyes and see?"

"Why did you want to know what those words mean? What are you hiding from me, Odo Whitley? Are you a Roman spy?"

"What? No, I'm not hiding anything, I just… well… was wondering. It's kind of a long story."

"I have a long story, too."

"Oh… well… maybe we could tell our long stories to each other sometime."

"Not if you call me Creepy Crumb."

"I won't ever call you that. I promise. Not ever."

She studied Odo's head.

"Okay, we can be friends, but I can't tell you my long story right now. We're almost at the mystery house."

"That's it there, that creepy old Victorian mansion. It looks haunted."

"Maybe an angry ghost will give you a Roman solidus."

Odo laughed. Sephie was funny.

"Here we go." He swung open the creaky front gate and walked up the steps, rapping gently on the ornately carved door.

There was no answer.

He rapped again.

No answer.

Sephie stepped up to the door.

"If it's a haunted house, we probably have to wake

the dead."

She pounded on the door with both fists.

Odo stepped back, his eyes wide.

A moment later they heard the latch rattle. The door creaked open a few inches.

"Yes?"

"This package came to our house by mistake. It was supposed to go to this address, to someone named Wikerus Praevian."

There was no reply.

"Hello?"

"Are you from Serendipity Salvage?"

Odo froze.

"What did you say?"

"You are from the Serendipity Salvage Company?"

"Yes, I'm Odo Whitley from Serendipity Salvage."

"And I'm his trusted associate, Sephie Crumb." Sephie grinned at Odo.

The door swung open. The package fell from Odo's hands, hitting the porch with a thud.

Wikerus Praevian was the man in the gray hat.

Sephie picked up the parcel and handed it to the old man. She smiled brightly.

"May we come in? Are there any angry ghosts here? Do any of them collect Roman coins?"

The man in the gray hat motioned them in, a broad smile on his face.

"Odo Whitley, it is a great pleasure to see you again. The boy has been transformed into a handsome young man. And I see you've brought a friend with you.

Excellent. Please come in. Young lady, you may rest assured there are no angry ghosts here, and consequently none who collect Roman coins. I am Wikerus Praevian, and the package is for me."

Wikerus led them down a long hallway to a magnificent sitting room lined with deep maroon carpeting, tastefully furnished with lustrous antique tables and chairs. He motioned for them to sit on an exquisitely embroidered pale blue couch.

Wikerus opened the drawer of a heavy mahogany sideboard, taking out a large box of chocolates. He set it down on the glass table in front of Odo and Sephie.

"Please help yourself. They are the most delightful chocolate creams, imported from Belgium."

Sephie studied the chocolates. "I'll eat them with my eyes. That way they'll last forever."

Wikerus laughed. "I like your friend, Odo. Very clever."

Odo took two chocolates and popped one into his mouth.

"Mmm, good."

Sephie grabbed his arm. "Odo, he might be trying to poison us!"

Odo choked, trying not to swallow the chocolate.

Sephie burst out laughing.

"Not funny, Sephie."

Wikerus took a seat in a comfortable stuffed chair, his expression becoming one of concern.

"Odo, I know life has been extremely difficult for you. I am well aware of the many adversities you have faced growing up translucent, how lonely it must have been. I'm truly glad you have found a friend in Sephie."

"We kind of just met. Sephie is in my science class at school."

"A falling marble seeks the ground."

"Right." Odo had no idea what Wikerus meant.

"Shall we find out what's in the mysterious package?"

Wikerus set the parcel on the glass table, carefully unwrapping it, revealing an object covered in white tissue paper. He picked up a pencil, gently moving the paper to one side.

"Whoa, that's a fancy old watch."

"Quite so. Very old indeed."

"Can I look at it? I've read a few books on horology. I know a lot about how they used to make the old watches." Odo reached for the watch.

Wikerus' hand was a blur, grabbing Odo's arm before he could touch the watch. His grip was incredibly strong.

"You know better than that. It's a raw waystone."

Odo looked at Wikerus, then at Sephie, then back at Wikerus.

"It's a what?"

"Sorry, it's best if you don't touch it." Wikerus gingerly picked up the watch with the pencil, carrying it over to a glass cabinet, gently setting it down.

"My cabinet of curiosities."

He sat down again, leaning back in his chair, drumming his fingers together.

53

"Where to begin? There is so much you don't know, but as they say, the time has come to open your eyes and see."

"Those are the words on my Serendipity Salvage ring. How did you– wait, what kind of things don't I know?"

Wikerus studied Odo's hand.

"You are wearing your work ring, so it's clear Sephie is meant to be here. She is part of your story now, part of the fabric of your life."

Odo glanced at Sephie. He liked having her be part of his story, whatever that meant.

Sephie grinned. "This is way better than an angry ghost handing out Roman coins."

# Chapter 11

# Shifting

Wikerus absently adjusted his gold watch chain.

"Translucency is not what you think it is."

"What do you mean?"

"What do you know about pottery?"

"What?"

"How is it made?"

"From clay?"

"Correct. Clay is taken from the ground, mixed with water, strained, cleaned, and shaped into a pot. Then what happens?"

"They heat it in an oven, a kiln. That dries it out and makes it hard."

"Correct again. The heat from the kiln removes all the water from the clay, inducing certain chemical reactions which increase strength and hardening, setting the pot's permanent shape."

Odo glanced at Sephie. She looked as puzzled as he did.

"A translucent person is a pot which was never fired in a kiln. Your permanent form has not been set. You are here and you are not here."

"I'm like a ghost?" Odo did not like this at all.

Sephie poked his ribs. "You don't feel like a ghost, Odo Whitley. Do you collect Roman coins?"

"You're not a ghost, you're translucent. That means you are also a shifter."

Odo decided at that moment that Wikerus was lacking a wide variety of vital nuts and bolts. He tried to think of a graceful way for them to make their escape.

Wikerus continued. "You use a waystone to shift to another dimension. The watch you brought me today is a waystone, but I don't know what dimension it's from. Those are called raw waystones, and it's not a good idea to touch them."

Odo nodded politely. "Got it. Raw waystones." He looked at his watch, feigning surprise. "Whoa, it's getting late, we should probably get–"

"The six-wheeled sailing truck I gave you for your birthday is a waystone from Plindor. Tell me what happens when you touch it?"

Wikerus now had Odo's undivided attention.

"It tingled, like an electric shock. You gave me the six-wheeled sailing truck?"

"Only a translucent can sense the deep vibrations of a waystone."

"How could a toy truck be one of those waystone things?"

"A waystone is simply a physical object from anoth-

56

er dimension. When a translucent touches the waystone and aligns the vibrations of his physical body to the waystone's deep signature vibrations, he shifts to the original home dimension of the waystone. More concisely, translucents can shift to other dimensions and back again."

Odo could not deny there was a weird kind of logic to what Wikerus was saying.

"How do you get back?"

"With your own homestone. Shifters carry a registered homestone from their own world, usually in the form of a small medallion. When you wish to come back, simply align your vibrations to those of your homestone."

"Where do I come back to?"

"To the very same spot you left from."

Sephie's eyes were bright. "You should try it, Odo Whitley."

Odo frowned. "Not a chance. No way."

Wikerus gave a sympathetic smile.

"This is a great deal of information for anyone to process in a short time. Think about it, do a little research. Come back when you are more comfortable with the concept of dimensional shifting. I will be here. It's far easier than it sounds, not scary at all."

"How do you know about this stuff? You're not translucent."

"All that will come later. Go home and think about what you've learned today. I am here if you have any questions."

Odo looked at the glass case. "You're saying if I touch that watch, my hand will tingle?"

"You may try it, but only for a moment."

Odo walked over to the curiosity cabinet, Sephie behind him. He touched the gold watch, jerking his hand back.

"It's a lot stronger than the six-wheeled truck."

"Waystones vary in power."

Sephie reached out and tapped the watch. She shrugged, turning to Odo. "We should go, Odo Whitley."

Wikerus walked the two friends to the door.

"Take care, my young friends. I hope to see you soon."

"Thanks."

Wikerus closed the door behind them.

The two friends walked silently along the wide sidewalk.

Sephie stopped abruptly, turning to Odo.

"I have something to tell you, Odo Whitley, but I'm afraid to. I'm afraid I'll sink to the bottom of the sea and never come back."

"You can tell me anything. We'll still be friends, no matter what."

Sephie looked away. "I was in a special clinic when I was little."

"What kind of clinic? Were you sick?"

"Sephie isn't my real name, it's a nickname the doctors gave me. It's short for Encephalo Girl."

"What does that mean? What was wrong with you?"

"When I was two years old I told my parents I could see lights around people, mostly around their heads. The lights would change and move, sometimes bright, sometimes soft and wavy. They took me to an eye doctor, then they took me to another kind of doctor."

"What were the lights?"

"The doctors at the clinic said I could see the electrical fields around people. I could see their brain activity, like an EEG, an electroencephalogram. They started calling me Encephalo Girl."

"I've read about EEGs. They show what parts of your brain are active when you think about different stuff. How could you see brainwaves?"

"I don't know. I was there for four years while they ran all kinds of experiments. They started calling me Sephie, but I didn't realize until later it was short for encephalogram. I didn't like being there. I didn't like the experiments and I didn't have any friends. When I was six I told them I couldn't see the lights anymore. They kept me for another month, then sent me home. I kept my name because I liked the way it sounded."

"But you still see the lights?"

"That's why I was staring at your head. 'It's not your hair, it's what's under it'."

"I don't understand what that means, exactly."

"It's called brain mapping, and I know a lot about it, probably more than most neurophysiologists. I know what parts of the brain light up when people are happy, when they're sad, when they're lying, when they're sincere, when they like me, or when they're afraid of me and call me Creepy Crumb. I know when they want me to go away."

Odo did not want Sephie to go away.

# Chapter 12

# A Nice Old Dead Lady

For the first time in his life, Odo woke up every morning looking forward to school. More precisely, he was looking forward to seeing Sephie. They had become friends, passing notes in science class and in the hallways, eating lunch together, walking home after school.

He had also been reading voraciously about deep theory, matrix mechanics, and string theory, coming to believe that shifting between dimensions might be possible.

Sephie had revealed another secret.

They were sitting under the oak tree in the schoolyard, talking about Wikerus.

"Maybe he's from another planet, some kind of weird alien or something, like from a UFO."

Sephie rolled her eyes. "A weird alien who wears a tweed suit and imports chocolate creams from Belgium? You need to adjust your brain cells, Odo Whitley."

"You're right, aliens don't like chocolate creams, they prefer chewy caramels. Besides, he's not gray and doesn't have giant black eyes."

Sephie laughed. "His hat is gray."

Odo liked it when she laughed.

"Odo Whitley, there's something I didn't tell you, something that happened."

"When you were at the clinic?"

"No, when we were at Wikerus Praevian's house. When I touched the gold watch a jolt of electricity shocked me."

"How is that possible? Wikerus said only translucents can feel it."

"I was reading his brainwaves, and he's hiding something. There's a lot he's not telling us."

"Do you think he could have used the gold watch like a trail of bread crumbs, luring me to his house?"

"I didn't think about that. He could have put the watch in your mailbox, knowing you'd bring it to him. You have a devious bright brain, Odo Whitley."

"I've read a lot of spy novels."

"We need to go back and see him. Find out more about mysterious Wikerus Praevian, and find out if dimensional shifting is real."

"I'd like to know who put the ad in the paper and if Wikerus knows Mrs. Preke. Her name plate said she was the administrative assistant, but she didn't say who her boss was."

"Let's go see him on Saturday morning. You can tell your parents you're working all day."

"I will be working. I'm putting the ring on the minute I get up."

As they strolled along, Sephie noticed an elderly woman standing at the bus stop ahead of them. She was holding a large map, looking confused. She waved to them.

"I do hate to bother you, but I'm afraid I'm quite lost. Would either of you happen to know where I might find Girard Station? It's supposed to be right next to a big triangle shaped building."

Odo shook his head. "I've never heard of it. Are you sure you're in the right part of town?" He glanced at Sephie.

Sephie's face was white.

"I've never heard of it either. You should ask one of the bus drivers."

"Thank you, dearie, that's exactly what I shall do." The old woman smiled pleasantly, waving to them as they turned to leave.

Sephie was looking straight ahead, her eyes wide.

"What is it? What's wrong? Do you know her?"

Sephie shook her head. "It's not good."

"What's not good?"

"That lady didn't have any brainwaves. None. Zero. Zip. Not a flicker, and there was a weird crackling noise, like static. I've never felt anything like it. Ever. I think she was dead."

Odo gulped. "She seemed alive to me. Maybe your

brain vision thing isn't working right."

"I can see your brainwaves just fine. There's nothing wrong with me. She didn't have a brain."

Odo stopped in his tracks. "She saw me! She was looking right at me, at my face. That's not normal. You're right, this is definitely weird."

"Girard Station. Don't forget that name. And a building shaped like a big triangle."

Odo pulled a pad and pencil from his backpack and wrote it down.

"What do you think it means?"

"Are you wearing your work ring?"

"Yes."

"Then it means something, we just don't know what."

"We need to talk to Wikerus and find out what's going on."

"We can ask him if he's ever heard of Girard Station."

"Or a nice old dead lady with no brain."

"The plot is thickening, Odo Whitley."

# Chapter 13

# The Wooden Spoon

The following Saturday morning found Odo and Sephie at Wikerus Praevian's front door.

This time Sephie didn't have to wake the dead, the door swung open after the second knock, Wikerus clearly delighted to see them.

"I was hoping it was you. Odo, are you ready to give dimensional shifting a try?"

"I'd like to know a little more about it first."

Sephie added, "And we want to ask you some questions."

"I thought you might have a few. Shall we go to the sitting room?"

When they were comfortably seated, Sephie said, "How do you know so much about shifting when you're not translucent?"

Wikerus thought for a moment.

"Would anyone care for chocolates?"

Odo nodded. "Sure, they were really good."

Wikerus flicked his wrist. There was a flash of blue light and a box of chocolates appeared on the table.

Odo gave a start. "You're a magician?"

Wikerus shook his head. "It's not magic, I'm afraid. It is energy obeying the laws of deep physics and consciousness."

"I'm pretty sure I know magic when I see it."

"It's called shaping, using the power of the mind to compress energy into physical objects."

Sephie's eyes narrowed. "Odo was right, you're from another world."

"I am a Fortisian."

"What's a Fortisian?" Sephie had been monitoring his brain activity, and it was definitely not human.

"Fortisia is the name of my home world. It is an extraordinarily old world where the inhabitants have evolved in ways quite unlike humans."

"Like shaping?"

"And other abilities, such as non-translucent dimensional shifting."

"What about Mrs. Preke? Is she a Fortisian?"

"All in good time. The first step is to understand the basic mechanics of dimensional shifting."

"How does it work? I'm not going to do it if it turns me into a ghost."

"You have my word you will not become a ghost. Quite to the contrary, when you shift to another dimension you will no longer be translucent, and the physical matter of that dimension will no longer shock you."

"I won't be translucent? People will be able to see me? Hey, when I was having my interview with Mrs. Preke I was solid. Was I in another dimension?"

"You were. The rippling wall you stepped through was an interdimensional gateway."

"That wasn't so scary, it was just like walking through an open doorway."

"Precisely. It is the idea of dimensional transitioning which is frightening to you, not the actual process. This fear will vanish once you experience it. Another relevant point is that physical matter in certain dimensions is less dense than in this world. In those particular worlds you will be able to shape matter just as I shaped the chocolates. You will also be able to formshift, to alter your physical appearance. Of course, skills such as that come only after intensive study and training.

"Your first dimensional transition will be a delightful venture into the world of Pacalia, a pastoral landscape dotted with quaint towns and villages, inhabited by friendly beings nearly indistinguishable from humans."

Sephie's eyes narrowed. "What do you know about a nice old dead lady who was looking for Girard Station?"

Wikerus turned to Sephie, clearly puzzled. "A nice old dead lady? Why do you think she was dead?"

Sephie hesitated, not wanting to reveal her ability to see brainwaves.

Odo jumped in. "Her eyes looked dead, like a weird zombie. She asked us how to get to Girard Station."

"I'm afraid I am quite unfamiliar with any such location, and likewise have no explanation for the curious state of this elderly woman's eyes. Perhaps she was nearsighted and forgot her glasses."

Wikerus' brainwaves revealed something quite unexpected to Sephie. He was terrified of the nice old dead lady.

He turned to Odo. "Are you warming up to the idea of dimensional shifting?"

"I guess so. I did a lot of research."

"How does a nice trip to Pacalia sound?"

"Just a quick visit so I can see what it's like."

"I want to go with him. I want to try it too."

Wikerus nodded agreeably, making no mention of the fact that Sephie was not translucent.

"Of course."

He stepped over to his cabinet of curiosities, picking up an old wooden spoon, setting it down on the glass table in front of Odo and Sephie. Reaching into his pocket he pulled out two small gold medallions on silver chains, handing one to each of them.

"These are your homestones. Wear them around your neck and guard them with your life. They are your tickets back to this world. This wooden spoon is a waystone from the world of Pacalia. Once you match the deep vibrations of your physical being to those of the spoon, you will find yourself in Pacalia, a most charming and bucolic world. If I remember correctly, you will arrive in a lovely meadow."

Odo and Sephie slipped on the medallions, tucking

them under their shirts.

"What now?"

"The process of transitioning is far simpler than you might think, but it does take a little practice and patience. Odo, I want you to visualize an old fashioned radio dial. Imagine yourself slowly turning the dial, tuning in to a particular station's broadcast frequency. Rotate the dial slowly in your mind while you are touching the wooden spoon. The closer you get to the right frequency, the more solid your body will become. Once you are completely solid you will instantly shift to Pacalia. To get back, repeat the process with your personal homestone.

Sephie said, "What about me? I'm already solid."

"In your case the procedure is slightly different, but just as simple. Hold the spoon, and turn the black dial in your mind until you see the spoon changing color. When it becomes the color of budding spring leaves you will also find yourself in Pacalia."

Sephie studied Wikerus' brain. He was sincere.

She grinned. "Are you ready for our first big shifting adventure, Odo Whitley?"

Odo did his best to sound confident. "Ready when you are, Sephie Crumb."

Odo and Sephie placed their hands on the wooden spoon.

"You may begin. Take your time."

Odo furrowed his brow, visualizing the black dial, turning it slowly in his mind. Four minutes later he gave a startled laugh.

69

"Hey, my fingers are turning solid! I can see my–"
He disappeared in a flash of blue light.

Ten seconds later Sephie was gone.

Wikerus leaned back in his chair, drumming his fingers together.

"Every atom is precisely where it should be at every moment in time. It can be no other way."

# Chapter 14

# Pacalia

When Odo vanished, he didn't feel like he had vanished. It felt as though Wikerus Praevian's house had instantaneously been replaced by miles of glorious sunlit rolling grass covered hills peppered with great swaths of brilliant wildflowers, a brilliant azure sky above dotted with puffy white clouds.

Sephie gaped at the stunning vista.

"Odo Whitley, are you seeing this?"

"I've never seen anything this beautiful."

"I feel like I'm in heaven."

Sephie flopped down on the soft grass, watching a pair of orange and yellow butterflies zig zag their way across the meadow.

Odo sat down next to her.

Her jaw dropped.

Odo gave a start. "What is it? What's wrong?"

"You're solid! I can see you. Your eyes are looking at me."

Odo held up his hands. "This is so weird. Look at my skin."

"It's hard to look at you, I don't know if I can."

"Am I ugly? Am I too ugly to look at?"

"No, it's not that. You're nice looking. You have kind eyes." She glanced awkwardly at Odo's face, quickly turning away. "You're kind of handsome. It's just... I've never actually looked into your eyes before. It's a little scary to see you looking back at me."

"Why is that scary?"

"It's one of my secrets, but I don't like it when people look at me. A lot of times I wish I was translucent so no one would see me, stare at me."

"Why don't you like people to look at you?"

"I don't know, I just don't."

"There must be some reason."

"Maybe people would be thinking things about me that would embarrass me. Maybe they'd say things. Make fun of my orange hair. Say I eat funny or I walk funny. Say my ears are too big or my legs are too short or my eyebrows are too dark."

As Odo was processing this information, four completely unexpected words popped out of his mouth. Words that shocked him more than they shocked Sephie.

"I think you're beautiful."

Sephie turned away sharply. She stood up, pointing to a small white building in the distance.

"Let's see what's over there. It looks like a farmhouse."

Odo felt sick.

"I'm sorry, I don't know why I said that, it just came out. I didn't mean to…" His voice trailed off to silence.

"It's okay. It gave me an ice cream headache, that's all. I don't want to talk about it."

"I'm so dumb. I didn't mean to upset you. Those wildflowers smell nice, don't they?"

"They do smell nice. Like summertime."

Sephie gave Odo a sideways glance as they strolled along through the meadow. She knew she wasn't beautiful. Her mirror told her that every day. Her orange hair, her eyebrows. Odo was being nice to her because they were friends. He was trying to make her feel better, saying what he thought she wanted to hear. That's what friends do. So why was his brain saying he was sincere? That he really thought she was beautiful. Maybe she read it wrong, maybe he was sincerely trying to be nice to her, make her feel better.

Her thoughts spiraled endlessly around and around as they made their way across the stunningly beautiful landscape.

"Sephie, look! Sheep! There's a bunch of sheep grazing on that hill."

"They look like clouds. Sheep clouds drifting across a grassy sky."

Odo laughed. "You say the best things. Sometimes I write them down so I won't forget."

"You write them down? Why? The things I say are why people call me Creepy Crumb."

Odo thought carefully before answering.

"When I was six years old, Wikerus Praevian stopped in front of my house while I was playing with my six-wheeled sailing truck. I had no idea who he was, so I called him the man in the gray hat. I told him my dad didn't want me to play with the truck because he thought it was weird. Do you know what he said?"

"How would I know that, Odo Whitley?"

"You wouldn't know. He said sometimes weird things turn out to be the most precious things in our lives, the things we cherish above all others."

"Oh."

The two friends trekked silently across the meadow, basking in the warmth of a radiant Pacalian sun, the sweet scent of wildflowers permeating the air.

Odo gave Sephie a quick glance. She was looking at him.

"It doesn't bother me when you look at me, Odo Whitley. I know you're not thinking the things I'm afraid of.

"Thanks. It's weird, I never noticed it until now, but your ears are a little big."

Sephie punched his arm.

"Ow! Hey, someone's at the farmhouse. Wikerus said the people here look just like us."

"I'd like to live on a farm."

Ten minutes later Odo and Sephie approached the rustic split rail fence surrounding the farmyard. A plump woman wearing a blue flowered cotton dress and white apron was tossing feed to a flock of clucking chickens.

Sephie called out, "Hello?"

The woman turned in surprise, then smiled and waved.

"Can I help you folks? Are you lost? We don't get many visitors this far from town."

"We were just out hiking and spotted your farm. It's beautiful."

The woman laughed. "Not quite so beautiful when you have to clean up after a flock of chickens. Where are you folks from?"

"Pretty far away. This is our first time in this area. You said there's a town nearby?"

"Burton-On-Guster is seventeen miles east of here. Plenty of shops and taverns, if that's what you're after. Are you sightseeing, or looking for something special?"

Odo looked at the woman curiously. "Just sightseeing, hiking through the meadows. We're not really looking for anything."

"Lots of shops in town if you're interested. All sorts of different things you might find there. I go in every two weeks for supplies. If you like antiques you'll find some nice ones."

"That sounds nice, thanks."

"What kind of antiques are you looking for?"

"Um, we don't really collect antiques, we're just out for a stroll." Odo decided the woman needed to spend more time around people. She was nice enough, but definitely odd.

"I've got some chilled lemonade if you'd like. Mighty nice on a hot day like today."

Odo smiled. "That sounds great, I'd love a–"

"We should go, Odo Whitley. I want to get to Burton-On-Guster before dark. We need to go."

"Oh, okay. Bye! Nice to meet you." Odo smiled and waved to the woman as they turned to leave.

When they were far enough away that the woman couldn't hear him, Odo said, "That was a little rude, Sephie. She was just being nice, and I am kind of thirsty from all the walking."

"Odo, she's one of the dead people! She didn't have any brainwaves and I heard that weird crackling noise."

"Are you sure? Wikerus said there was nothing scary about Pacalia. Maybe it's just the way people's brains are here. Maybe they have a different kind of brainwave you can't see."

"The chickens and sheep had brainwaves, but that lady did not. She was dead, Odo. Brainless and dead. As a doorknob."

"She was asking some weird questions. What was all that stuff about collecting antiques and looking for something special?"

"I don't know, but it's not a coincidence that these dead people started showing up right after our first visit with Wikerus. I didn't say anything to you, but when I mentioned the nice old dead lady to Wikerus, his brainwaves spiked fear. Wikerus is deathly afraid of these creatures, whatever they are."

"That's not good. They'd have to be really bad for him to be afraid of them. I wonder what they want? What do you think Girard Station is?"

Sephie shook her head. "It's a big scrumbly mystery, Odo Whitley. And we're the ones who have to unscrumble it."

"Unscrumble it?" Odo grinned. "Let's head for the village. It sounded like the dead farm lady wanted us to look for–"

"We have to go back to the farm! If the dead lady was a weird brainless alien, where are the farmers?"

"You're right! We need to go back."

# Chapter 15

# Sephie's Surprise

Odo and Sephie turned around, hurrying back to the sheep farm. When they got there, the brainless dead farm lady was nowhere to be seen.

Odo swung open the front gate, pushing through the flock of squawking chickens to the farmhouse, peering through a murky glass window. A woman wearing a pale green dress was handing a plate of food to a dark haired man in a red plaid shirt and blue coveralls. Odo studied them, his insides turning to ice.

"Sephie! Come look at this!"

Sephie stepped up next to Odo, gazing through the window.

"Hurry! We have to go in!" She darted to the front door and pushed it open, the rusty hinges squealing. They stepped into the cool interior of the farmhouse, their eyes on the two farmers. What had caught Odo's attention was not the current activity of the farmers, but the current inactivity. They were living statues, their vacant eyes staring straight ahead into nothingness.

"What happened to them?"

"The dead farm lady must have done this."

"Is there any brain activity?"

"They're alive, but in some kind of coma. They have brainwaves I've never seen before, coming from deep inside the hippocampus and spreading out across the cortex. It's not normal."

"You know a lot about that stuff."

"I've studied it most of my life. Another reason they call me Creepy Crumb."

"You're not creepy, you're amazing. I'm going to read about brain mapping when we get home."

Sephie smiled. "We have to get them out of the coma. What I don't understand is how they can still be standing. They should have fallen over."

Odo gently shook the man's arm.

"Hello?"

There was no response.

Odo whipped around when he heard Sephie's anguished cry.

"My head!" She moaned, leaning over, her hands pressed tightly against her temples. "It's bad, Odo! It hurts! It's really bad!"

Odo put his arms around her, holding her steady. "What is it? What can I do?" He was terrified.

As quickly as it had started, Sephie's pain stopped. She stood up, her eyes on the farmers, a ghostly calm about her.

Odo backed away. She held out one hand, palm facing outward, directing it at the motionless couple.

A rippling beam of pale green light shot out from her

hand, enveloping the farmers. When it stopped, her arm fell limply to her side. Her breathing was fast and shallow.

"I don't know what I did."

The plate of food tumbled from the farmer's hand, shattering on the stone floor.

"Who are you!? What are you doing in our house?"

The man in the blue coveralls grabbed a heavy shovel from the wood stove, raising it.

"What do you want? How did you get in here?"

Sephie held up her hands. "We mean you no harm. We were walking past your house and peeked inside to see if anyone was home. You were both standing there, frozen like statues. Odo shook your arm and you woke up."

"That's crazy talk, we weren't frozen, we're having breakfast. What kind of– " The farmer stopped when he glanced through the open front door, his jaw dropping. "Look at the sun, it's late afternoon. It can't be. I just got up and you were handing me breakfast."

The farmer's wife turned to Sephie, her eyes wide. "What happened to us?"

"I don't know. We just saw you and tried to help."

"Thank the heavens above for that. Who knows how long we would have been standing here. You saved our lives. Are you headed for town?"

"Yes, we went for a long hike since it was such a beautiful day."

"Stay with us. It will be dark soon and it's seventeen miles to the village. Have dinner and spend the night.

It's the least we can do. You can start out fresh in the morning. I'll make up beds for you. Are you married?"

Odo's face turned a remarkable shade of crimson.

"We're just friends."

# Chapter 16

# Burton-On-Guster

Bright and early the next morning Odo and Sephie bid their farewells to the farmer and his wife, thanking them for their generous hospitality. Odo was carrying a heavily laden lunch basket the farmer's wife had packed for them.

"Bless you both. Come back and visit anytime you want. You're always welcome here."

The pair of adventuring friends headed off across the rolling emerald green hills. Sephie stopped to pick wildflowers, weaving a colorful necklace from the blossoms.

"The flowers here are beautiful, aren't they?"

Odo stared at the blossoms.

"What is it, Odo Whitley? There's a question trying to jump out of your mouth."

"Do plants have brainwaves like people and animals?"

"They have bioelectric fields, but they're weak.

They're hard for me to see."

"I've read a lot of biochemistry books. It's all really interesting. Living creatures are so amazing and so complex."

"I'm glad we're friends, Odo Whitley."

"So am I, Sephie Crumb. Let's stop for lunch. This basket is getting heavy."

Odo sat down and flipped the lid open.

"Whoa, that's a lot of food, no wonder it weighs so much. Yum, half a chocolate cake."

"Sandwiches first, Odo Whitley. You know the rules."

"I don't quite remember that rule."

"Sandwiches first, chocolate cake second. That's the rule."

"Right. Sandwiches first."

After lunch Odo and Sephie lay on their backs, staring up at the clouds.

Odo was pointing to a puffy cloud directly above them.

"I think it looks more like a horse carrying an umbrella. That pointy part is the umbrella and that long thing is–"

"The girls at school tell each other how cute they look, but they never say it to me."

Odo nodded. "I know how that feels. No one ever says anything to me."

"Sometimes I get tired of being Sephie Crumb. I wish I fit in more. I wish girls would say how cute my outfit was, or how cute my hair was, or ask me if I was going to the dance."

"Sephie, I hear a lot of things at school. It's not eavesdropping, I just hear things because people don't realize I'm there. I've heard girls tell someone how cute they look, then five minutes later make fun of them behind their back. I'm glad you're not trying to be someone else. They always say be true to yourself, be who you are. You're Sephie Crumb, and there's no one else in the world like you. Be Sephie Crumb."

"I should write that down so I don't forget."

Odo laughed. "We should go. We have some serious antique shopping to do."

Four hours later they were approaching the bustling little village of Burton-On-Guster.

"Now that's what I call a quaint village. It looks like a postcard. Look at those thatched roofs."

"It's lovely, so peaceful."

"Cobblestone streets. I've never actually walked on these before. Kind of bumpy. I wouldn't want to run on them."

"Their clothes are old fashioned. I like that. I like old fashioned clothes."

A lovely woman carrying a green silk parasol stopped and turned, studying Sephie's hair.

She placed a white gloved hand on Sephie's shoulder and said, "I love your hair, young lady. It's exquisitely beautiful. You are truly blessed." She continued on her way with a quick wave.

Sephie's mouth was hanging open.

"Did you hear that? Did you hear what she said,

Odo?"

"I did."

"I want to tell her how much that meant to me. I want her to know." She watched the woman making her way down the cobblestone street, then gave a sudden yelp.

"Odo, we have to go! Now!"

Sephie grabbed Odo's hand and pulled him into a narrow alleyway.

"What is it? What's wrong?"

"Two of them, coming this way! A tall man in a black suit and a lady in a blue striped dress. They're dead people, no brainwaves. I hear the crackling noise."

"Who are these people? What do they want?"

"We have to hide."

"Through that door! Hurry!"

They ran across the alley and flung the green door open, darting into the building.

"Okay, this is weird. We're in an antique shop."

"My goosebumps have goosebumps."

Odo walked to the front of the shop, peering through the front window, watching the two dead people walk past.

"They're gone. Let's look around. Maybe this is where we'll find whatever it is we're supposed to be looking for."

Sephie breathed in the musty aromas of the shop.

"It smells like the old books in my grandpa's house." She glanced at Odo. "My adopted grandpa's house."

"I like antique shops. Everything in them has such

an amazing story. Look at those oil lanterns, the kind miners used back in the old days. And those tools, weird old hammers and saws. I don't even know what that thing is."

"There's some jewelry." Sephie stepped over to a glass case, eyeing a display of sparkling necklaces. Odo stepped up next to her.

"That's a nice one." He pointed to a lovely necklace with an ornate silver chain, two small iridescent green gems mounted on either side of a large brilliant blue translucent stone.

"Looks expensive. It would be perfect for someone else, but not for me."

Sephie turned, her eyes on a rack of old clothes against the far wall. "Let's look at those clothes. I'm getting a funny feeling."

"What kind of funny feeling?"

"I don't know exactly. It's new."

"Sephie, what happened at the farmhouse? What did you do? I saw a green light come out of your hand. That's what pulled the farmers out of the coma."

"I don't want to talk about it."

"Oh, sorry. Um... did you want to buy a new coat or something?"

Sephie walked over to the rack of old clothes, running her hand across them. She closed her eyes, her head moving slowly back and forth. It reminded Odo of a cobra listening to a snake charmer.

"What are you doing?"

"Quiet."

86

She moved down the rack of clothes, her hand stopping on a dark brown roughly woven coat that had clearly seen better days.

"This one."

"It's ten sizes too big and smells funny."

Sephie reached into one of the coat's enormous pockets, pulling out a wrinkled envelope. She handed it to Odo.

"What is it? How did you know that was there?"

"Open it."

Odo flipped open the envelope and pulled out two small discolored rectangular pieces of paper. He studied them, then stepped back, his eyes wide. "This can't be real."

"What is it?"

"Tickets. Two tickets to a place called Plindor. The train leaves from Girard Station."

Sephie's face was pale.

"Something pulled me to that coat. It pulled me. I don't like this. What's happening to me?"

Odo had no answer.

# Chapter 17

# **The Doll**

Odo tucked the tickets into his pack and they headed for the back door. He stopped, turning to Sephie.

"You're not the only one who does weird stuff. If I show you something, will you promise not to run away?"

"What is it?"

"Something I've never shown to anyone else. Ever."

"Can you fly like a bird?"

"What? No, of course not, it's nothing like that."

"Are you a werewolf? A vampire? A Roman emperor?"

"No, it's not something crazy, it's just something I can do. First we should check if the two dead people are in the alley."

"I'll open the door and peek out."

"No need for that."

Odo touched his finger to the wall.

"What are you doing?"

"Wait for it."

The wall around his finger glimmered. Ten seconds

later a small circular section of the wall was translucent. Sephie's eyes widened.

"How did you do that?"

"I'm not exactly sure, but I think I make the wall become part of my body. I started doing it when I was little. I used to peek through the wall in the morning to check the weather."

Sephie peered through the translucent circle.

"They're out there, both of them! They're standing right next to–" Sephie didn't finish her sentence because the brainless dead aliens were no longer there. They had rippled with a strange iridescent orange light, transforming into something that made Sephie's skin crawl.

"Odo, what are they?"

Odo peered through the wall at the two gaunt creatures with dark violet skin and burning yellow eyes. They had faces of a sort, but no nose or ears, their long white hair moving slowly back and forth like a thousand tiny snakes. One of them opened its mouth, revealing a row of dark blue pointy teeth.

"It's them! It's the creatures Mrs. Preke asked me about in my interview! I thought she was being funny. She asked what I would do if I saw them."

"Did she say what they were?"

"No. Do they have brainwaves?

"None, and I hear the crackling noise."

"Remember when Wikerus told us about formshifters? That's what these things are. They're not dead people, they're brainless aliens formshifting into people."

"Why are they following us?"

"I don't know, but it can't be good."

"Let's think about it. The one at the farm didn't try to kill us or put us into a coma, but it did keep asking us if we were looking for a special antique."

"You're right, that's a good thing, they're not trying to kill us. Not now, anyway. There's something they want, and they think we know where it is."

"What are we supposed to be looking for?"

"I don't know. It must be an antique though. Maybe the train tickets to Plindor?"

"Why would they want old train tickets?"

Odo skittered back from the wall.

"Whoa!!"

"What happened?"

"The brainless aliens vanished."

"They're shifters. Let's go before they come back. I'll keep an eye out for them."

Odo swung the back door open and they peered outside, looking up and down the narrow alley.

"No sign of them. What now?"

"Let's look around. Maybe we'll find whatever it is we're supposed to be looking for in one of the other shops."

Sephie walked to the end of the alley, peeking around the corner, scanning the streets.

"No brainless aliens. It looks okay." She exited the alley, Odo behind her.

"There's a lot of shops here. How do we know

90

which one to go to? Hey, can you do that thing where you get pulled, like when you found the tickets?"

"I don't want to do it again."

"I made the wall translucent. Now it's your turn to do something weird and spooky."

"Making the wall translucent wasn't weird and spooky, it was kind of cool, like a super X-ray vision power."

"You're the one with the amazing powers. You brought the farmers out of the coma and saved their lives."

"We could be superheroes, Odo Whitley. Translucent Boy and Encephalo Girl, saving the universe from creepy purple brainless aliens."

Odo burst out laughing. "I like it. We could have our own comic book, maybe a movie."

"All right, Translucent Boy, I'll do it."

"Encephalo Girl to the rescue."

"Maybe." Her head swayed back and forth like a cobra as she turned slowly. "That way, near the end of the street."

"This is incredible."

The two friends made their way down the cobblestone street, Sephie on the alert for brainless aliens. She was also looking for the woman who told her she had exquisitely beautiful hair. She really wanted to thank her. She stopped in front of a small shop.

"In here."

"It's a toy shop. What would be in a toy shop?"

"Toys?"

A small brass bell jingled when Sephie pushed the door open.

Odo studied the interior of the shop.

"It's definitely a toy shop. Need a big snuggly teddy bear?"

Sephie's head was swaying again.

"That way."

She strode down a narrow aisle, stopping in front of a wall of dolls.

An elderly man wearing round gold spectacles shuffled out from behind the counter, making his way toward them.

"Good afternoon, friends. Is there anything I might help you find?"

Sephie smiled. "I was just looking at the dolls."

"Are you a collector, or buying for your little one?"

Odo snickered.

Sephie glared at Odo. "I'm more of a collector. Just browsing to see what's here."

"Feel free to look as long as you wish. Let me know if you find anything you can't live without."

Sephie smiled her thanks, turning back to the dolls.

"I know there's something here. This is where I'm supposed to be, but I don't see anything. None of the dolls seem special. Maybe I'm wrong. I don't know."

Sephie's thoughts were interrupted by the shopkeeper clearing his throat. He was holding a ten inch long white cardboard box.

"I almost forgot about this one. We got her in yesterday, purchased from an itinerant peddler. It's quite old and has never been played with. I have no idea who made it, or where it's from."

When he lifted the lid, a jolt of recognition shot through Sephie. Her hand was shaking as she ran her fingertips over the doll's blue felt dress, feeling its familiar texture. It was a rag doll with red and white striped legs and large black button eyes. The memory was overwhelming.

"How much is it?"

"I'm afraid it's quite costly due to its rarity. I'm asking nineteen silvers, one silver more than I paid for it."

"I'll have to come back, I don't have enough money right now."

"I would be happy to put it aside for you."

"It's beautiful, but I need to think about it."

"Of course. I can't guarantee it will be here when you return."

"I understand. Thank you so much. Odo, we should probably go, it's getting late. Time to head home."

"You found everything we need?"

"I did, Odo Whitley. I found everything we need."

# Chapter 18

# Advenus Bandiir

Much to their surprise, when Odo and Sephie shifted back to Wikerus Praevian's sitting room they discovered less than an hour had passed in their world.

"That's not possible, we were gone for two days."

Wikerus motioned for them to sit on the blue sofa.

"It ceases to be a paradoxical event once you understand that time passes at different rates in different worlds, depending upon gravitational pull and the relative velocity of the worlds in question. Think of time as a river, sometimes narrow raging rapids, sometimes wide and calm and meandering. Now, tell me about your visit to Pacalia. Is it not a gloriously resplendent world?"

"We saw the purple creatures with white hair and yellow eyes that Mrs. Preke talked about in my interview."

Wikerus was clearly rattled by Odo's revelation.

"Atroxians on Pacalia? Are you absolutely certain?"

"What are Atroxians?"

"Tell me exactly what happened. Do not leave out a single detail."

Sephie described their encounters with the formshifting aliens that Wikerus called Atroxians. She also revealed to Wikerus her ability see the energy fields surrounding living creatures. Wikerus was pacing anxiously, his eyes on the two friends.

"You are quite correct in your assumption that the brainless dead people are formshifting aliens. They are Atroxians, and trust me when I say they are extraordinarily dangerous. They are desperately searching for a certain object, but for me to reveal its precise nature at this time would put your lives in dire jeopardy. You are safe for now, but the Atroxians are watching you. Sephie, don't show your hand, don't let them know you can see them. I will tell you that the potential consequences of our actions are staggering, far beyond what you can imagine."

Odo's eyes were wide. He did not want to be responsible for staggering consequences beyond his imagination.

"Um... so what do we do now?"

Sephie hopped up from the couch.

"I know exactly what we do, Odo Whitley. I talk to my parents about something that happened a long time ago."

The following afternoon found the two friends in the school cafeteria, Odo setting his tray down on the table across from Sephie.

"What did you ask your parents?"

"When I saw that doll in the toy shop, it brought back a memory. I had a doll exactly like it when I was little. I vaguely remember someone giving it to me, but it's hazy, I don't know who it was. I played with it all the time before I went to the clinic, but when I came home it was gone."

"Did your mom know who gave it to you?"

"She said I had the doll when they found me. They sold it to an antique dealer when I was in the clinic, thinking it might hold bad memories for me, that getting rid of it might help me stop seeing the lights."

"What's so special about an old doll?"

"It's special because the universe went to a great deal of trouble restoring my lost memory, sending us all the way to a toy shop on Pacalia. The doll is part of our story, a piece of the puzzle. That's all I know."

"Wikerus knows what's going on, but he won't tell us."

"He doesn't want to put us in danger. I also have a feeling he's afraid that telling us too much will alter the course of events, change the future."

"How could he know what's going to happen?"

Sephie shook her head. "One thing is certain, Wikerus Praevian is far more than he appears to be. He might even be a formshifter."

"That's kind of scary. Are we supposed to find the doll?"

"We are."

"Is that thing pulling you toward it?"

Sephie removed a small wrinkled business card from her pocket, setting it on the table in front of Odo.

"Not exactly, but I do have a clue."

Odo picked up the card and read it.

## Jonathan L. Morse
*Antiques & Curiosities*
*12158 Debra Avenue*

"This is who bought the doll?"

"He left the card with my mom in case she had more antiques to sell."

"He probably sold it a long time ago."

"We have to start somewhere, and this is the only clue we have."

"We can take the bus there after school. Debra Avenue is at the south end of Asper Street. Do you think the doll is what the Atroxians are looking for?"

Sephie shrugged. "Maybe, but we're missing a lot of the story. I think things are going to get complicated."

Odo grinned. "It's kind of fun being detectives and tracking down clues."

When the last bell rang, Odo and Sephie headed for the bus stop. Half an hour later they were walking down Debra Avenue.

"These buildings are old, the paint's all cracked and peeling. It's not the best section of town. Maybe the antique dealer moved. It's been ten years."

Sephie stopped, pointing to a black weathered door with barely legible painted gold letters.

## J. Morse
### Antiques & Curiosities

Yellowing newspaper covered the inside of the windows, concealing the shop's interior.

"Doesn't look like anyone's home."

Sephie reached for the brass doorknob, twisting it.

"It's locked."

"They must be closed. I don't see a sign with store hours. He probably went out of business, or maybe–"

"Or maybe we need to wake the dead."

Sephie pounded on the door with both fists.

The two friends heard shuffling footsteps on the other side of the door. Someone pulled back a corner of the newspaper and peered out. Seconds later the door creaked opened.

"Shall I assume you are searching for a book on door knocking etiquette?"

Odo couldn't help but notice the unsmiling antique dealer was aiming an ancient bronze blunderbuss directly at them.

"Uh... sorry, we weren't sure if you were still in business. The windows were... um... all the newspapers... we couldn't..."

Sephie stepped in front of Odo. "We're looking for a doll you bought from my mom ten years ago. We need to find it."

"You have my attention. Enter."

The two friends stepped into the shadowy shop, their

eyes scanning the dim interior. A single overhead bulb revealed long wooden tables and shelves jammed with thousands of dusty antiquities.

"Whoa, you have a lot of stuff here. Is that skull real? What's that thing?"

"Describe the doll."

Odo's eyes were glued to the deadly blunderbuss.

"Is that thing loaded?"

Jonathan Morse did not answer, but set the ancient firearm down on a table.

"The doll. Describe it."

"I had it when I was little, but my mom sold it to you when I was about five years old. It was a rag doll, nine inches long with a blue felt coat, red and white striped legs, and big black button eyes."

"I remember it."

Sephie raised her eyebrows. "You remember it? That was ten years ago, how could you remember–"

"I can name every item in my shop and tell you precisely where and when I bought each one."

Odo blinked. "Whoa, I wish I had your memory."

"No you don't. There are plenty of things I'd like to forget. Plenty of them."

"Oh, right, I see what you mean."

"Do you still have the doll?"

"I sold it four years ago on a drizzly Saturday morning to an elderly gentleman with a foreign name wearing a long dark green coat. Strange old man, paid with a small ingot of silver."

Sephie frowned.

"He didn't leave an address, did he?"

"Wait here, don't touch anything." The antique dealer gave Odo a dark look.

Jonathan Morse turned, shuffling to the rear of the shop, disappearing into a back room. A light blinked on. They could hear him rummaging around for almost five minutes.

Odo pointed to the huge blunderbuss and grinned. He pretended to pick it up and shoot it.

"Beware the dread pirate Odo!"

"You need to have your neuronal synapses adjusted, Odo Whitley."

Odo was about to reply when the antique dealer called out.

"Found it!"

He returned with a large dusty black ledger, setting it on the table in front of them.

"Here it is. The man's name was Advenus Bandiir. Told you it was a strange name. Not from around here."

Odo scanned the ledger, reading the hastily scrawled address next to Advenus Bandiir's name. His eyes widened, but he said nothing.

"We should go, Odo. Thank you so much for your help, Mister Morse."

"Call me Jon. Leave your name and number and I'll contact you if I see the doll again."

Sephie knew that would never happen, but she jotted it down anyway. "Thanks again for your help, Jon."

"I hope you find it. It must mean a lot to you."

"It was my favorite toy when I was little."

100

"I understand. Memories. Days gone by. Things that might have been."

Odo and Sephie stepped into the bright sunlight.

Odo grabbed Sephie's arm. "Did you see it? The address?"

"I saw it with my own two green eyes, Odo Whitley."

"Advenus Bandiir was from Plindor. Wikerus called the yellow octopus in my six-wheeled sailing truck a Plindorian."

"And it's the destination on our Girard Station tickets. These are not coincidences."

"We need to find Girard Station. I have a strange feeling it's not going to be like any train station we've ever seen."

# Chapter 19

# Ten Balloons

Odo and Sephie were walking home from school, the ground covered with yellow and orange leaves. Their search for Girard Station had come to a dead end. Two weeks had passed and they were no closer to finding it than when they started.

"I like the crunchy sound the leaves make when I step on them."

Odo laughed. "It is a nice sound. I like the fall, not too hot and not too cold. Plus we have crunchy leaves to walk on."

"I'm not being pulled anywhere."

"You mean to Girard Station?"

"I don't think I'm the one who's supposed to find it."

"Um, that kind of narrows it down to one person."

"I think you're supposed to find it."

"What else can I do? We've talked to Wikerus and he's never heard of it. We checked the library, did a computer search, looked up every train station in the country. No Girard Station, nothing even close."

"I think we should stop looking. It's like when you're trying to remember a name. The harder you try, the worse it gets. If you do something else for a while and take your mind off it, the name just pops into your head out of nowhere."

"That's true, and a break would be nice. We haven't done anything except search for this crazy station."

"Think of something you always wanted to do, but never did."

"I've never been to Girard Station. Maybe we should go there."

"I'm going to thump your head with a big stick, Odo Whitley. We have to do something you've always wanted to do, something that would make you happy. That's how it works."

"Okay, let me think... something I've always wanted to do, but never did."

Sephie studied Odo's head. "Why are you thinking of something sad?"

"There was a birthday party when I was in the fifth grade. All the kids in my class were invited except me. They talked about it for days, how they'd gone to Lost Lake Amusement Park. I heard all the stories about the rides they went on, how exciting they were. It sounded like the most fun you could ever have, a whole park full of rides and games."

"I'm sorry you didn't get to go."

"It was a long time ago."

"We'll go to the park. It will be a happy story, the adventures of Translucent Boy and Encephalo Girl at Lost Lake Amusement Park."

Odo grinned. "That sounds really fun. I picked up my pay envelope from Serendipity Salvage so we'll have lots of money for rides and games. And snacks."

"When are you going to get your new bike?"

"I decided not to get one. I'm saving my money for college. My parents can't afford to pay for it, and I want to go."

"Are we growing up, Odo Whitley?"

"I think we are, Sephie Crumb."

\* \* \* \*

Odo had a broad grin plastered across his face. Sephie's hands were pressed against her ears.

"It's so loud here!"

"There must be a million people, and look at all the rides. We should definitely go on the ferris wheel. It's really big. I've always wanted to ride on one. I bet it's like flying."

"I have another secret, Odo Whitley. I don't like heights."

"We don't have to go on it if you don't want to. Let's try that ride over there, the Monster MegaWheel of Spinning Death."

Twenty minutes later Sephie had her arm around Odo's waist, holding him steady.

"Can you walk? You're not going to barf, are you?"

"I'm not going to barf, I'm just dizzy from all the spinning. Maybe we should try a ride that doesn't have the words *spinning* or *death* in it."

Sephie snickered. "Here's the midway, we can play some games until you feel better. Maybe we'll win a doll with red and white striped legs and big black button eyes."

"Why does that sound so familiar?"

"There's a dart game. You just have to pop the balloons. How hard can that be?"

"Very hard if the balloons are half filled and the darts are dull."

"Odo, look! One of the prizes is a plush yellow octopus. That can't be a coincidence."

"Maybe I'm supposed to win it."

Odo stepped over to the booth.

"How many balloons do I have to pop to win the octopus?"

Odo had never seen anyone as bored as the man in the blue jump suit slouched behind the counter reading a magazine. He didn't bother to look up at Odo.

"Ten in a row, dollar a throw. Good luck. Have a great day."

Odo dropped a ten dollar bill on the counter and picked up ten darts. He grinned at Sephie. "Watch and learn, Sephie Crumb."

As Odo turned toward the balloons, a searing pain shot through Sephie's head. She leaned over, pressing her hands to her temples. It was like Pacalia, but the pain didn't last as long this time. She stood up, the same unnatural ghostly calm on her face.

She watched as Odo picked up the first dart and aimed it. A barely visible blue light shot out from her hand the moment he threw it, the dart flashing through the air toward the first balloon, popping it.

"Whoa, I did it! I popped one!"

The curious sensation of controlling objects with her mind felt strangely familiar to Sephie, almost as if she was remembering how to do it.

Nine more balloons popped. The man in the blue jump suit never looked up, tossing a plush yellow stuffed octopus onto the counter.

"Congratulations. Have a nice day."

Odo handed the octopus to Sephie, a wide grin on his face.

"Ten balloons in a row! How awesome was that?"

"You're amazing, Odo Whitley."

Sephie studied Odo's head. She had never seen him this happy.

# Chapter 20

# Proto's Taste-E Kakes

"Odo Whitley, I think we should go on the ferris wheel."

"We don't have to go if you don't like heights. There's plenty of other stuff we can do."

"I want to go because it's something you always wanted to do. That's why we're here. Besides, I have my friendly yellow Plindorian to protect me. I think he has magical powers."

"It won't be as scary as you think."

The two friends wove their way through the crowd toward the towering ferris wheel.

"Are you having fun, Odo Whitley?"

"I am. Going with you makes it even better."

"I came here with my parents when I was nine. This is way more fun."

Odo looked up at the gleaming ferris wheel. "I bet I can see my house from up there."

"Your house is thirty miles away. You'd have to

have super eagle vision."

A few minutes later Odo and Sephie clambered aboard the swaying ferris wheel gondola. They took their seats, the operator locking the metal safety arm in front of them.

Sephie scooted over next to Odo. "How high does it go?"

"About two hundred feet I think."

"That high? That seems really high. Are you sure?"

"We'll be fine. I was watching the people get off and they all looked happy."

"Maybe they were smiling because the ride was over and they didn't die."

Odo gave a cackling laugh.

Sephie jumped when the gondola jerked forward, the gigantic wheel groaning.

"Is it supposed to swing this much?"

"Some people rock the car back and forth just for fun."

"Don't even think about it, Odo Whitley."

"I won't, I promise. Sephie, thanks for doing this. It means a lot to me."

As the gondola rose, a grin crept across Sephie's face.

"This isn't so bad. I can see the whole park and we're only halfway up. Imagine what it will be like when we're two hundred feet up. This safety bar seems really strong."

"It is. We'll probably see the whole city."

The swaying gondola rose higher and higher until it

finally reached the top. That was when the ferris wheel jerked to a halt, the gondola swinging wildly back and forth.

Sephie yelped, grabbing the safety bar. "What happened? Why did we stop?"

"I think it's just part of the ride, so we can look around while we're up here."

Sephie looked across the sprawling cityscape, still gripping the safety bar, her knuckles white. "It is an amazing view. The afternoon sun makes everything sparkle."

Odo nodded, studying the gleaming buildings.

"It kind of makes me wish I was a–"

Odo Whitley never finished his sentence. He never finished it because he was staring at the last thing he had expected to see from the top of a two hundred foot tall ferris wheel in Lost Lake Amusement Park.

"Sephie, I think that name we were trying to remember just popped into my head. Look over there."

Odo pointed to a gleaming golden roof three miles away.

Sephie gave a low gasp. "It's a triangle."

"The nice old dead lady said Girard Station was right next to a huge triangular building."

"You found it, Odo Whitley. You found Girard Station."

Odo grinned. "You're the one who said if we stopped looking for it we'd find it, that we should do something I always wanted to do. And that this would be a happy story."

On the bus ride home Odo and Sephie decided to visit the triangular building on a weekday in case Girard Station was closed on weekends.

"If we don't find it, we can always ask someone in the triangle building where it is."

Sephie looked dubious. "I don't think this is an ordinary train station. We should bring backpacks with extra clothes and anything else we need."

"Need for what?"

"For our trip to Plindor."

Two days later Odo and Sephie hopped off the city bus across from the enormous gleaming triangular building.

"Yum, all those food trucks are making me hungry."

"No time for snacks, Odo Whitley. Time is money. The Translucent Boy and Encephalo Girl are on a top secret mission to save the universe."

Odo laughed, but couldn't take his eyes off the food trucks.

The pair of friends crossed the street, studying the massive glass and steel triangular structure.

"It's so big, a lot bigger than I thought it would be. I can't imagine how many people work there."

Odo eyed the huge silver letters running across the front of the building.

## Proto's Taste-E Kakes Corporation

"That's a weird coincidence, Proto's Taste-E Kakes is my dad's main competitor. I'd never say it in front of him, but they're way better than Silver CrunchCakes."

"They are good. We should start looking."

Odo and Sephie made their way around the massive Taste-E Kakes building, searching for anything even vaguely resembling a train station.

"I'm not seeing anything. It's just a big industrial park with factories and warehouses and office buildings, no bus stations or train stations. The brainless alien lady said it was right next to the triangular building. I don't get it."

"Let's walk around it again. We must have missed it."

It wasn't long until Odo and Sephie were sitting on a bench in front of the Taste-E Kakes building.

"This is hopeless. There's nothing here. Did you spot any brainless aliens?"

"Not one, Odo Whitley."

"I'm getting hungry. Let's get something to eat. There's a lot of people at those food trucks. Aren't you hungry?"

Sephie glanced over at the row of colorful trucks and the lines of customers. Her eyes narrowed.

"As a matter of fact, I'm starving. I'm in the mood for some Captain Freddie's Fish n' Chips. Nothing else will do."

"I didn't know you liked fish and chips. That sounds good. There's a really good fish and chips place near my house. We should go there sometime. I like them with tartar sauce, lots of ketchup on the chips. They never give you enough ketchup, just those little packets, and you have to tear each one open and–"

"Snap to it, Odo Whitley. Time is money."

Sephie darted toward the fish and chips truck, taking her place in line.

Six customers later they were looking up at a portly bearded man wearing black rimmed glasses, a bright yellow rain slicker and matching floppy rain hat, both festooned with the colorful Captain Freddie's Fish n' Chips logo. He gave them a cheery smile.

"What'll it be, folks? Fish and chips, or chips and fish?" He gave a great booming laugh. Odo was pretty sure this wasn't the first time he'd made that joke.

Sephie slapped the two Girard Station tickets down on the counter.

"Two tickets for Plindor. It's supposed to be lovely this time of year."

# Chapter 21

# Supervisor!

The fish and chips vendor turned and hollered, "Two Captain Freddie's Specials!"

He pushed the tickets back across the counter to Sephie.

"Don't see your kind around here much."

Sephie frowned. "My kind?"

The vendor shrugged. "Not looking for trouble, just sayin'. Love your hair, by the way."

Sephie did not smile. She was quite certain the vendor did not love her hair.

He pushed two small styrofoam boxes across the counter.

"Enjoy, my orange haired friend. Next in line, please!"

Sephie grabbed the two food containers and they headed to a nearby bench.

Odo looked confused. "What just happened?"

"At first I didn't realize what I was seeing. The

Captain Freddie's Fish n' Chips truck is the center of a massively powerful energy field. I've never seen one like it."

"Are you saying the food truck has something to do with Girard Station?"

"That's exactly what I'm saying. I also have my doubts whether Captain Freddie is human."

Sephie handed Odo one of the styrofoam boxes.

"Why is it so light? There's nothing in it."

"Open it."

Odo flipped the lid, staring curiously at the contents.

"It's a silver card. What's it for?"

"I think it opens the door to Girard Station."

"What door?"

"The Fish n' Chips truck is the door. Follow me."

Sephie slung on her pack and stood up, pointing to the back of the truck.

"The center of the energy field is at the rear of the truck. Are you ready, Odo Whitley?"

"I guess so, but I don't exactly understand what's happening.

Sephie pointed to a small silver slot on the rear of the truck, a tiny blinking violet light next to it.

"The card goes in, we go to Girard Station. I'll go first."

She grinned at Odo, inserting her card into the slot.

Sephie was there, and then she was not. Odo stood gaping at the empty space where she had been.

"Not what I was expecting."

He took a deep breath and slipped his card in.

The world around him vanished, replaced by a hundred foot wide gleaming white corridor. One side of the massive hallway was adorned with colorful murals of unfamiliar landscapes and extraordinary creatures. The mural directly behind Odo was an artful rendering of Captain Freddie's Fish n' Chips truck.

The opposite side of the corridor was lined with floor to ceiling windows, two blazing orange suns in a violet sky.

"Two suns, violet sky? What is this place?" Odo turned to see a wide eyed Sephie pointing at an eight foot tall yellow octopus wheeling a large blue travel bag down the hallway, its wheels making a rhythmic clicking sound as it rolled along.

Odo let out a yelp.

The creature stopped in its tracks, looking behind it to see what Sephie was pointing at. It turned back, glaring at Sephie. Raising one of its arms, it pointed directly at her while making a series of incomprehensible sounds. For some reason it made Sephie think of a burning hot desert. The creature lowered it's arm and continued down the corridor, averting its eyes as it walked past them.

"A giant yellow octopus just pointed at you."

"We just saw our first Plindorian. We're definitely not on Earth anymore, Odo Whitley. What I'd like to know is why he was glaring at me, and why it made me think of a desert. You're solid, by the way."

Odo looked at his hands. "Whoa, this time I have to find a mirror, maybe a camera. Is this Girard Station?"

"No, but I think this hallway takes us there."

Odo grabbed Sephie's arm. "Don't look, four huge insects behind us. Yellow and orange, really tall, big bug eyes."

Sephie ignored Odo's advice and turned, gazing curiously at the creatures.

"They look like praying mantises. That weird noise must be how they talk to each other."

Odo attempted a casual demeanor, leaning back against the wall, discreetly directing his gaze toward the four enormous insects.

"They're pushing red travel bags and have long blue capes, almost like uniforms. Do you think they work here?"

As the creatures walked past, one turned, eyeing Sephie, making a scratchy whistling sound. The others turned to look at her.

Odo waved to one of them. It nodded, tapping its head with a long spiky arm, then turned, continuing down the corridor.

"They didn't seem too scary. You know, for giant praying mantises wearing blue capes."

"Let's see what's outside. It's so strange to see two suns in the sky." Sephie ran to the windows. "Odo! Come see this!"

He darted over next to her. "Whoa, we're in the middle of an ocean, no land anywhere. Do you think we're on an island?"

"Maybe Girard Station is a big floating platform in the middle of an ocean."

"How would anyone get here?"

Sephie raised her eyebrows. "Adjust your brain cells, Odo Whitley."

"Oh, right, Captain Freddie's food truck. Let's keep going. Girard Station must be incredible.

The two friends followed the gently curving corridor for almost a mile, stopping occasionally to look at some of the more interesting travel murals.

"Look at the weird trees on that one. They look like they're walking. I hope I never run into a walking tree. Or one that talks. How weird would that be? Hey, maybe the tree doesn't talk, it barks. Get it? Barks?"

"I think we're here."

The corridor ended abruptly at a gleaming silver wall lined with six magnificent arched doorways. Next to each door was a cylindrical guard station, only one of them currently occupied.

Odo studied the stern looking guard bedecked in a crisp maroon uniform, a single row of gold buttons running down his chest. A glowing violet disc was clipped to his breast pocket.

"Please don't tell me that's a giant mouse."

"Okay, I won't."

"Or a giant blue mouse. I don't like mice."

"Adjust your brain dials. We're going to be seeing a lot of creatures who don't look like us. We both know what it's like to look different. Pretend it's Halloween and he's your best friend wearing a giant blue mouse costume."

"You're right. He seems nice enough. Maybe a little

crabby."

The uniformed guard watched with interest as Odo and Sephie approached, his eyes focused on Sephie's orange hair.

He held up one hand, motioning for them to stop.

When he opened his mouth, a series of shrill squeaks and squeals emerged.

Odo glanced at Sephie, then back at the guard. "Are you talking to us?"

The guard's eyes narrowed.

"Sorry, we don't know what you're saying. We don't understand... um... mouse languages. We're not from around here."

The guard sighed, reaching into a drawer and pulling out two gold discs. He stepped out from his booth, sticking one disc on Odo's left temple, the other on Sephie's.

When he spoke again Odo could understand his words.

"World of origin?"

"Whoa, that's amazing! How does this thing work?"

"Let me guess, you're from Earth. Have you guys invented fire yet?"

"What's that supposed to mean?"

"The gold discs are universal translators. They've been around for millennia. Everyone uses them."

He turned to Sephie.

"World of origin?"

"Earth."

He rolled his eyes.

"*Original* world of origin?"

"I'm from Earth. I was born there."

He studied her face, then motioned for her to place one hand on a circular silver disc set into the counter.

"Original world of origin?"

"Earth, I'm from Earth."

The silver disc glowed with a violet light.

The guard shrugged.

"Destination?"

"Plindor. We're going to Plindor."

"Touch your travel rings to the green pad."

"Our what?"

"Touch. Travel. Rings. To. Green. Pad."

"I don't know what travel rings are. This is our first time here."

"They really do not pay me enough. Do you have proof of purchase for your transition?"

"You mean tickets?" Odo pulled the two paper tickets from his pocket and set them on the counter.

The guard looked at the tickets, then at Odo.

"What are these?"

"Our tickets to Plindor."

The blue mouse tapped the violet disk on his uniform. "Supervisor!"

A second blue mouse stepped out of the guard station, this one with two rows of gold buttons running down the front of his jacket.

"What seems to be the problem?"

The first blue mouse pointed to the paper tickets.

His superior picked one up, studying it closely.

"Is this some kind of joke?" He tapped the violet disc on his jacket. "Supervisor!"

A third mouse emerged, this one a distinguished looking older mouse, three rows of buttons running down his jacket.

"How may I be of assistance?"

Both guards pointed to the paper tickets.

The elderly mouse held the tickets up to the light, turning them slowly.

"These bring back memories. They might be worth something to a collector. What's the problem?"

Sephie did not want to see another supervisor. "Can we use them to travel to Plindor?"

"Use them? An unusual request, but I see no reason why not. I'll transfer the ticket data to a set of travel rings for you. You may keep the old tickets. You might be able to sell them to an antique dealer for a substantial amount."

"That would be great. Thank you so much. This is the first time we've been here."

"It can be overwhelming if you're not used to it."

He pressed the tickets against the green pad, rewarded by a whirring sound and the appearance of two silver rings. He handed one to Odo and one to Sephie.

"Wear these during your travels. They will simplify your passage through the transition terminals. Have a pleasant journey."

The door to Girard Station slid open.

# Chapter 22

# Girard Station

Odo and Sephie slipped on their travel rings and stepped through the doorway.

Neither of them spoke for a full minute, trying to absorb the extraordinary spectacle that was Girard Station.

They found themselves on the outer edge of a titanic sparkling glass dome, fifteen hundred feet tall and nearly a mile across. The floor of the dome was covered with thousands of towering violet tinted glass cylinders, their purpose unknown to Odo and Sephie. It wasn't the dome or the violet cylinders which had stunned the two friends, however, it was the sea of otherworldly creatures walking, flying, slithering, hopping, and rolling across the monumentally vast pavilion of Girard Station.

"I think my head's going to explode."

Sephie nodded, unable to remove her eyes from a group of three bulbous headed gleaming white creatures strolling past them.

"Odo, their feet aren't touching the ground."

"They don't have eyes."

"Or a mouth."

"Look at their arms, they're like white ropes."

"Did you see the ones that look like black butter-flies?"

"More like bats with little backpacks. I feel like I'm trapped in a dream, like I should try to wake up."

Sephie gave Odo's arm a sharp and painful pinch.

"Ow! What was that for?"

"Just a test, to see if you'd wake up. I guess this isn't a dream, Odo Whitley. Is this more fun than Lost Lake Amusement Park?"

"It doesn't compare to anything in our world. I could sit here for a month and watch all the weird creatures walk past. Or slither past."

Four undulating scaly snake like creatures with two arms wriggled past them.

"Look at those three green blobby things. Two big ones and one little one. Are those eyes? Or maybe ears?"

"Do you think the little one is their kid?"

"There's some of those praying mantises. These ones have red capes, not blue ones, and their travel bags are different colors. Eww, giant striped worm thing."

"It's wearing clothes. Or something sort of like clothes."

"What do you think all the big violet glass cylinders are?"

"I saw two orange lizardy creatures step inside one and vanish. They must be doorways to other worlds."

"There are thousands of them. How do we find the one that goes to Plindor?"

"Let's look for an information booth. There must be one around here somewhere."

Odo and Sephie slung on their packs, weaving their way through the bustling crowd.

"Oops, sorry!" Odo almost tripped over a line of ant creatures wearing brown robes and hats. The largest ant was carrying a bright yellow flag. He gave Odo a wave, calling out, "No problem. Have a grand day out."

"Sephie, did you hear that?"

"Very polite."

"I saw a talking ant, Sephie. A talking ant."

"It was a sentient being who resembles an insect that we call an ant."

"I think I know a talking ant when I see one."

"Life is life, no matter what shape it is."

"That's true. It looks like they all get along pretty well. They're not pointing at each other and saying how weird everyone looks. Can you imagine if one of those praying mantises walked through a train station back home?"

"People would be terrified. They're so scared of anything that doesn't look like them. And when they're scared they say mean things. Things that make you wish you were translucent so they couldn't see you."

Odo set his pack down, leaning back against a post. "They're the ones with the problem, Sephie, not you. You're fine. You're more than fine. You're amazing."

"Thanks, Odo."

"I don't see anything that looks a like an information booth."

Sephie glanced up and gave a yelp, grabbing Odo. "Watch out!" Odo looked up, giving a shriek. He was not leaning against a post, he was leaning against the leg of a gigantic black beetle.

"Sorry! I thought your leg was a post. Not that your leg looks like a post, it's just I've never seen a–"

The creature glanced down at Odo, its three red eyes blinking.

"No worries. Safe travels, friend."

Odo grinned at Sephie. "For a giant beetle he seemed really nice."

Sephie pointed. "Look! Over there, a Plindorian! Let's ask him where we're supposed to go."

"Are you sure? Look at the giant suckers on his arms."

Sephie darted through the crowd after the huge yellow octopus, finally catching up with it.

"Excuse me! You're a Plindorian?"

The enormous creature stopped and turned, it's expression grim.

"I'm not looking for trouble. Probably best if we went our separate ways."

"I was wondering if you knew where the big violet cylinder is that goes to Plindor. We have tickets on our travel rings but we don't know where to go."

The Plindorian studied Sephie's face, its eyes pulsing with a curious pale blue light.

"Where are you from?"

124

"I'm from Earth. My name is Sephie and this is my friend Odo. We're both from Earth."

"You were born there?"

"Yes, both of us."

"Curious. Why do you wish to visit Plindor? That seems an unlikely place for a... for a young lady to visit."

"We're trying to find someone, a Plindorian named Advenus Bandiir. He has something we're looking for. We want to buy it from him."

"This is your first time in a transition station?"

"I guess it's pretty obvious we don't have any idea what we're doing."

"Are you hungry? I was just going to grab a bite to eat before I transition. We could have lunch together and chat. My name is Juvo, by the way. "

Odo grinned. "That sounds great, I'm starving. What kind of food do they have here?"

"Anything you want. They have a state of the art CFS."

"What's a CFS?"

"Sorry, a Cerebral Feedback Synthesizer. You tell it what you want and it searches your memories for that particular food, then synthesizes it. It's real time, and none of your memories are recorded."

"It searches my memories? That's creepy."

"Universal Law strictly prohibits duplication or viewing of memories accessed by cerebral feedback devices."

"It's still kind of weird. Will I feel anything?"

"No, it takes two seconds for the scan, another fifteen

seconds or so for the food."

"I don't have much money."

"All the food is included in the price of your transition fee."

Odo grinned at Sephie. "I guess there is such a thing as a free lunch."

Sephie turned to Juvo. "Are there other transition stations besides this one?"

Juvo did a poor job of hiding his smile. "There are millions of them spread across the dimensions, maybe billions. Girard Station is tiny, a little blip of a backwater station."

"Millions of them? That's not possible."

"I don't think anyone has ever tried to count them."

"I used to think I knew a lot about the world."

The Plindorian rested the end of a tentacle on Sephie's shoulder. "You're from Earth, you can't be expected to know these things. It's a most remarkable feat that you found your way to Girard Station. That alone is astonishing and says a great deal about you and your friend Odo."

"Thanks. I feel like a little kid."

"Everyone does. The universe is far too vast and complex for any one being to fully understand it. Here's the food emporium. Just walk up to one of the violet panels and tell it what you want. It has to be something you've had before, so it can find the memory. I always get the vegetable medley."

# Chapter 23

# Lunch with Juvo

Odo watched Juvo order his meal from the CFS.

"He's really nice for a giant yellow octopus."

"You mean a Plindorian."

"Right, a Plindorian. Did you see how he walks on his back two legs and uses the others like arms?"

"Just like you do?"

"I'm not saying he's weird, he's just different from anyone I've ever met. Now, if you'll excuse me, I'm going to walk over there on my hind legs and get some lunch."

Sephie snorted.

Odo approached one of the CFS panels, giving a start when he heard the friendly voice.

"Hi, Odo. What can I get you today?"

"Um… you know my name?"

"I performed a shallow memory scan, just getting to know you a bit. What do you feel like having for lunch today?"

"How about a grilled cheese sandwich, fries, a frosted brownie, and cranberry juice."

"May I search your memory for your favorites?"

"Sure."

"Done. We'll have your meal in thirty seconds. Would you like to listen to your favorite music while you wait? Or maybe answer a few neurophysiology trivia questions?"

"No thanks, I'll just–"

The violet panel rippled, now translucent.

"Your meal is ready, Odo."

Odo's lunch blinked into view behind the panel. He reached through and grabbed the silver tray.

"Enjoy your lunch and have a great day. Say hi to Sephie for me, okay?"

"Right. I'll say hi to Sephie. This looks delicious."

"Thanks, Odo. It was great to meet you. Hope to see you again soon."

"I'm chatting with a food machine."

He turned around, spotting Sephie and Juvo next to an empty table. Juvo took a seat on a wide bench, setting his tray down. Odo grinned. "I don't know how he keeps track of all those arms and legs." He hurried over and sat next to Sephie.

"Is that a tuna sandwich?"

Sephie nodded. "It's the kind my grandma used to make when we would visit. She always packed lunches for our drive home."

"This is the grilled cheese sandwich I get at Madam Beffy's Diner. See how it has the letters MBD toasted into the bread? Oh, the food machine told me to say hi to you."

"It told me to say hi to you too, and it hopes you enjoy your grilled cheese sandwich."

Juvo laughed. "Those food synths are way too chatty for me. Most creatures like it though."

Odo took a bite of his sandwich. "Sooo good, just like Madam Beffy's Diner."

Juvo turned to Sephie with a look of concern.

"Tell me why you're going to Plindor."

"We have to find someone named Advenus Bandiir. He has something we're looking for."

"I won't ask what it is, but I'm glad you stopped me. There are some things you need to know before you go."

"What kind of things?"

"Have you ever heard of the Fortisians?"

"Wikerus Praevian is a Fortisian. We know him. He's helping us."

Juvo was trying to process this new information.

"I see. Does your friend Wikerus have orange hair?"

"No, it's gray. He's old."

"Remember that things are not always as they seem to be in this world. There are beings who can alter their appearance in any way they wish."

"Formshifters. Wikerus told us about them. He said in some worlds we would be able to do it."

"You are translucents?"

"Odo is."

"I see. Sephie, you need to dye your hair black before you go to Plindor."

"Why?"

129

"There is bad blood between Fortisians and Plindorians."

"I'm not a Fortisian, I'm from Earth."

"You still need to do it. All Fortisians have bright orange hair. If the wrong Plindorian were to see your hair, your life would be in jeopardy."

"Just because I have orange hair? That's crazy."

"I am a Plindorian, but was not born there. My great grandparents left Plindor after the Atroxian invasion. Most of the population was wiped out, their technology destroyed. There was anarchy after the war. My great grandparents managed to escape on a Fortisian freighter. They were lucky."

"Why are the Plindorians angry at Fortisians?"

"Imagine you and Odo were walking down the street and a creature jumped out from behind a tree, attacking you. How would you feel if Odo just turned and walked away?"

"He wouldn't do that. Odo's my friend."

"The Plindorians and Fortisians were friends. When the Atroxians invaded Plindor, the Fortisians retreated to their world, doing nothing to help. Plindor was devastated, and is still a very dangerous place. I would strongly advise you not to go there."

Sephie looked at Odo, then back at Juvo.

"We have to go. We don't have a choice. I'm being pulled there."

"By your deeper self?"

"I don't know exactly what it is. It just started happening."

130

Sephie studied Juvo's brainwaves. It was hard to read them, but she thought he wanted to tell her something.

"You want to tell me something, but you're afraid to?"

"You can read brainwaves?"

Sephie nodded.

"That's what I needed to hear. Sephie, you may have been born on Earth, but you're a Fortisian."

# Chapter 24

# Welcome to Plindor

When they had finished their meal Juvo stood up, motioning for Sephie and Odo to follow him.

"We're going to need some help." He scanned the crowded floor, spotting three of the tall white creatures with the bulbous heads. "Follow me."

The white beings stopped, turning toward Juvo as he approached them.

Juvo bowed his head. "Greetings and blessings. This is a moment unlike any other, to be cherished for eternity."

The creatures nodded.

"I need your help."

Three minutes later one of the creatures wrapped its ropey white arm around Sephie's head. An instant later her hair was jet black.

Juvo said, "Your hair will be this color until you return to Earth."

Odo grinned. "You look kind of cool, Sephie."

Sephie watched the curious white creatures disappear into the crowd.

"How do they walk without touching the ground?"

"They are Sinarians, no one understands them. Not a chatty bunch, but their wisdom and kindness is infinite. They are more than remarkable."

Odo said, "When I first saw them I thought they were kind of spooky. To be honest, I was a little scared of you too."

Juvo smiled. "May we never stop learning and growing. Please be careful on Plindor. Watch out for each other. Sephie, keep your powers hidden and trust no one, no matter how friendly they may seem. It is a far different world from the one you are used to."

Odo and Sephie waved to Juvo as he stepped into one of the violet transition cylinders. He tapped his ring and was gone.

"We were lucky to meet him. I'm glad you stopped and asked for his help."

"I was pulled to him. The moment I saw him I knew we had to talk to him."

"Cool power, Encephalo Girl."

"Maybe it isn't. It's the power that's sending us to a scary and dangerous world. I've never done anything this dangerous before."

"Neither have I. Maybe things aren't as bad as Juvo thinks they are. A lot could have changed since the Atroxians invaded Plindor."

"I hope so."

"Juvo said we can use any transition cylinder? Just go in and tap our travel rings on the gold sphere?"

"It's as easy as that."

"I can't believe we're going to Plindor."

"I can't believe Juvo said I'm a Fortisian."

"You might be a Fortisian, but you're still Sephie. That hasn't changed."

"Thanks, Odo Whitley."

"Ready to go?"

Sephie nodded, the two friends stepping into a violet transition cylinder.

A soothing voice greeted them.

"Good afternoon, Sephie Crumb and Odo Whitley. Please touch your travel rings to the gold sphere when you are ready to transition to Plindor. Your current destination is Plindor. Please exit the transition station if Plindor is not your final destination."

Odo took a deep breath. "Let's go on three."

"Okay. One... two... three!"

They tapped their rings on the gold sphere.

Girard Station vanished, replaced by an infinite blackness.

"Sephie? Sephie??"

"I'm here, Odo."

"Why is it so dark? Where are we?"

"Maybe it's nighttime on Plindor."

"I don't see any stars."

"The ground feels flat, like a floor. I think we're inside."

"Hold on."

Odo rummaged around in his pack, feeling for his flashlight. He flicked it on, illuminating their surroundings.

"What is this place?"

The room was a tangled mass of steel beams, shattered concrete, and long shards of violet glass.

"It looks like an old transition station, but the cylinder is smashed to pieces."

"Maybe there was an earthquake or something."

"More likely an Atroxian invasion. This happened a long time ago. Remember how Juvo said the Atroxians destroyed all their technology? The bad news is we can't transition back to Girard Station from here."

"We have our homestones if we need them. We can be back on Earth in two minutes. Let's look around."

Odo shone his light across the room.

"Over there, through that open area behind the metal beam."

They squeezed under an enormous steel girder, clambering over piles of rubble.

Odo stopped. "Did you hear that?"

"Hear what?"

"I thought I heard something."

"Turn off your light."

Sephie scanned the area, searching for electrical fields.

"There's a bunch of small creatures up ahead. A lot of them. Their energy fields are about the same as a small mouse."

"Did you have to say mouse? I don't like mice."

Odo flipped on his light and heard the creatures scatter.

"I guess they're afraid of light."

"That looks like an elevator, but the door is smashed in."

"We must be underground. Maybe we can climb up the elevator shaft."

"Does it go up really high?"

"I'll check."

Odo peered up the open shaft. He could see a glimmer of light thirty feet above him. When he aimed the light down he could not see the bottom of the shaft.

"It's about thirty feet to the top. The cables go all the way up."

"I can do that. Thirty feet is okay."

Odo did not mention the bottomless shaft below them.

"Here we go." He clenched the small flashlight in his teeth and began to climb, Sephie right behind him.

"It's not bad, the cables aren't greasy, they're easy to grip. We should be able to–"

The flashlight slipped from his mouth and tumbled down the shaft.

"I dropped my flashlight!"

Sephie watched it fall. And fall. And fall. Ten seconds later the light blinked off.

"Odo, did you see how far down it fell? The shaft goes way down. Way down."

"Just keep climbing and imagine you're two feet above the floor."

"I feel a little dizzy."

That was the moment Odo heard the scrabbly scratchy sound of uncountable little legs clawing their way up from the darkness below.

"Are you sure those are mice? They don't sound like mice."

Sephie looked down and gave a yelp.

"I can see their brainwaves, there's thousands of them! They're coming up the cables! Odo!!"

"Hurry! Keep climbing!!"

"They're coming too fast! We'll never make it!"

"Do you have a flashlight? They're afraid of light!"

"I didn't bring one."

The creatures were making crunchy snapping noises.

"Try to kick them off the cable!"

Sephie let out an agonized moan. "My head! It hurts! It's happening again!"

Odo could feel the cables vibrating as the horde of creatures scuttled up toward them.

"Sephie! Are you okay?"

A brilliant beam of purple light blasted down toward the mass of creatures. Sephie was enveloped in a violet glow, the powerful beam streaming out from her hand, ten thousand black clawing vicious insect creatures ripped from the cable, tumbling down into the darkness.

Odo gaped at Sephie.

"What did you do??"

"I don't know. It was like the darts at Lost Lake except way stronger. I don't know what's happening to me."

"The darts at Lost Lake? What do you mean?"

"Nothing, I'll tell you later. Keep climbing before those things come back."

"We're almost there."

Two minutes later they swung off the cable onto a small landing illuminated by light from a narrow vertical crack.

"It's a door!"

Odo scrambled over and forced it open, the platform flooded with daylight.

"Stairs!"

The two exhausted friends scrambled up the long staircase, stepping into the crumbling foyer of a devastated building.

"Whoa, look at this place. That whole wall is gone, completely destroyed. It looks like it used to be a big hotel or something."

"That ceiling looks unstable. We should keep moving."

They climbed over the piles of rubble, down a grand curving staircase, and across a shattered marble floor. The entrance to the once magnificent building was gone, leaving massive chunks of white marble covered with gritty yellow sand.

The two adventurers stepped out into the blazing Plindorian sunlight, Odo shielding his eyes from the blinding glare.

"This is bad. Really bad."

# Chapter 25

# The Magician

Sephie scanned their blistering sunbaked surroundings.

"We're in the middle of a desert. And it goes on forever."

Sephie squinted in the blazing sunlight.

"It's so hot. Just a few spiky plants and flat sandy ground. This wind is awful, like a giant hair dryer blasting me."

"Why would they put a big hotel in the middle of a desert? It makes no sense."

"Maybe they lived underground. You saw how far down the elevator shaft went."

"It's possible. Juvo didn't mention anything about that."

Sephie pulled a pair of binoculars from her pack, studying the horizon.

"We might be in luck, Odo Whitley. I think I see a city. Or maybe it's a forest. It could be a mountain range."

"Are you being pulled toward it?"

"We should start walking."

"We can't walk across a scorching hot desert without water. We'll die of thirst if this crazy wind doesn't kill us first."

"We should go anyway."

"You're sure?"

"I'm sure. The feeling is getting stronger."

Odo pulled two shirts from his pack, tossing one to Sephie. "Put this over your head to block the sun and the blowing sand."

The two adventurers set off on their trek across the burning sands of Plindor, the wind howling around them.

"How are we going to find Advenus Bandiir?"

"I don't know how, but we will. Something is telling me to keep going."

Odo tried to look optimistic. Two hours later he was parched, but he said nothing to Sephie. The wind was getting worse.

It was a curious rumbling sound that caused Odo and Sephie to turn around. Odo froze when he saw them, an astonishing, terrifying, and yet strangely familiar sight. Three gigantic six-wheeled sailing trucks were streaking across the desert toward them.

"Sailing trucks like the one Wikerus gave me! How weird is that?"

"They might be bandits. We should hide!"

"We're in the middle of a desert, where are we going to hide? Maybe they're friendly."

Odo waved his shirt at the rapidly approaching

sailing trucks. He spotted a huge yellow Plindorian on the bow of the nearest ship.

"They're not slowing down!"

One of the ships veered toward them.

Odo and Sephie didn't see the long wooden pole flip down from the deck of the sailing truck, or the enormous net on the end of it. Before they knew what was happening they were yanked from the desert floor forty feet into the air.

Odo was hanging upside down, tangled up with Sephie in the coarse netting. He gave a shriek when he saw the desert floor shooting past beneath him.

"Sephie, are you all right?"

"I'm okay! This is good, Odo Whitley, this is where we're supposed to be!"

"We're supposed to be dangling upside down in a net, screaming across a desert at fifty miles an hour?"

Sephie watched three Plindorians maneuver the pole back toward the ship. The two friends landed on the deck with a dull thud. One of the Plindorians released the net, eyeing their catch.

"What are they?"

"They look like Fortisians but they don't have orange hair. I don't know what they are."

Odo gave his friendliest smile.

"We're from Earth. We're looking for someone. I like your sailing truck. I used have a toy one when I was little. Are you pirates?"

A powerful suckered arm lashed out, knocking Odo across the deck into a cabin wall.

"Silence! One more word and it's the noggle box. It takes them a week to finish you. They start with your feet."

Odo was dazed from the blow, having trouble focusing on the huge Plindorian, but he was aware enough to know being fed to noggles was something he wanted to avoid.

The two Plindorians studied him. "Never seen clothes like that. Maybe these two are valuable, worth a good ransom."

"They don't look like much. Throw them down below, pedal till they die."

"We should tell the Magician. He'll know what they are. They could be worth something."

"He gives me the creeps. They should have left him in the desert to die."

"Talk like that will get you put in the noggle box."

"Do whatever you want. It's a waste of time, scrawny little beggars won't last a week down below."

Odo's mind was racing. He knew two things; he wanted nothing to do with noggles, and they needed to get off this ship. He scanned the deck, watching the Plindorian sailors work the rigging. The ship was enormous, two hundred feet long, with three masts. The other two ships were smaller, with two masts. The wind was howling, the three ships thundering across the hard packed desert sands at over fifty miles an hour. The crew looked like a rough bunch, most had scars and carried an odd assortment of daggers and old fashioned flintlock pistols strapped to their arms. Odo thought about grabbing Sephie and jumping off the ship, but a forty foot fall at fifty miles an hour would kill them both.

He looked at Sephie, attempting to smile at her thumbs up sign. He wanted to trust her deeper feelings about where they were supposed to be, but this felt very wrong. Their captors could be vicious pirates or bloodthirsty bandits. Juvo said there were a lot of bandits on Plindor.

When the Magician stepped out from his cabin, Odo's heart sank to a place it had never been before, even in his darkest moments. He knew evil when he saw it, and this was a darkly evil and sinister creature, far different from the Plindorians. Its form was basically human, but with mottled dark blue skin, peppered with thousands of tiny yellow bumpy protrusions. Black matted and tangled hair fell to his shoulders from beneath a pointed maroon hat, his body concealed by a heavy purple cape covered with indecipherable blue symbols. What frightened Odo most of all were his pale yellow watery eyes, eerily distant, as though he was watching the world from some faraway realm.

The Magician ambled slowly across the deck with a strange awkward shuffling gait, sailors jumping out of his path, clearly disturbed by his presence. A deep and profound fear took control of Odo's body. He managed to turn his head toward Sephie. He knew she was studying the Magician's brainwaves. Her face was grim and pale.

The Magician stood seven feet tall, but when he stared down at Odo with his pale yellow vacant eyes, he seemed twenty feet tall. He was silent, his cold distant eyes moving slowly across Odo. Without a word he turned, shuffling toward Sephie. The sailors stood motionless, the only sounds being the howling wind and snapping canvas sails.

The Magician stood over Sephie, his breathing raspy and low. He raised one arm, a sleeve sliding back to reveal a seven fingered blue hand with short yellow claws. He drew three invisible symbols, a pale cloud of blue light enveloping Sephie.

Odo felt sick. If the Magician discovered Sephie was a Fortisian, he would kill her.

Without thinking, Odo cried out, "Wait!"

There were muffled gasps from the sailors. The Magician turned slowly toward him, his head tilting, studying Odo like a peculiar little insect that had scurried out from a rotten log. He extended one arm, his thumb pointing downward.

Two burly sailors grabbed Odo, dragging him across the deck to an open hatchway, a crude wooden ladder descending into the shadowy bowels of the ship.

One of the Plindorians gave a nervous laugh.

"Welcome aboard the *Canthus*, boy. Today's your lucky day. You could be screaming in the noggle box, now you just pedal till you die. He shoved Odo roughly toward the ladder.

"Down the hatch, boy. Best not to think about what the Magician is going to do with your little friend.

She's small, it will only take the noggles four or five days to finish her."

Odo climbed partway down the ladder, crying out to Sephie as the heavy hatch door slammed down above his head.

# Chapter 26

# The Question

"Odo! Odo!!"

Sephie tried to run for the hatch but found she could not, the cause of her immobility being a heavy rope which appeared in a flash of blue light, binding her ankles tightly. The Magician flicked his wrist again, ropes binding her arms. A murmur ran through the Plindorian sailors. The crew of the *Canthus* was a superstitious lot, and dark magic did not sit well with them. A number of them backed away, unnerved by what they had witnessed.

The Magician grabbed Sephie's face with a clawed hand, twisting it toward him, looking into her eyes.

"You will obey, girl." It was not a question, it was a command, low and ominous, the deadly rumblings of a wolf before it attacks.

Sephie nodded mutely. She didn't want anything to happen to Odo.

"Come."

The ropes vanished. Sephie followed the Magician across the rough wooden deck to a large windowless cabin. A murmur ran through the crowd of sailors. Sephie heard the word *noggles* more than once.

The cabin door swung open of its own accord. They stepped inside and it slammed shut, the lock clicking. A few sailors stood outside, waiting for the screams.

The Magician had once told them the noggles were his demon children, that he had taught them well, taught them to take small bites, chew slowly and thoroughly. One sailor had leaped to his death when the Magician threatened to put him in the noggle box.

The interior of the cabin was not what Sephie had been expecting. There were no skeletons chained to the wall, no vile venomous serpents slithering about, flicking their black tongues, no vats of bubbling potions spewing out noxious fumes. To her surprise, it was filled with opulent furniture and luxurious hand woven rugs. More surprising was the seven foot long heavily reinforced black iron box sitting in the center of the room, its lid secured with half a dozen stout metal chains and great iron padlocks.

The Magician pointed to the box. His voice was low and malevolent, a paralyzing chill rolling through Sephie.

"There be noggles, girl."

The color drained from Sephie's face.

"Please don't. Please."

"Silence."

The Magician pointed to an elegant stuffed chair in

the corner of the room.

"Sit."

Sephie sat in the chair, her eyes frozen on the noggle box.

The Magician stepped over to a heavy mahogany bookcase filled with dusty volumes, their titles formed from incomprehensible symbols.

He tapped one yellow claw against a glittering crystal vase sitting on the top of the bookshelf.

"This vase is worth the treasures of a thousand worlds. If any harm befalls it, your life and the life of your friend shall be held forfeit."

Sephie was having a hard time breathing.

As the Magician turned, his sleeve caught on the vase, pulling it off the shelf. Time slowed to a crawl as Sephie watched it tumble end over end toward the floor. Before she realized what she was doing, a beam of blue light flashed out from her hand. The vase stopped, floating harmlessly six inches above the floor.

The Magician flicked his wrist and the vase vanished.

"That was easier than I thought it would be, Fortisian."

"I'm not Fortisian. I was born on Earth."

"Sad child, I could feel your pitiful attempt to read my brainwaves."

Sephie's jaw tightened.

The Magician gave a mocking smile.

"Because I hold such great fondness for Fortisians, I will grant you one favor. If you can answer a simple question, I will spare your life and the life of your little translucent friend."

"How did you know he–" Sephie stopped in mid sentence. She was no match for the Magician.

"You will agree to answer my question?"

"I have a choice?"

"You always have a choice, girl. You may answer the question, or you may witness your friend being devoured by noggles. That is your choice. An incorrect answer will likewise result in your friend being eaten by noggles. You may take as much time as you wish to compose your answer, but any longer than five minutes, and your friend will be… well, I don't suppose there's any need to say it again."

Sephie felt a deep burning rage building inside her, her eyes narrowing. She did not like this evil creature. "Your demented games make me sick."

"Excellent. Let us begin." He stepped over to the enormous iron box, flicking his wrist. One by one the massive iron padlocks vanished.

"What are you doing?"

He flicked his wrist again and the heavy chains were gone. Three great iron latches fell open.

"Before you answer my question, I would ask you to think carefully. Be aware that a perfunctory, shallow answer will result in a painful and prolonged death for your friend. Seek assistance from your deeper self."

Sephie glared with dark fury at the Magician. What would a despicable evil creature like this know about deeper selves?

"Approach the box, girl."

Sephie rose from her chair and stepped over to the Magician.

"My question is a simple one. What is in the box?"

With one fluid motion the Magician raised the heavy lid.

# Chapter 27

# Aisle Seat

Fortunately, Odo had not heard Sephie's desperate cry as he climbed down the wooden ladder. He could barely see, the only illumination being a few flickering oil lanterns dangling from the central beam of the ship. A scaly blue creature with four arms stepped out of the shadows, a disgusted look on its face.

"This is what they give us? Sad. Section two, seat eleven."

"What am I supposed to do?"

"Simple enough, even for worm food like you. When the wind stops, you pedal. When the wind blows, you rest. We stop when the sun goes down and everyone gets a pillow to sleep on."

"Oh, that's not so bad."

The creature let out a shrieking laugh. "The sun never sets on Plindor, worm food! You really are a nimmy."

"Right, a nimmy. Where is section two?"

"Section one, fore axle. Section two, mid axle. Section three, aft axle. Twenty rows in each section. Go. Now."

Odo headed down the narrow center aisle, glancing at the assortment of shadowy creatures, most of them leaning back in their wooden seats, eyes closed.

"The wind must be blowing. Okay, section one ends here, next section is mine, mid axle."

Another forty feet and he was in section two. A tall furry creature with a bear like face was staring at him.

"Um... section two, seat eleven?"

"Third row, right side, aisle seat."

Odo nodded. "Thanks."

The bear creature leaned back and closed its eyes.

Odo stuffed his pack under the seat, eyeing the large wooden pedals in front of him.

"This is like one of those sit down bicycles. No chain and sprocket system though, just wooden gears and belts. Not very efficient."

He took a seat, glancing at the creature next to him, a large praying mantis who appeared to be sleeping.

"Looks like they have different sizes of seats and pedals for different creatures. A little padding would be nice. This seat is kind of hard."

A dreadful ache washed through him when he let himself think about Sephie and the evil Magician. He tried to convince himself she would be all right.

"She's really smart and has those powers. Maybe she'll read his brainwaves and trick him into letting us both go."

He gave a long sigh. This was very bad, definitely not where they were supposed to be.

His eyes were drooping when the bell clanged, a voice from the front of the ship roaring out, "PEDAL!! PEDAL!! PEDAL!!"

Odo groaned, placing his feet on the two heavy wooden pedal blocks, pushing one, then the other.

"This is harder than I thought it would be. That praying mantis is pedaling twice as fast as I am."

The huge orange insect was watching Odo.

"Pace yourself, friend. It will take time to gain the strength you need."

"Thanks. My name is Odo."

"I am Volu. We are fed every eight hours. It is dreadful food, but nutritious. Sleep when you can. There is a latrine between sections two and three. You are free to walk around when the wind is blowing."

"Okay, thanks." Odo's legs were already burning.

* * * *

Sephie blinked when the Magician opened the box, trying to make sense of what she was seeing. There were no noggles in the box, it was completely empty. She remembered the Magician's warning about a hasty and simplistic answer. She would not state the obvious, that the box was empty.

"You have five minutes, Fortisian."

Sephie studied the great iron box. There were supposed to be horrific flesh eating noggles in it, but it was

153

empty. The box was empty. There were no noggles, and yet the Plindorians were terrified of them, choosing death as an escape from the horrific creatures.

She closed her eyes. "Deeper self, please help me. What is in the empty box?"

She waited patiently, trying to relax. Two minutes passed before she heard the soft voice. It was her own voice, but it came from far away.

"The box is not empty. You know this."

"What is in it?"

"Think. What does the box do? What would cause such a thing?"

The clouds vanished, a radiant sun appearing in her mind. She knew what was in the box.

A cold smile flickered across the Magician's face. "Yes?"

"Fear. Fear is in the box."

"Congratulations, Fortisian, you have saved your life and the life of your friend. I will make certain no harm comes to him. After a great deal of training you will become my assistant. You are Fortisian, but lack even the most rudimentary skills. I will teach you all that I can in the time that we have."

"Why would you choose me? I'm nothing like you."

"Sit at the table, Fortisian. Let us begin."

# Chapter 28

# The Red Ball

The Magician flicked his wrist and a red ball appeared in front of Sephie.

"What do you see, girl?"

"A red ball."

"How are you seeing it?"

"I don't understand."

"What is the physiological process which allows you to see the red ball?"

"I've studied that. Light bounces off the red ball and goes into my eyes through the cornea, pupil, and the lens. The lens focuses the image on my retina, and my optic nerve carries signals to my visual cortex, the part of my brain that creates images in my mind."

"Excellent. Now look at the ball."

The ball was bright green.

"How did you do that? How did you change the color of the ball?"

"I did not change the color of the ball, I changed the color of the image being produced by your visual cortex. The ball itself has not changed, only your perception of it."

"You can make me see things that aren't there?"

"Watch the ball, tell me what you see."

Sephie watched the green ball transform to a small yellow bird, then to a glass of water, and finally to a crystal vase, the same one which had tumbled off the bookshelf.

Sephie shook her head. "It's not possible."

"Pick up the vase."

When she tried to grab the vase her hand passed through it.

The Magician smiled. "There never was a red ball. It was all in your mind."

"You can make people see whatever you want them to."

"Child's play compared to what a highly skilled Fortisian can do."

The magician flicked his wrist and the red ball appeared on the table. "Pick up the ball."

"It's not there, it's only a thought."

"Pick up the ball."

Sephie reached out and picked it up.

"It's real. I don't understand."

"I will reveal to you a grand and simple truth. The universe is composed of two things, and two things only; energy and mind. Physical matter is made of compressed energy, and mind is consciousness, mind is life. Your deeper self is mind, Fortisian, and it is far more powerful than you can fathom. When I created the illusion of the red ball I was manipulating energy in your visual cortex. When I created the ball you now hold, the process was more complex, but still founded in the manipulation of energy. I used my mind, my deeper self, to compress energy into matter, in this case, the red ball."

Sephie studied the pale yellow watery eyes of the Magician. She laughed when she heard the words from her deeper self. She knew what the Magician was.

"You're a Fortisian. The Plindorians would kill you if I told them." She instantly regretted threatening him.

"Mind yourself, girl, there are far worse things in this world than noggles. Close your eyes and imagine a red ball. When you see it clearly, turn it slowly until it becomes sharp and focused, solid. Take that clear thought and send it to my visual cortex."

Sephie closed her eyes, imagining a red ball.

Over the next three months Sephie trained eight hours a day under the strict tutelage of the Magician. She was a quick learner and highly motivated. When her powers were strong enough, she and Odo would use them to make their escape.

The Magician arranged for Odo to visit Sephie every few days for an hour, leaving them alone in the cabin to talk.

"You can make people see things that aren't there?"

"He's teaching me how to do it. I had to make a Plindorian chase a thought chicken around the *Canthus*. It was kind of funny but I felt a little bad for tricking him. The Plindorians are a little rough around the edges, but they're pretty nice once you get to know them. They're not pirates or bandits, they're nomads. The landsailers are their home."

"Volu is nice too. He's the praying mantis who sits next to me. They call him Volu because he's a Volucrian but no one can pronounce his real name. It sounds like a squeaky door when he says it. He talks a lot about his world, it's really interesting. He was kidnapped by Atroxians and managed to escape, then got captured again and sold to the *Canthus*."

"Odo Whitley, what do you miss most about home?"

"I don't know, the food I guess. You can't believe what we have to eat. It's like gray oatmeal pudding with crunchy black things in it. I don't even want to know what they are. So bad. I guess it's nutritious though. I haven't lost any weight and I'm getting really strong. I can pedal for hours now and not even feel it. I chat with Volu while we're pedaling."

Sephie flicked her wrist and two boxes of Proto's Taste-E Kakes appeared on the table in front of Odo.

"Whoa!! Are those just in my mind?"

"Pick one up."

Odo grabbed one of the boxes. "They're real! How did you do that?"

The Magician calls it shaping. I use my mind to manipulate energy, compressing it into physical objects. He calls them thought forms."

"Is he totally evil and scary, some kind of creepy alien?"

"I don't think he's anything like that. Don't tell anyone, but I think he's a Fortisian. He's either a

158

formshifter or he's manipulating everyone's thoughts so they see the scary blue lizard creature."

"What do you think he really looks like?"

Sephie shook her head. "I don't know. He has total control over his brainwaves. When I look at his head everything is a big soft blur. He does it on purpose."

"I wonder why he's here? He could escape any time he wanted to."

"I don't know. He doesn't tell me much. He won't even admit he's a Fortisian."

"Have you thought any more about... you know what?"

She leaned across the table, whispering, "I think I'll be ready in another month. The Magician says he has a few more things to teach me before I become his assistant. He said they're important. Once I learn those we can escape."

"I'm so ready to go. The pedaling isn't as bad as I thought it would be, but it's still pretty hard. Volu said this is a windy time of year so we get a lot of breaks. He said summers are the worst, almost no wind. We're supposed to stop at some secret place in a month or so and dig up a weird mineral called duplonium. They trade it for supplies in the cities. Volu said it's used to power big steam engines."

"We'll be gone before then, I promise."

# Chapter 29

# A Glass of Water

"I'm thirsty, Fortisian. Walk to the end of the board, pick up the glass of water and bring it to me."

Sephie stared at the ten inch wide board running the length of the cabin.

"Why?"

"Walk the board, get the glass of water, bring it to me."

Sephie shrugged, strolling down the board and picking up the glass. It didn't seem like much of a lesson. She walked back along the board and handed him the glass.

The Magician frowned. "This isn't the glass I wanted, girl. I want the other one."

Sephie turned to see a second glass of water sitting at the end of the board.

"Walk the board, get the glass of water, bring it back to me."

Sephie tried not to roll her eyes.

Unfortunately, the moment she stepped back on the board was the moment the cabin vanished, Sephie finding herself standing on a ten inch wide board two hundred feet in the air, the ground below her a jumble of deadly jagged rocks.

She gave a weak moan and sank to her knees, afraid she was going to faint. She managed to lie down, pressing her face against the board.

"Please... make it stop. Please, I'm begging you."

"What was in the box?"

Sephie turned her head slightly. The Magician was standing on the board in front of her.

"Fear was in the box."

"When the board was on the ground you strolled right down and got the glass of water. What has changed?"

Sephie could scarcely breathe, her eyes on the jagged rocks far below. "Fear. You knew I was afraid of heights."

"Watch, please." The Magician stepped off the board, standing in mid air next to it.

"How are you doing that?"

"Reach out, touch the air."

Sephie pressed her hand against it. "It's solid. We're not up in the air."

"Stand up, walk the board, get the glass of water."

Sephie stood up. She gingerly tapped the air next to the board with her toe. It was solid. She returned with the glass of water.

"Again."

Fifteen times Sephie walked up and down the board in the sky, each time returning with a glass of water.

161

The sky vanished, the cabin floor returned.

"Sit, girl."

Sephie took a seat at the table.

"The last five times you walked the board, the floor was not there. You were two hundred feet above the jagged rocks. If you had fallen, you would have died instantly."

Sephie's eyes were wide, her mind racing. "Fear was in the box."

"Yes. Most creatures are controlled by their fears, not by reality. Remember this the next time you find yourself staring into a deep and unfathomable abyss of any kind."

Sephie nodded. "I will."

"There is one final lesson, my gift to you."

"What is it?"

"You will see the world through my eyes. You will see what I see."

"Why?"

"Are you ready?"

"I guess so."

Sephie gave a shriek when she found herself on the other side of the room watching herself sitting at the table.

"What's happening?"

"You are seeing what I see. I am watching you, looking at you. This will be tricky, but I want you to stand up and walk around the room. Pick something up, turn toward me and smile."

"How do I..." Sephie watched herself rise awkwardly from the chair. She turned the wrong way, stumbling into the table. "This is hard, everything is backwards." She started laughing when she collided with the chair. There was something really funny about this.

"What do you see? Describe yourself to me."

"It looks like someone else, but it's me. It's so strange, not at all like looking in a mirror. My hair is black. Odo was right, it is sort of cool. I'm a little short, but just a little. I have a nice smile, a nice laugh, a friendly face. If I was walking down the hall at school and saw me, I'd want to make friends with me. I don't walk funny, it's just a normal walk. I look like a normal girl. I don't look creepy at all. Not even a little. I'm not Creepy Crumb. I never was."

Sephie found herself seated at the table again.

"Do you understand the gift?"

Sephie nodded, fighting back tears.

"I never wanted people to look at me, to see me, to see who I really was."

"And now?"

"I'm not afraid. The box is empty."

The Magician sat down at the table, his pale yellow eyes on Sephie.

"That was your last lesson."

"I'm your assistant now?"

"No, you're not going to be my assistant."

"Why not? Did I do something wrong?"

"You never were going to be my assistant."

"I don't understand."

"You have wondered why I arrived at this place,

why I stay. The answer is simple, I was waiting for someone. I didn't know who until you and Odo arrived. You may tell your translucent friend we will be leaving in two days. I will accompany you. I am supposed to help you find what you are searching for."

# Chapter 30

# Escape

Sephie leaped up from her chair when she heard the screams outside the cabin, the deck shaking as sailors thundered past, heading toward the stern of the ship. The Magician swung the door open and peered inside.

"Time to go! Grab your pack! Your friend is waiting for us."

"What's happening? Are we being attacked?"

"Hurry!!"

She slung on her backpack and darted outside. Dozens of sailors were racing wildly across the stern of the ship, screaming to each other, waving daggers, stabbing into the air.

"What are they doing?"

"They're fighting off a horde of terrifying bat creatures which exist only in their minds."

Sephie grinned. "That's kind of clever."

"Follow me! Hurry!"

The Magician's awkward shuffling gait was gone.

He raced toward the bow of the ship. Sephie spotted Odo pulling a heavy rope through a series of large pulleys.

"What's Odo doing?"

"Lowering the longboat."

Sephie called out to Odo as she raced toward him. "Odo!! We're here!

"It's ready to go! Jump in!"

She peered over the rail at a single masted longboat hanging from four ropes. She grabbed one of the ropes, sliding down into the craft.

Odo and the Magician climbed down after her. The wind was howling, the sand stinging Odo's face. He released the hawser line and the craft dropped, its wheels thudding onto the hard packed desert floor.

The Magician bellowed out commands. "Sephie, grab the tiller! Odo, help me raise the main!"

Odo and the Magician hauled the sail up and tied it off, the canvas billowing out, snapping taut in the pounding wind. The little ship leaped forward. Sephie jammed the tiller to the right, veering them away from the *Canthus*.

"She's way faster than the big ships! They'll never catch us!"

The Magician turned, watching as they pulled away from the three landsailers. He drew a symbol in the air with his hand. "The bat creatures are no more."

An hour later the three landsailers were specks on the horizon. Sephie was gripping the tiller with both hands as they raced across the desert at almost sixty miles an hour, the wind roaring in their ears.

Odo shouted, "This is incredible! We're free!!"

Sephie grinned. He was right, this was a moment to remember.

The Magician pointed to a massive outcropping of green rock in the distance. "Head for that outcropping, we can hide there. It's time we had a talk."

"Take us in over there!"

Despite the powerful wind, Sephie managed to maneuver the heavy longboat into a narrow hidden cave.

Odo hopped out of the ship. "This is perfect, they can't see us in here. What kind of rock is this?"

Sephie picked up a chunk of the lustrous green stone. "It looks like jade. It's beautiful."

"Whoa, can you imagine how much it's worth? We should take some back to—"

The Magician scowled. "We are not treasure hunters. I need to know why you are here."

He flicked his wrist and three wooden chairs appeared. He flicked it again and there was a roaring campfire in the center of the cave.

Odo's jaw dropped. "Whoa, that's amazing!"

The Magician slumped into a chair, motioning for Odo and Sephie to do the same.

"Speak."

Sephie glanced at Odo, then began the story of how and why they had come to be in Plindor. She left out nothing, telling the Magician about Wikerus Praevian, their trip to Pacalia, Girard Station, the Atroxians, the doll with red and white striped legs, the antique dealer, and their quest to find Advenus Bandiir, the man who had purchased the doll.

When she finished, the Magician folded his hands together, deep in thought. Finally he spoke.

"You're certain Wikerus Praevian is a Fortisian?"

"Yes, I trust him. He knows more than he told us, but I trust him. His brainwaves showed sincerity."

"You have no idea where the doll came from?"

"It was lying next to me in the snow when my adopted parents found me. They sold it to the antique dealer."

"Your deeper self is pulling you toward the doll? The pull is strong?"

"It is. I know am supposed to find it, but I don't know how to find Advenus Bandiir."

"That is where I will be able to help you. By tradition, the second name of a Plindorian is the name of the village where they live. Advenus lives in a village called Bandiir. That much I know for certain."

He studied Sephie and Odo's faces. Odo shivered. It felt like ants were walking around inside his brain. Finally the strange feeling stopped.

"As you suspected, I am not what I appear to be. I can locate Bandiir, but in doing so I will be forced to revert to my true form. It could prove to be… most unsettling."

Sephie nodded, her face grim. Odo gulped. What could possibly be more unsettling than a seven foot tall blue lizard creature with big watery yellow eyes and a long purple cape?

"Okay."

"So it shall be." The Magician raised one hand, moving it rapidly, drawing a symbol in the air. There was a brilliant flash of green light.

Odo's jaw dropped. "No way."

Sephie gaped at the chair where the Magician had been sitting. "No. Way."

Sitting in the chair was a young girl with bright orange hair, an enormous grin on her face.

# Chapter 31

# Cyra

"I'm Cyra. It's nice to meet you."

Odo and Sephie stared at the orange haired girl.

"You're a little girl."

"I'm not little, I'm ten and a half years old."

"How could you... all those powers... you were so scary, so evil, those big creepy yellow eyes."

"I got the idea for the Magician from a scary book I read. It seemed like a good way to keep the Plindorians from clobbering me. I'm not allowed to harm living creatures, so I had to find other ways to protect myself while I was waiting for you."

"How could you possibly be so powerful when you're so young?"

"All the kids on Fortisia can do the stuff I do. We start our training when we're two years old." She raised one hand, drawing an invisible symbol. There was a blinding flash of lightning outside the cave followed by an earsplitting crash of thunder that rolled across the desert.

Odo was stunned. "Whoa. Did you just... that lightning?"

"It's not that hard, just manipulating a lot of energy at once. My mom used to say I show off too much."

Sephie felt a wave of sadness roll through her.

"She used to say it?"

"My mom and dad are gone. Our ship crashed. That's how I got here. We were trying to get back to Fortisia before they powered up the spectral moat, but the Atroxians spotted us. Plindor was the closest planet, but they hit us with a pulse beam as we entered the atmosphere. It killed my mom and dad instantly. I managed to get into an escape pod. That's how I survived."

"I'm so sorry."

"It was two years ago. A Plindorian family found me and took me in even though I was a Fortisian. I stayed with them until my deeper self told me to find the *Canthus*, to wait for someone there. You don't know who your birth parents are?"

Sephie shook her head. "I have no memories of them, just a vague feeling of someone giving me the doll."

"Only one of your parents was Fortisian. Your dad was Fortisian, but your mom was from Earth. Your powers aren't as strong as a full blooded Fortisian's would be."

"How do you know about my parents?"

"I did a deep scan of your physiology and neurology back on the *Canthus*. There's no doubt your dad was Fortisian and your mom a human. It's all there in your genome."

"Are you sure you're only ten years old?"

"Ten and a half years old."

"This is a lot to think about. My dad was a Fortisian. What could he have been doing on Earth?"

"We used to travel everywhere before the invasions. It was easy to change our form, blend in with other species on other worlds. We studied them, learned about their history and culture."

"You said something about powering up a spectral moat? What is that?"

"It's technical, and I don't understand a lot of it, but the moat creates an artificial spectral barrier around the planet, a spherical gap in the universe. Nothing can get through because there's nothing there to get through. It's like trying to break a glass that's not there. You can't do it."

"That's kind of spooky."

"It's just deep physics. But it also means I can't go home. The only way to get through the moat is to shift there with a secure homestone, and they collected them all before powering up the moat. We'd been fighting off Atroxian invasions for almost a hundred years. We're safe now, but we're also prisoners of our own world."

"How are you going to find Bandiir?"

Cyra slipped off her backpack, rummaging around inside it, pulling out a shiny green metallic cube. "This is an IMS, Interdimensional Mapping System."

She tapped a small violet button on the side of the disc and a translucent three dimensional holo map

172

popped up around her.

She pointed to a small red dot. "We're here. I'll zoom in to show Plindor."

"Whoa, that's amazing."

"This brown area is all desert. Half the surface of Plindor is desert, always in sunlight. The other half is dark and frozen. The family I lived with said nothing lives there. Well, nothing you'd ever want to meet."

She squeezed the violet tab, holding it down.

"Searching for Bandiir on Plindor."

The map whirled quickly, a bright blue dot appearing.

"That's it. Bandiir is in the borderlands, the area between the light and dark sides of Plindor. It's not so hot there, more like your world. They have rivers and lakes, lots of water."

"How far is it?"

"We head east for two thousand three hundred and eighteen miles."

Odo glanced at Sephie. "That seems really far."

"It won't be so bad." Cyra pulled an iridescent blue sphere from her pack. "This will help. It's a MAMPS, a Micro Antigrav Multidirectional Propulsion Sphere."

"A what?"

"Hop in the ship and I'll show you."

The three adventurers climbed into the longboat. Odo's eyes were on the blue sphere. "What does it do, exactly?"

Cyra gingerly twisted the top of the sphere. "Not too much, we don't want to wind up in dark space." She grinned at Odo.

Odo did not like the idea of being in dark space.

The longboat began rocking gently.

"What's happening?"

Cyra adjusted the sphere.

Odo gave a yelp. "We're floating!"

"It's a mini anti-gravity device. Comes in very handy. My dad gave it to me for my seventh birthday. It's multidirectional, which means I can control the pull of gravity. The ship is actually falling, but I can make it fall in any direction I want."

Odo was gripping the side of the little boat, the ground now ten feet below them. "You're saying we can fly? Anywhere we want?"

"That's pretty much it. Ready?"

A huge grin appeared on Odo's face.

"Ready!!"

# Chapter 32

# Help From Above

Cyra was attempting to maneuver the landsailer out of the narrow cave. "Kind of tricky in tight spaces, it's a no frills MAMPS. Use that pole to steer us."

Odo grabbed a long wooden pole from the boat to guide the ship along the rocky cave.

"That's it! We're out!"

Cyra pointed across the vast desert. "That's east. I'm going to keep us low, you never know what might be flying around. The Atroxian invasion was a long time ago, but they still send out raiding parties from time to time, mostly slave traders. We definitely don't want them to find us. They have some very dangerous weapons."

"Slave traders?"

"They kidnap Plindorians, sell them as slaves on Atroxia."

"That's horrible."

Cyra shrugged. "It's nothing compared to the other things they do. That's why we built the spectral mote. The Atroxians are pure evil."

"Why do they keep trying to invade Fortisia when there's so many other worlds they could attack?"

Cyra looked puzzled. "Your friend Wikerus didn't tell you about the Glow?"

"The Glow? What's that?"

"It's what the Atroxians want. It's a natural resource, but it's alive."

"I don't understand. What is it?"

"It's hard to explain because there's nothing like it anywhere else. It's everywhere on Fortisia, like dust in the air, but it's alive and has a blue glow. We have no idea where it came from. My teachers said it's halfway between a physical life form and pure life force. Sometimes it's energy and sometimes it looks like glowing dust. If you touch it, it becomes energy. You can't grab it, or put it in a bottle. It's in all the creatures on the planet, and it's what caused us to evolve the way we did. It's why we have these powers.

"The Atroxians know about it, and they want it. The problem is they can't steal it or take it with them. Their solution is to kill everyone on the planet and move in."

"We've seen four Atroxians, three of them on Pacalia. They didn't have any brainwaves. I thought they were dead at first."

"They're not like us, they don't have their own brain. They're a little like insects, with a central brain that controls the members of the hive. There can be thousands of Atroxians in one hive. The hive that's invading all the different worlds has millions of members, most likely the biggest hive on Atroxia."

"I can't imagine not being able to do my own thinking. That would be horrible."

"I agree. Okay, let's get moving."

Cyra twisted the dial on the MAMPS and the little craft shot forward across the desert.

Odo sat at the bow, the whistling wind blowing through his hair.

"Whoo hoo! This is fun! Can you take us up higher?"

"Just a little higher, I don't want anyone to see us. Besides the Atroxians, there are pirates and bandits. There was a lot of talk on the *Canthus* about pirates. Their weapons are primitive, but we still need to keep our eyes open. We're not exactly riding in a shielded interstellar battlecruiser."

Cyra reached into her pack and pulled out a pair of dark green sunglasses, handing them to Odo. "Put these on."

"Thanks, the sun is kind of bright. Plus they make me look cool." He grinned at Sephie.

"That's not what they're for. Turn the silver dial on the left side."

"Whoa! They're like binoculars. This is amazing, they're really powerful. I just saw a little critter running along the sand next to a tall spiky plant at least a mile away."

"Keep an eye out for landsailers. We don't want any surprises."

Sephie watched Cyra as she guided the ship across the desert, adjusting the MAMPS to keep them on course. She looked too young to be on her own in a world filled with pirates and bandits and slave traders. She might be powerful, but underneath it all she was a young girl.

"Cyra, what will you do after we find the doll? Where will you go?"

"I don't know. I could go back and stay with that Plindorian family. They were nice to me."

"I was thinking you could come back to Earth, stay with my family. My parents would love to have you. They're always saying they wish I had a sister."

"Nothing against Earth, but it's a bit primitive."

"I know, but it's still a nice place to live. It can be really beautiful. Lots of green trees and flowers and rivers. Don't you get lonely here?"

"I miss my mom and dad. Sometimes I can't think of anything else. Mostly when I'm trying to sleep. I imagine my mom kissing me good night."

"I always wonder who my birth parents were, and why they left me alone in the snow, why they never came back for me. Maybe they died, or just didn't want me."

Cyra was silent for a long time, her eyes on the desert floor passing beneath the little ship.

"I'll think about it."

"Landsailers! A group of them about two miles ahead!"

Cyra grabbed the MAMPS and twisted the dial. The longboat shot up into the sky.

"I'm taking us up to five thousand feet. Their weapons won't be able to reach us. I doubt they'll even notice us way up here. It's going to get cold."

Sephie was shivering as she peered over the side of the ship at the desert floor almost a mile below them.

The Magician's raspy voice rolled out of Cyra's mouth.

"What's in the box, Fortisian?"

Sephie laughed. "The box is almost empty, Magician."

Odo looked puzzled. "What box is empty? Whoa! Puffs of smoke coming from one of the ships! They must be firing cannons. Definitely pirates, the three big ships have black sails. They're chasing two other landsailers, smaller ones. The pirates are catching up to them!"

"Time for a little help from above."

Cyra leaned over the side of the ship, drawing a symbol in the air. The largest pirate ship, a four masted behemoth, veered suddenly, skidding sideways across the desert floor, coming to a grinding halt in a massive cloud of swirling dust. The other two pirate ships dropped their sails, slowing down.

"That should do it."

"What did you do?"

"Jammed their steering. It will take them about half a day to repair it. No one got hurt and the two little ships got away."

"You're amazing."

Cyra grinned. "Thanks, Odo.

# Chapter 33

# An Unexpected Visitor

Odo was mesmerized by the desert passing below them as they sailed eastward toward Bandiir.

"This is like one of those old a fairy tales, flying through the air in a wooden boat. How long will it take us to get there?"

Cyra scrunched her face. "The distance to Bandiir is two thousand three hundred and eighteen miles. If our cruising speed is thirty-five miles an hour we'll be flying for sixty-six hours.

Four hours later everyone was hungry and tired of sitting.

"We should stop and have dinner, set up camp."

"There's a bunch of trees way over there, and a little pond."

"Our own oasis."

Cyra brought the ship down next to the trees.

"Nice landing, Captain Cyra." Odo jumped out and ran to the edge of the pond. "I don't see any sharks. He took off his shoes, rolled up his pants and waded into the water. "Nice, just the perfect temperature."

Cyra let out an earsplitting shriek, sprinting across the sand and cannonballing into the water next to Odo. Sephie was right behind her.

Odo glared at them. "You got my clothes all wet."

Sephie cackled, "So sorry, Odo." She and Cyra proceeded to splash him mercilessly.

"You will pay for your insolence!"

An hour later the three soaking wet friends climbed out of the pond and flopped down on the warm sand.

"Best beach ever."

"It won't take any time at all for the sun to dry our clothes."

"It is kind of weird how the sun never sets here."

Cyra looked up at the sky.

"Plindor is in a synchronous orbit around its sun. One side of the planet is always facing the sun and the other side always in darkness. That happens when one side of the planet is heavier than the other. It's a little like swinging a ball around you on the end of a string, one side is always facing you."

"Our moon back home is like that. I wonder what kind of creatures live on the other side of Plindor?"

Odo grimaced. "I don't even want to know. Have you ever seen the creepy stuff that lives in the dark at the bottom of the ocean? Scary looking."

"It's just life adapting to its environment, Odo Whitley.

"Creepy life that wants to eat me."

Sephie snorted. "Speaking of eating, let's have some dinner."

Cyra drew three symbols and a roaring campfire blinked into existence, a black kettle simmering above it.

"Yum, that smells good. I'm starving."

Odo leaned back against a tall swaying palm tree, his eyes half closed. "Plindor's not half as scary as Juvo made it sound. Except for that scary evil Magician." He grinned at Cyra.

After dinner Cyra shaped tents and sleeping bags.

An exhausted Odo Whitley crawled into his tent. "Last one to fall asleep has to make breakfast!"

Odo awoke to the sound of murmuring voices outside his tent, still half asleep when he saw the barrel of a flintlock pistol poke through the tent flaps.

A huge tentacle ripped the flaps open, another one grabbing Odo and dragging him out. He staggered to his feet, gaping at six heavily armed Plindorian pirates.

"What do you want?"

"Where's your valuables, boy?"

"We don't have any valuables. Just our little landsailer. You can take it if you want."

"Such a generous lad, warms my heart."

The pirate stepped closer, the barrel of his pistol two inches from Odo's nose.

"Where's your valuables, boy?"

"Really, we don't have anything that–"

Odo turned to see Sephie crawl out of her tent, eyes wide at the sight of the pirates.

"Get her!!" One of the pirates grabbed Sephie.

The pirate holding the pistol gave a dreadful smirk.

"Only seen a few of your kind. A matching pair will fetch a good price at the slave market. Or maybe at the butcher shop."

He let loose a high pitched terrifying laugh, a laugh cut short by the sudden appearance of the last person Odo and Sephie were expecting to see.

All six pirates jumped back, pulling out an impressive array of swords, daggers, and pistols.

The pirate holding Sephie put a pistol to her head.

"Back off, Magician, or your little friend dies."

The Magician stared at the pirate with pale yellow watery eyes, saying nothing. His silence scared the pirates even more.

"I'll kill her where she stands, Magician."

The pirate screamed when his heavy pistol turned into a hissing red serpent with long black venomous fangs. He stumbled back, letting go of Sephie, trying to escape the deadly nightmarish snake.

The pirates looked at each other, then at the Magician. One of them lowered his weapon, the others following suit.

"Keep your friends, Magician. Too scrawny anyway. No good for work and no good for food. We'll leave you be."

"No."

The word seemed to squirm out of the Magician's mouth and crawl across the sand into their thoughts. They tried to run, but couldn't, watching in horror as ten thousand slippery black centipedes crawled up from the sand, swarming over them, waving razor sharp mandibles. One of the pirates collapsed when a centipede wriggled across his eye.

Sephie was trying not to laugh. Whatever Cyra was making them see must be really scary. She had no idea how Cyra could keep a straight face.

One of the pirates groaned. "No more, Magician. We'll give you whatever you want."

The centipedes vanished.

The Magician stared silently at the pirates with his pale yellow watery eyes.

"What do you want? We'll give it to you, whatever it is. Your words shall bend our will."

"East. We wish to travel east in your vessel."

He flicked his wrist and a dozen gold coins landed on the sand in front of the pirates. "You will be well paid, but if you think of causing harm to my two apprentices you will not live long enough to regret it. You do not wish to see the demons I call forth from the depths of the Sixth World."

The pirates had never heard of the Sixth World and had no desire to find out what kind of demons lived there.

"Of course, of course, no harm shall come to them. You will each have your own cabin, traveling with us as long as you wish. We will set sail to the east this day. Is there a name attached to your destination?" The pirate's attempt at a friendly smile looked more like a pained grimace.

"I will tell you when the time comes. I am being hunted by five blood demons from the Third World. Only my spells keep them at bay. Remember this well."

A collective shiver ran through the pirates.

Sephie had to turn away, her hand over her mouth. There was something extraordinarily funny about bloodthirsty pirates being terrified of a ten and a half year old girl.

"Take us to your ship, and tarry not. Bring our land-sailer, I have become quite fond of her. Set it by my cabin. It shall, on occasion, be necessary to feed it."

The pirates' eyes widened. The largest pirate bellowed at the others. "You heard the Magician, bring his landsailer! Follow me, Magician, I will take you to our ship."

The Magician turned to Sephie, hissing, "What's in the box, girl?"

"Fear is in the box, Magician."

# Chapter 34

# Puero

Sephie and Odo had no idea why Cyra wanted to travel with the pirates when they already had a marvelous flying landsailer. The two friends were huddled together in the single masted scout sailer carrying them to the pirate ship.

Odo whispered to Sephie, "Maybe her deeper self told her to do it. There must be some reason why we're supposed to be on the ship."

"Maybe we're going to meet someone."

The Magician sat alone at the prow of the ship, staring into the distance. None of the pirates would sit near him, or even make eye contact with him. One brave soul had looked into his eyes, but stopped when his insides suddenly felt like a bag of angry vipers.

The desert wind was howling, the small sailer racing along the sand, veering to avoid rocks and the spiky red plants with dagger shaped leaves.

Odo spotted the three pirate ships when they were

almost a mile away, studying the massive six wheeled landsailers.

"Those are the same three ships that were chasing the two little landsailers. See how they're working on the big one? The rear wheels are off. Remember how... um... the Magician said he jammed their steering? He must have done a good job, they're still trying to fix it."

When they were a few hundred feet from the largest ship one of the pirates cried out, "Furl the sheet!"

The billowing sail dropped and they coasted toward the huge pirate ship.

Two of the pirates grabbed a heavy wooden lever in the center of the craft, pulling up on it. With a loud squealing sound the ship ground to a halt next to the four masted pirate ship. Four heavy ropes dropped down from above, the pirates quickly lashing them to heavy iron rings. One waved his arm and the ropes jerked taut as the little craft was winched upward.

The Magician stepped onto the main deck of the pirate ship. Odo and Sephie watched the pirate crew slowly back away, giving each other nervous glances. One of them ran to a cabin, pounding on the door. A huge Plindorian with a massive silver sword strapped to one arm stepped out, his demeanor slow and deliberate. He made his way across the deck, his calculating eyes on the Magician.

The Magician said nothing, staring into the distance, purposefully ignoring the captain.

"I am the captain of the *PV Latro*. Why does your shadow darken my decks, Magician?"

The Magician turned slowly, as if he had heard a small dog barking in the distance.

"I journey to the east with my two apprentices. Your ship suits my purpose."

"And why would I risk an encounter with the Mavorites for a paltry venture such as that?"

The Magician drew three symbols in the air. With a blinding flash of light a heavy iron box appeared on the deck.

The captain took a step back, studying the box.

"What's in the box?"

The Magician turned to Sephie. "Think carefully before you answer, apprentice. What is in the box?"

Sephie closed her eyes, listening to her deeper self.

"Greed is in the box, Magician."

The Magician flicked one gnarled blue finger and the box tipped over, hundreds of gold coins spilling out onto the rough wooden deck.

The captain turned to one of the pirates. "Take our guests to their cabins. Set sail for the east once repairs are complete. Eyes on the ship, laddies, we head into the realm of the Mavorites."

An anxious murmur ran through the throng of villainous pirates, though none dared to question the captain's order.

The captain raised one tentacle. "Three gold coins for each of you, more upon our safe return."

The murmuring stopped, the pirates forming a line in front of the mound of gold coins.

Odo's cabin was only slightly larger than his bedroom closet at home, wide enough for a narrow wooden cot and a single oil lantern dangling from an overhead beam.

Sephie peered in through the open door.

"My cabin is way bigger, and I have a refrigerator and a television."

Odo snorted. "Maybe Cyra just wanted a big fluffy bed to sleep in. The longboat was a bit cramped. We should go ask her."

"You mean *him*, ask the Magician. We have to be careful, no one can know the truth about him."

"Oops, I wasn't thinking."

"Let's go talk to him."

Odo and Sephie walked across the deck toward Cyra's cabin, the pirates hastily moving aside. Word had spread rapidly about the presence of the Magician. Whispered tales of ten thousand black centipedes, a venomous red serpent, and blood demons from the Third World passed like lightning from sailor to frightened sailor.

Sephie rapped gently on the Magician's door.

They waited for almost a minute before the door opened.

The Magician stepped onto the deck, his face dark, wrapped in a dreadful scowl. The pirates froze, their eyes locked onto the frightening blue creature.

He extended both gnarled blue hands, flames shooting out from his fingers. Sephie and Odo were surrounded by a great swirling mass of orange fire, lifted three feet into the air.

"Do not test me, apprentices!"

He flicked one finger and the flames vanished, Sephie and Odo tumbling to the deck. The Magician pointed with one bony finger to the open door. The two friends staggered to their feet, stumbling into the cabin. The Magician followed them in, slamming the cabin door behind him.

The pirates looked at each other in frozen silence. This was dark magic of the worst kind.

"Are you okay? I wanted to put on a good show for the crew. They won't bother us now."

"We're fine, it didn't hurt. How did you make us float up in the air like that?"

"You weren't floating in the air, you just thought you were. So did the pirates."

Odo grinned. "I was actually kind of scared when I saw the look on your face. I can't imagine how scared the pirates must be."

"I've been using the age old combination of punishment and reward to induce a particular behavior. Terrify them with one hand, give them gold with the other."

"Sephie and I were wondering why you wanted to travel on the pirate ship?"

"It's a vital link in this chain of events. That's all I know."

"Are we supposed to meet someone?"

"Maybe."

"Who are the Mavorites? The crew seems really scared of them."

"I don't know. We'll let events play out and see where it takes us. In the meantime, I've decided to continue your training, Sephie. Teach you how to project complex illusions to large groups of people, like the show I just put on for the pirates. You have a lot to learn. Most Fortisians train for a minimum of ten years, some their whole lives."

The *PV Latro* hoisted her sails when the ship's steering mechanism was again functional, the low rumbling of the six gigantic wheels rolling across the desert sand waking Odo from a deep sleep. He stepped onto the main deck, spotting Sephie next to the starboard rail, her eyes on the horizon.

"We're moving again. Any sign of the Mavorites?"

"I've been here for an hour and haven't seen anything. I don't know if that's a good sign or a bad one."

"I hope the Magician knows what he's doing. The pirates are really afraid of Mavorites, whoever they are."

"Odo, don't look, but there's a young Plindorian peeking out from behind that cabin. He's been watching me the whole time I've been here."

"Why?"

"I don't know, maybe he's just curious."

"Let's find out." Odo turned and waved to the Plindorian, motioning for him to approach.

The Plindorian ducked behind the cabin.

"He's afraid of us. Don't forget we're scary Magician's apprentices."

"Let's go see what he wants."

191

Odo and Sephie walked across the deck to the cabin. The Plindorian skittered back when they stepped around the corner, clearly terrified by their presence.

"Why were you watching us?"

The young Plindorian's mouth opened and closed, but no words came out.

Sephie said, "There is no need to fear us if you have done no wrong. Were you simply curious about us?"

"You are magicians?"

"Apprentices. The Magician is teaching us."

"Can you use magic to send creatures far away?"

"What do you mean?"

"If a creature was far from home and wanted to return, would you be able to send him home with magic?"

"Are you far from home?"

The Plindorian nodded.

"You're not one of the pirates?"

"A raiding party captured me in the borderlands. They kidnap young Plindorians and turn them into pirates. Even if I could escape, I don't know how to get home."

"How long have you been on the ship?"

"Almost a year. My parents must think I ran away or was killed."

"What is your name?"

"I am Puero Bandiir."

Sephie gave a low gasp. "You are from Bandiir?"

"Yes, that is the name of my village. You know of it?"

192

"Have you ever heard of someone called Advenus Bandiir?"

Puero shook his head. "It is vaguely familiar, but there are many in the village I do not know. He is a friend of yours?"

"We're looking for him."

"You are traveling to Bandiir? You could take me with you. I could help you find your friend."

Sephie studied Puero's brainwaves.

"Not a word of this to the pirates." She held out one hand, orange flames sprouting from her fingertips.

Puero took a step back, shaking his head vehemently. "On my life, I will say nothing."

"Do not speak to us or approach us until we reach Bandiir. Go now."

Puero turned and ran.

# Chapter 35

# Mavorites

The *PV Latro* was on high alert, sailors in the crow's nests scanning the horizon with long spyglasses, searching for Mavorite landsailers as they raced toward Bandiir.

Odo had just woken up when the ship's bell started ringing and did not stop. He leaped out of bed and threw on his clothes, darting out onto the deck. The pirates were at their stations, the captain bellowing commands from the quarterdeck. All twenty-six sails had been raised, the landsailer careening across the desert at close to forty-five miles an hour, leaving a great swirling dust trail in its wake.

Odo's jaw dropped when he spotted the titanic ten masted land sailer behind them.

"Whoa, look at all those sails! There's no way we can outrun that!" He scanned the decks, spotting Sephie and the Magician near the bow of the ship. He sprinted toward them, calling out to Sephie.

She turned at the sound of his voice, waving to him.

Odo skidded to a halt in front of her.

"Is that a Mavorite ship?"

Sephie nodded. "Yes. The captain said the Mavorite empire controls half of Plindor. They're highly trained and well organized. The people they conquer have a choice between Mavorite citizenship or death. Most choose to be citizens, the young men conscripted into the military. They're not slaves, they're well paid and well fed."

"Just like the Roman Empire."

"Exactly like it, and just as successful."

"Can we outrun them?"

"The captain says no, they have three times our sail. It will take a few hours, but they'll catch us."

"What happens then?"

"The pirates fight. The Mavorites give no quarter to pirates, no choice between death and citizenship."

"Can you use shaping to stop them? Jam their steering?"

"Not now."

"Why?"

"It's not time."

Odo glanced anxiously behind them. The distance between the two ships was shrinking rapidly.

Six heavy bronze cannon had been rolled to the stern of the *PV Latro*, cannonballs and kegs of black powder stacked next to them, ready to fire on the Mavorite vessel when it came into range. Cauldrons of bubbling black tar were being heated over roaring fires on the port and starboard sides of the main deck. The boiling tar would be poured onto the sands below in an attempt slow the Mavorite ship, the hot tar sticking to the ship's gigantic wheels and axles.

It was Sephie who saw the errant canister of black powder rolling across the deck toward the blazing fire beneath a cauldron of tar, the pirate standing next to it oblivious of his impending doom.

A stream of purple light shot out from Sephie's hands, forming a field of energy around the cauldron just as the canister hit the flames. There was a massive explosion, but the force of the blast was directed upward thanks to Sephie's energy field. The pirate next to the cauldron staggered back at the sound of the blast, realizing instantly what had happened. His eyes went from the shimmering violet cylinder of energy to Sephie, her glowing hands still extended.

He ran across the deck, falling to his knees in front of her.

"You saved my life!"

"I saw the powder rolling toward the flames and created a... magical barrier around it."

The pirate lowered his head, removing a gold chain and a brilliant green stone from his neck.

"This is my most valuable possession, a green star-fire stone from the fabled lost mines of Atroxia. I give this to you freely as equal exchange for my life." He held out the necklace.

"There's no need for that. I'm just glad I could help."

Fear washed across the pirate's face. "Magician, if you refuse my gift, the next battle will be my last. This is well known among all sailors."

Sephie took the necklace.

"Thank you for your generous gift. I will treasure it always."

"Bless you, Magician. I will not forget what you have done this day."

Odo turned at the sound of the captain's booming voice.

"Shot the cannon, laddies!"

The gun crews loaded powder and ball into the heavy bronze cannons, seating it firmly and placing a short fuse in the touch hole.

Odo gaped at the titanic ten masted Mavorite monstrosity, now less than a mile behind them.

The captain stood on the quarter deck, his eyes on the approaching ship. His voice roared across the decks.

"Loose the tar, laddies!"

Eight great iron cauldrons of molten burbling tar were dumped off the port and starboard sides of the ship.

Two minutes later the great behemoth hit the smoking black tar, its wheels turning black. The pirates let out a great cheer, a cheer that faded when the Mavorite ship showed no sign of slowing down.

"Sight the cannon!"

The ship was now only a half mile away, a monstrous trail of dust behind it.

"Fire!!"

The pirates touched off the fuses, all six cannon firing simultaneously. Odo watched the heavy cannonballs flash through the air. A split second before they hit the Mavorite ship a massive rippling wall of energy appeared, the cannonballs bouncing off, falling harmlessly to the desert floor.

"What happened? What was that?"

The Magician frowned. "Most unexpected. The Mavorites have their own magician, more than likely a Fortisian mercenary. They're rare, but not unheard of. It's time to go. Into the longboat, and be quick about it!"

"What about all the pirates and—"

"Now, apprentice! Run!"

The three adventurers dashed across the deck toward their small longboat. The Magician pulled the MAMPS from his cloak pocket, leaping into the ship.

"What about Puero? We said we'd take him."

"There he is! Puero! Puero Bandiir!!"

Puero looked up at the sound of his name.

"Over here! Get in!!"

He didn't need to be told twice. Puero raced to the longboat and clambered in."

"How are we going to get your landsailer onto—"

"Hold tight, here we go!" The Magician twisted the top of the MAMPS and the little craft rocketed up into the sky.

They looked down at the sound of cannon fire coming from the Mavorite ship, a massive iron harpoon ripping through the air toward the *PV Latro*, a heavy metal cable trailing behind it. The Magician blinked up an energy wall, the harpoon smashing into it, tumbling to the ground. The Mavorites reeled the harpoon back to their ship, now only a quarter mile behind the pirates.

The Magician cried out, "Sephie! Six wheels on their starboard side, each secured with a massive wooden pin. I'll take the bow, you take the stern! Vaporize the pins!"

They both stood up, extending their palms toward the ship. In the space of four seconds, six blinding vermillion beams of light flashed out, all six pins vanishing.

Odo watched the wheels of the Mavorite ship wobble wildly, then fall off one after another, the titanic craft listing hard to starboard, skidding sideways across the sand, sending up a gigantic cloud of dust and debris. Twenty seconds later the great behemoth came to a grinding halt, their captain listening to the raucous cheers of *PV Latro* as they made their escape.

# Chapter 36

# Fetch

Puero was clinging to the sides of the longboat with all six arms. "Your landsailer is flying! You are a great and powerful wizard."

The Magician rippled with a blue light, transforming back to orange haired Cyra.

Puero gave a shriek of horror. "A Fortisian!" His tentacles were shaking. "Don't kill me, please don't throw me out, I'll do anything you want."

"No one is going to hurt you, Puero. We're taking you home. I am a Fortisian, but I mean you no harm. The stories you have been told about us are not true. We are a peaceful race, wishing only to be left alone."

"You will take me to Bandiir?"

"Yes, and you will be free to go anywhere you wish. We will continue our search for Advenus Bandiir."

"Why do you seek him?"

"He has something that belonged to Sephie, something we need to find."

"I could help you. I have friends who might know him, might know where he lives."

TOM HOFFMAN

"We would appreciate your help, Puero. It's very important that we find the missing item."

Odo leaned back against the side of the boat.

"Say, Puero, how do you know when to go to bed when it's always daytime? In our world, half the day is dark and half is light. We sleep when it's dark."

"You live in the darkness? I've heard stories of the creatures who dwell on the dark side of Plindor, too terrible to think about. I would never be able to sleep in darkness."

"So when do you sleep?"

"We sleep when we are tired, eat when we are hungry."

"I guess that makes sense. Speaking of hungry, isn't it about time for lunch?"

Sephie snorted. "You just had lunch, Odo Whitley."

"That was more of a late morning snack than lunch."

Sephie flicked her wrist and a tray of sandwiches and drinks appeared. She grabbed one of the sandwiches.

"Tuna sandwiches, just like my grandma used to make. Help yourself, Puero. I can make you something else if you'd like. A salad maybe? "

"I will try one of these. They are called sandwiches?"

Odo nodded. "They are, and they're tasty. Say, Sephie, maybe our good friend Puero would like a box of Proto's Taste-E Kakes for desert."

Sephie rolled her eyes. "Odo Whitley, always putting the needs of others before his own."

201

Odo grinned.

Cyra's eyes were on the distant landscape.

"We're approaching the borderlands. It won't be long now."

Odo peered over the side of the ship. "Long grass and scrubby trees down there."

"The IMS says we're about four hours from Bandiir. I zoomed in on the holo map to look. It's a small town, a farming community. Three or four hundred homes, lots of cultivated fields. One section is in ruins. I recognized the craters, definitely from Atroxian weapons. Not a recent attack though, maybe a few years ago."

Puero nodded. "Yes, the Atroxian slave traders came two years ago and took some of the children, two of my friends. They destroyed part of the town with terrible fire weapons."

"I hope Advenus didn't get hurt. I'm looking forward to meeting him. He's a formshifter, right?"

Cyra nodded. "He was in human form when he was on Earth. I've only heard of a few Plindorian formshifters, but most would not reveal their ability. Speaking of formshifting, you need to learn how, Sephie. It comes in handy, especially if you want to be a terrifying magician."

Sephie did not look entirely enthusiastic. "Suppose I can't change back?"

"What's in the box, girl?"

"Fear is in the box, Magician."

"Exactly, the idea of formshifting scares you be-

202

cause you've never done it. It's not as hard as you think, and it's fun. You can transform into a bird and fly around. I love doing that. We should land outside the village. If we set down in the middle of town they might think we're Atroxian invaders."

Puero nodded. "Yes, after the Atroxians came everyone grew fearful of outsiders."

"I'll formshift into a Plindorian and say I found you two wandering in the desert."

Puero looked confused. "You are going to become a Plindorian? This is a joke?"

"No, it's not a joke. It's what Sephie and I were just talking about, formshifting. I know it sounds like magic, but it's not. It's just very advanced science, using the power of my mind. The Plindorian we're searching for is also a formshifter. More than likely he hides this skill from the villagers."

"Just like I do on Earth. Can you imagine if I told kids at school I could shift between dimensions?"

"That's why I never told anyone I could read brainwaves. It's the same everywhere, creatures are scared of things they don't understand."

Two hours later Cyra spotted a clearing in the middle of a small forest. "We can land there."

She brought the ship gently down on the soft forest floor.

"Welcome to Bandiir." Sephie tucked the MAMPS into her pack. "Ready?"

Everyone jumped out, Puero breathing in the earthy aromas of the lush forest.

"I have missed the forest."

"The trees smell lovely. If they didn't have the little blue flowers I'd think they were pine trees."

Odo pointed to a stand of green saplings. "Did you see that? A little critter ran through there, kind of like a blue squirrel with a really long tail."

"Puero, I'm going to formshift now. Don't be afraid, it's not dark magic, it's just deep physics." Cyra raised both arms, drawing six symbols in the air. She vanished in a blink of light, transforming into an enormous yellow Plindorian.

"What do you think? Is this a good look for me?"

Sephie laughed. "You look really cute in a giant yellow octopus sort of way."

Puero's mouth was hanging open. "Dark magic."

Cyra climbed out of the ship.

"Let's go find Advenus. Puero, you said you could introduce us to some of your friends?"

"Yes, that trail over there will take us past several farms."

The three adventurers followed Puero through the forest.

Odo whispered to Sephie, "It's weird seeing Cyra as a Plindorian. It's still her, but she's a giant octopus. And it was her when she was the Magician. What's the part of her that doesn't change when she's in different forms? The part that's always her."

"Her true self, the self that exists outside of space and time. That part of us is constant, no matter what physical form we take."

"I still don't get how it works."

"I don't really understand it either, but it's all deep physics, laws of energy, dimensional stuff."

"She was so scary when she was the Magician."

"I bet she was laughing the whole time. I thought I was going to faint when she showed me the big iron noggle box. When I think about it, she was probably stimulating a fear response in my amygdala."

"Doing what?"

"The amygdala is the part of your brain responsible for fear. When I look at it I can tell if someone is afraid. That's how I could tell Wikerus was afraid of the Atroxians. I think she was elevating my fear response."

"Whatever it was, she was terrifying. I could hardly breathe when she looked at me."

Puero held up a tentacle, motioning for them to stop.

"There are two farmers ahead, but I don't know them."

"I'll talk to them. Odo and Sephie, walk behind us and do exactly what I tell you. Do not hesitate, no matter what I say."

Odo glanced at Sephie. She shrugged.

Cyra and Puero stepped out of the forest, waving at the two Plindorian farmers.

Cyra approached them. "Greetings, friends. A glorious day, one to be cherished."

The two farmers nodded, eyeing Cyra with obvious suspicion. "What brings you to our humble farm, friend?"

"I am searching for a villager named Advenus

Bandiir. I promised a friend that I would visit Advenus, and I am hoping today will be that day."

Puero added, "I am Puero. I live only a few miles away, and these are my friends. I am trying to help them find Advenus. They saved my life."

"Your friends have become our friends, Puero."

The larger of the two Plindorians pointed a tentacle at Odo and Sephie. "What are those things?"

"They are humans. I found them wandering in the desert. They make excellent pets, docile and quick learners."

"What can they do?"

Cyra picked up a stick and threw it.

"Odo! Fetch! Fetch, Odo!"

Odo stared blankly at Cyra.

"Odo, fetch the stick!"

Odo ran and grabbed the stick, bringing it back to Cyra, dropping it at her feet.

"Clever. I could use them to help with the harvest. You said you're looking for Advenus?"

"Yes, Advenus Bandiir."

The farmers gave each other knowing looks.

"We know of him. He lived with his daughter until she was taken by Atroxian slavers. He lives alone now, seldom coming to town. He is a friend of yours?"

"I don't know him, but I told a mutual friend I would check on Advenus, see how he's doing."

"I should warn you, he's a strange one. There are rumors about him and dark magic."

"Dark magic? I don't like the sound of that. Do you

think he could be dangerous?"

"Not dangerous, just peculiar."

"Where does he live?"

"Follow this trail for about eight miles, turn right at the egg shaped boulder. Follow that trail for a few more miles until you reach a small lake. His cabin is on the far side of the lake. It's the only cabin there. He greatly favors his privacy."

"My deepest thanks for your kind assistance. I will take care during my visit. I hold no fondness for dark magic."

"A violation of the laws of nature, and an abomination on this world."

"I could not agree more. Good day to you, and may you have a bountiful harvest. Come along, humans! Follow! Follow!"

Odo gritted his teeth, following Cyra and Puero as they headed down the wide trail into the forest.

# Chapter 37

# Cyra's Storm

"Puero, thank you so much for your help. You can find your way home?"

"It's only five miles from here. It won't take any time at all."

"Your family will be so happy to see you safely home."

"They will be very surprised to see me. I imagine they gave up all hope for my return."

"Families never give up hope, Puero."

Odo grinned. "You'll get to tell your grandchildren you were a pirate."

Puero laughed. "First I shall tell my friends. Thank you again for bringing me home. It is a debt I can never repay."

"You already have."

After hugs and good byes, Puero headed home, the three adventures continuing on toward Advenus Bandiir's cabin.

Sephie kept a straight face for almost a full minute, then burst out laughing. "Fetch, Odo! Fetch the stick!"

Odo glared at her.

Cyra snickered. "Sorry, I had to make you seem as harmless as possible so you wouldn't frighten the farmers. They've seen what the Atroxians can do."

"You could have asked me to do something a little more challenging, like rolling over and playing dead, or shaking hands."

Sephie picked up a small stick and waved it back and forth in front of Odo, pretending to throw it.

An hour later, as they were strolling through the shadowy forest, Sephie said, "Advenus had a daughter. That's why he bought the doll, it was a gift for her."

"The farmers said she was taken by slave traders."

"I can't imagine the heartache it caused him, what he must go through every day. They say there is nothing harder than losing a child."

The adventurers trekked silently through the forest, turning at the egg shaped boulder. It was Odo who spotted the octagonal log cabin on the far side of the lake, a Plindorian seated on the front steps.

"I think we found Advenus Bandiir."

Cyra led the way, circling the lake. She waved to the Plindorian as they approached.

"Greetings, we are searching for Advenus Bandiir. Is he the one who stands before me?"

The Plindorian was aiming a silver cylinder directly at Cyra.

Odo studied the curious device. "What is that thing?"

Cyra's eyes were on the Plindorian. "It's a Mintarian

duster. It can vaporize a six inch hole in solid rock. They call them dusters because they turn you into space dust."

Odo took a step back.

The Plindorian's expression did not change.

"I see you in there, Fortisian. You think I don't know a formshifter when I see one?"

There was a flash of blue light and Cyra was an orange haired girl again.

"I'm guessing you and your two human friends want something?" The duster had not moved.

Sephie stepped forward. "A doll. I'm looking for a doll I had as a child. You bought it from Jonathan Morse the antique dealer when you visited Earth."

The Plindorian lowered his weapon.

"Why do you want it?"

"I am drawn to it by my deeper self."

"Come closer, girl."

Sephie approached the Plindorian. He reached out, touching her forehead.

"As I suspected. It's not every day I am visited by two Fortisians. Why is the doll important?"

"We don't know. You are Advenus?"

"I am. I bought the doll for my daughter Addy. I would give it to you without hesitation, but it's gone. Addy and the doll are gone."

He set the duster down on the steps.

"Your daughter had the doll when... they took her?"

"She was playing in the yard. She called out for me. By the time I got there it was too late. They'd taken her,

210

all of the Atroxians were gone except one. I shaped a force beam, knocked him into a tree. That surprised him, wiped the smile off his face. He grabbed his duster and shifted."

"I can't imagine how painful it must be for you."

"There are days when I wish the Atroxian had used his duster on me. Days when it's all I can do to get out of bed. Days when I stare at her picture, wishing I had been there when she needed me."

No one spoke. Odo could hear the leaves rustling in a soft breeze.

"Do you think they took Addy to Atroxia?"

"It's what they do. She's a slave now, somewhere on that vile world."

Sephie turned to Odo and Cyra.

"We're going to Atroxia."

Advenus shook his head vehemently. "No, I won't allow it. You have no idea what it's like, a dark and malevolent world filled with murderous creatures. I'm not sending three children to that evil place."

"I'm not a child, I'm ten and a half years old."

"Odo and I are fifteen. And don't forget that Cyra and I are both Fortisians."

"Don't sacrifice your lives for an old doll. I know you don't want to hear this, but you are still children, not much older than my Addy."

Cyra raised both arms, rapidly drawing half a dozen symbols in the air. The sky turned dark, trees swaying wildly in a sudden shrieking maelstrom, undulating curtains of rain pounding against the house. Odo tried to shield his face from the torrential stinging downpour, hollering, "What are you doing?? Stop!!"

She drew two more symbols and the roiling black clouds in the sky exploded with a hundred jagged flashes of white-hot lightning, violent crashes of thunder shaking the ground around them. Flocks of terrified birds rose up from the forest.

Cyra lowered her arms and the storm was gone, the sky once again a brilliant azure blue.

" I'm not a child, I'm ten and a half years old."

Advenus looked at Cyra with new eyes.

"How would you get there? You don't know where it is."

"And you do?"

"Not precisely. I've heard rumors, stories. If I knew where it was I would not be here, I would be searching for Addy."

Sephie touched the necklace given to her by the grateful pirate.

"We don't need to know where it is, we have a waystone. This starfire gem came from the lost mines of Atroxia."

Advenus studied the brilliant green stone.

"There's nothing I can say that will change your mind?"

Sephie shook her head. "Nothing. I am being pulled there by my deeper self."

Advenus turned, motioning for them to follow him.

"Come inside. I may be able to help you."

# Chapter 38

# The Basement

The interior of the cabin was just as Sephie had imagined it would be, cozy and warm, filled with hand crafted wooden furniture, illuminated by flickering oil lanterns. The basement, however, was another story.

Advenus pulled aside a colorful woven rug to reveal a heavily armored trapdoor. He twisted a hidden knob on the wall and the door whirred open.

He motioned to Odo. "Down the stairs."

Odo peered into the darkness, hesitating. "It's kind of dark."

With a flick of his tentacle Advenus sent out a brilliant orb of light, illuminating the stairway.

"Atroxia is far scarier than a dark basement. You're certain you wish to go?"

"I wasn't afraid, I just didn't want anyone to trip on the stairs. Stairs can be dangerous, everyone knows that."

"Everyone knows that? Really?" Sephie grinned,

poking Odo in the ribs. "You sound like your dad."

Odo glared at her, then turned and hurried down the creaky wooden steps.

"Whoa, what is all this stuff?"

The walls of the thirty foot wide room were lined with shelves holding hundreds of strange devices, their purpose unknown to Odo. He studied the perplexing contraptions, recognizing only the silver cylinders Cyra had called Mintarian dusters.

Sephie eyed the long metal shelves.

"You brought these things back from other worlds?"

"I did. My neighbors believe me to be a hermit, seldom leaving my home, but they are quite mistaken. I have visited many worlds, many dimensions."

"You're a shifter."

"And a shaper, converting energy into physical matter. I have some proficiency in these arts, but nothing compared to the powers of a Fortisian. Addy shaped her first thought form when she was five years old."

Advenus walked over to a gray metal box, flipping the lid open, removing two pale blue spheres.

"What are those?"

"These are immensely valuable, incredibly rare. They are called Mintarian time throttles."

"What do they do?"

"They stop time in a twenty foot wide radius for fifteen minutes."

Odo laughed. "They stop time?"

"Time is far more malleable than you might think,

flowing at different rates in different worlds."

"That's true, when we came back from Pacalia almost no time had passed on Earth. These really stop time?"

"They do. The Mintarians used them during the Anarkkian wars."

"How do they work?"

"Twist the top half of the sphere counterclockwise as far as it will go, then twist it back again. You have three seconds to throw it at least twenty feet away from you. Anything inside that twenty foot sphere will be frozen in time for fifteen minutes, giving you ample time to escape a life threatening situation."

Odo grinned. "It's a hand grenade that stops time."

"There are only two, so use them judiciously."

Advenus handed the time throttles to Sephie, then stepped over to a group of three inch long red cylinders.

"These are power shields. Pressing the top and bottom of the cylinder simultaneously will create a defensive energy sphere capable of blocking most weapons. Unfortunately, they offer no protection from Atroxian pulse beams."

Odo glanced at Sephie. He had no idea what a pulse beam was. "Do they have a lot of those pulse beam things there?"

"Enough that you should worry about them. Your best defense will be stealth. That is why I am giving you these."

He handed a small black disk to each of them. "Stick them on the back of your wrist. To activate it, press it for five seconds. Odo, would you like to try it?"

"What does it do?"

"Press it and find out."

Odo stuck the disk on his wrist. "So... um... I just press it?"

"For five seconds."

"And then... I..."

"And then you discover what it does."

"Right. Okay, here goes, pressing the disk now."

Five seconds later Odo vanished.

"Nothing happened. It didn't do anything."

Sephie laughed. "You're invisible, Odo Whitley. You're not Translucent Boy, you're Invisible Boy."

"I'm not invisible, I can see myself."

"You are surrounded by a sphere of light bending energy. Light rays do not reflect off you, they go around you, rendering you invisible for up to ten minutes at a time. Press the disk again to become visible. It takes eighteen hours for the disk to recharge, so use it prudently."

"I'm really invisible?"

"Watch." Sephie pressed her disk, vanishing.

"Whoa! That's amazing! Hey, we could use these to sneak into the movie theatre."

"I'm rolling my eyes, Odo Whitley. These are not for sneaking into the movies, they're for sneaking past Atroxian guards."

"Right, just kidding."

"I don't need one." Cyra drew three quick symbols in the air and vanished.

"Where did she go?"

"I shaped a light bending sphere around me."

"Everyone visible, please."

Odo and Sephie pressed their disks and reappeared. Cyra blinked off her invisibility field.

Advenus stepped over to the shelf that held the Mintarian dusters, picking up three of them.

"These are not defensive weapons, they are Anarkkian Model 14A Particle Beam Projectors. They dissociate physical matter. If you fire this at a living creature its physical form will become a vaporous cloud of atoms."

Odo frowned. "It kills them?"

"Instantly and completely."

Cyra shook her head. "I don't want it. Fortisians are forbidden to take the life of another living creature, no matter the form."

"They are also quite useful for vaporizing armored doors, locks, vehicles, and a host of other formidable obstacles."

Cyra slipped the projector into her pack. "We should get some rest before we go."

"Stay here until you're ready to leave."

"If we find Addy we'll bring her back to you."

Advenus picked up a framed picture from his desk.

"This is her. She's a little older now, but..." His voice trailed off.

"We'll do everything we can to find her, I promise."

After a restful sleep and a delicious breakfast prepared by Advenus, the three adventurers stood on the front porch bidding their farewells.

"Please be careful. Watch out for each other and don't take unnecessary chances. It is a truly dangerous world."

Sephie gave him a hug. "We wouldn't be here if you hadn't bought my doll. Maybe when you bought it you were saving Addy's life. We'll find her, I know we will."

Advenus nodded, tears welling up in his eyes.

"Are we ready?"

Odo held up one of the red power shields. "Just in case. We have no idea where we'll arrive. It could be in the middle of an Atroxian slave trader camp, or deep in some weird starfire mine."

Sephie nodded. "I have a time throttle ready. Don't forget your invisibility disks."

Cyra's face was grim. "Remember, Atroxians don't have brains like us, so we can't alter their perceptions. We can't make them see something that's not there. I can formshift, but they can probably see through that, just like Advenus did."

"Ready?"

Odo and Cyra touched Sephie's starfire stone.

Cyra grinned. "What's in the box, girl?"

"The box is empty, Magician. Let's go find the doll and bring Addy home."

The three friends vanished in a flash of white light.

# Chapter 39

# Atroxia

Odo pressed his invisibility disk the instant he arrived. After precisely six seconds he shut it off.

"Is this right? It doesn't look like Atroxia."

"It's definitely not how Advenus described it."

Sephie studied the endless lush rolling green fields and majestic shade trees stretching out to the horizon. A golden sun shone down from a brilliant blue sky.

"It's not what I'd call dark and scary and filled with murderous evil Atroxians."

"Maybe the starfire stone wasn't from Atroxia. Maybe it sent us somewhere else."

Cyra shook her head. "This is Atroxia. This is where we're supposed to be. Don't let your guard down, things are seldom what they appear to be."

"Do you think the Atroxians are making us see something that's not really here?"

"I'd know if they were doing that. This is real."

"What should we do?"

Sephie pointed to a low hill. "We see what's on the other side of the next hill. Then we do it again."

"Eyes open, everyone. Watch for movement."

Cyra led the way, Odo and Sephie behind her. She motioned them toward a stand of tall trees at the top of the hill.

"In there. Keep low, stay hidden."

Odo crept silently up the slope, slipping into the thicket, Sephie next to him. They ducked down, moving cautiously between the trees.

"Look! What's that?"

Sephie studied a low white building at the bottom of the hill.

"It looks like a farmhouse. See the fields? Something moving, maybe farmers."

"Or slaves."

"Maybe."

Cyra pulled the dark glasses from her pack. She twisted the silver dial on the side, magnifying her vision. "I was not expecting that." She handed the glasses to Sephie.

"They're Atroxians, and they're picking vegetables. Putting them in baskets."

Odo took the glasses from Sephie, studying the farmers. "This doesn't make sense. Why would murderous evil Atroxians be picking veggies on a farm?"

"Even Atroxians have to–"

"What are you doing here?"

The three friends whirled around. Odo's finger was on his invisibility disk, Sephie was flipping on a power shield, and Cyra had popped up a massive energy field around them.

They stood facing four very tall dark violet Atroxians, their long white hair moving like a thousand tiny snakes.

Odo vanished. Sephie and Cyra were surrounded by glowing energy fields.

The Atroxians studied them curiously.

"Where did your friend go?"

"What?"

"Your friend was here, and now he is not."

"I'm here, I'm just invisible."

"Why would you choose to do such a thing?"

"So you won't see me?"

"You don't wish for others to see you? Are you hideously deformed?"

" Um... I'm hiding from you because you're Atroxians?"

The Atroxians looked at each other, then back at Sephie and Cyra.

"We are not Atroxians, we are Stirpians. Atroxians have been gone for two thousand years."

Odo blinked back into view.

"I think I know an Atroxian when I see one. Violet skin, yellow eyes, white hair that wiggles? Sound like anyone you know?"

"You are describing a Stirpian, not an Atroxian. Atroxians were short, with green skin and red eyes. They are gone, poisoned by their own hand. So spoke the First Stirpian."

The four Stirpians bowed their heads.

Sephie and Cyra blinked off their energy fields.

Odo got to his feet, brushing the leaves and dirt off his shirt.

"Is anyone else confused?"

"You are welcome to stay with us as long as you wish. We seldom have visitors."

Cyra smiled politely. "Thank you for your kindness, but we have a long journey ahead of us and must be on our way."

The four Stirpians froze, their eyes blinking rapidly. As one, they turned and left, walking down the hill toward the farmhouse.

Odo picked up his pack. "Those guys were very weird. I'm confused about Atroxians."

Cyra looked at her two friends. "We were calling them by the wrong name. The invaders are Stirpians, not Atroxians. We are also guilty of judging an entire race by the actions of a few. Not all Stirpians are murderous slave traders, some are peaceful farmers. We need to find the ones who took Addy."

"What was all that about the Atroxians being poisoned by their own hand?"

"It wouldn't be the first time a civilization poisoned their own planet with toxic waste and deadly pollution, ignoring it until it was too late. It is not an uncommon fate for primitive civilizations."

"Scary. Who do you think the First Stirpian was? They bowed their heads after they said his name."

"He could have been the first one to arrive on the planet, maybe a famous explorer or something."

"They did a good job of cleaning up after the Atroxians. Clean air, lots of trees and plants."

"We should get moving. It will be dark in a few hours."

Odo strolled alongside Sephie, his brow furrowed.

"Did you see how the Stirpians froze, then turned at exactly the same moment? That seems off. "

"It's very weird, Odo Whitley. Something else is going on, but I don't know what. We're missing a piece of the puzzle."

It was Cyra who spotted the village through the trees. She stopped, holding up one hand. "We can stop, or we can go around it. There could be slave traders or Stirpian soldiers there."

Sephie said, "I'll check it out. If it's safe we can go in and ask them about the slave traders."

"It doesn't look very scary."

Sephie pressed her invisibility disk. "It could be filled with angry Roman ghosts, Odo Whitley." They could hear her footsteps as she set off for the village.

Odo dropped his pack and flopped down, leaning back against a tree. "Sometimes I wish I was a normal kid, not traipsing around another dimension looking for a lost doll. We don't even know why we're looking for it. Sephie is my first real friend, but that deeper self stuff seems kind of weird."

"Does it feel like an accident that you met Sephie?"

"It doesn't feel like an accident, but I don't know. It could have been a bunch of weird coincidences, like when the black scary dog made me cross the street and walk past her house."

"There are no coincidences."

"I'd like to think my deeper self was guiding me toward–"

Odo screamed when the cold hands grabbed his neck. He rolled over, trying to break their grip, stopping when he heard Sephie laughing.

"I'm an angry Roman ghost here to kidnap Odo Whitley!"

Odo jumped to his feet as Sephie blinked into view.

"That's not even funny at all, Sephie. You scared the daylights out of me."

"Sorry, Odo Whitley, I couldn't resist. I saw your neck and some strange force made me–" Sephie's grin vanished. "That's it! I know what's happening! The Stirpians are being controlled by an outside force."

"What?"

"Odo Whitley, stop and think. Why did all four Stirpians freeze, blink, and turn away at exactly the same moment? Something took control of them, something made them do it."

"So now we have to worry about some weird alien force controlling us?"

Cyra looked up at Odo. "There's nothing weird about it. Most Fortisians can control other creatures, but it's only allowed in life threatening emergencies."

"You're saying you can make me do something I don't want to do?"

"I can manipulate your cerebellum, the part of your brain that controls movement."

"You could make me scratch my nose even if I didn't want to?"

"Easily."

"Okay, do it."

Odo wrapped his arms tightly around himself and gritted his teeth. Three seconds later he reached up and scratched his nose.

"Whoa, that's completely weird."

"I'm just manipulating energy impulses in your brain. If you had an itchy nose and wanted to scratch it, you would create the same series of electrical impulses I just did."

"It's still weird. Suppose the weird alien force takes control of us?"

"And makes you do a funny dance?"

Odo glared at Sephie. "Um, it could make us murder each other?"

Cyra interrupted. "Sephie, how was the village?"

"It was fine, nice and peaceful. Everyone seems friendly."

"Let's find out what they know about slave traders."

# Chapter 40

# Karolus

"This reminds me of Pacalia, quaint and rustic."

Odo watched the Stirpians strolling along a wooden walkway in front of the shops, some with little ones in tow.

"They have kids, just like we do. They're kind of cute. Except for the wiggly white hair."

"Let's check out the shops. I could use a new pair of hiking boots."

"Did you notice no one is looking at us? That seems odd. If I saw a Stirpian walking through town I'd definitely be looking at them."

"It is odd. Maybe it's not polite to look at strangers. I like it that they're not looking at me."

Sephie swung open the shop door and stepped inside. "They have shoes. Way too big for me, though. I need the kid section."

Odo sidled over to a Stirpian and two children sitting on a bench trying on shoes.

"They're too big."

"They're big now, but you'll grow into them. Shoes are expensive. We get one pair a year. Stuff socks into the front of them and they'll be fine."

Odo grinned. It sounded like home.

Sephie and Cyra waved to him. "Let's go, Odo Whitley. We're going to try a different shop."

The friends stepped out onto the walkway.

Odo glanced up at the sky. "The sun's going down, it's almost dark. Maybe that inn has a restaurant. I'm hungry."

"We can ask the innkeeper about slave traders."

They crossed to the other side of the street.

"No cobblestones, just hard packed dirt roads."

Sephie swung the door open. "They're busy, they must have good food here."

"What do you think they eat? Maybe it's creepy stuff like ant pudding or something."

"They're eating fruits and vegetables."

"Oh, that's okay, I guess. I'm going to ask the guy at the front desk about slave traders."

"We'll get a table and order you something. It might take a while since it's so crowded. You said you wanted ant pudding?"

"Ha ha." Odo headed over to the Stirpian behind the long wooden counter.

"Good evening, young sir, how may I help you?"

"It's kind of a weird question, but we were wondering if you knew anything about slave traders who–"

Every Stirpian in the inn froze, the room suddenly

silent, filled with living statues.

"Whoa, I was not expecting that."

"Odo! What did you do?"

Sephie and Cyra jumped to their feet.

"I didn't do anything. I was asking the innkeeper if he knew anything about slave traders."

"They know nothing of such things, nor should they."

Odo gave a start. The new voice was coming from the innkeeper's mouth. His eyes were fixed, staring into empty space.

Sephie whispered, "I told you something was controlling them."

"I do not control them, I advise them. They are my children, free to live their lives as they wish, hopefully showing kindness and respect for each other and for the world they live in."

"So... you're their..."

"I am Karolus. Why do you search for slave traders? Sensus is sick, his children have been quarantined for two centuries. The slave traders are no more."

"Stirpian slave traders took the daughter of our Plindorian friend two years ago, bringing her to this world. We have seen Stirpians on Earth and on Pacalia."

"I was not aware of this. There have been rumors in the past that Sensus was sending his children to other worlds, but I thought them to be nothing more than fantastical tales. Perhaps he is using old Atroxian technology. You are trying to locate this missing

228

child?"

"Yes."

"What do you know of this world?"

"The Stirpians moved here after the Atroxians poisoned the planet and became extinct. I'm a little confused about who you are."

"I am Karolus."

"Right, but... who exactly are you?"

"You have one brain and one body, is that correct?"

"All creatures do."

"All creatures do not. Stirpians have one brain and many bodies. Our bodies are our children."

Sephie raised her eyebrows. "That's why I couldn't read their brainwaves."

"So, Karolus, where exactly is this one brain?"

"Far beneath the surface of the planet. The First Stirpian arrived two thousand years ago, burrowing deep into the ground. When the eggs hatched, its children made their way to the surface. The First Stirpian then divided, creating a second generation of brains who came to the surface, migrated across the land and burrowed down again. Eggs were hatched, more children rose to the surface. Those brains divided, and on and on, the never ending cycle of life. It took our children a thousand years to heal the planet. Today we live peacefully on a world we have nurtured for two millennia."

Odo stood silently, his eyes on the innkeeper.

"Do your children know you exist?"

"I am impressed, Odo Whitley. Few creatures would

think to ask this question."

"How do you know my name?"

"The children are my eyes and ears, my sensory organs. I see what they see, hear what they hear, just as your eyes and ears send electrical signals to your brain. I was told of your coming. The answer to your question is no, my children are not aware of my existence. I give them advice and they live their lives as they wish."

"Will you help us find our friend's daughter?"

"If you are able to enter the quarantine dome, what will you do? Will you kill Sensus? Kill his children?"

"No, we just want to find Addy and bring her home. What's wrong with Sensus? Why is he quarantined?"

"He suffers from an unknown malady. One hundred and ninety-five years ago he began to change, becoming quick to anger, aggressive, believing we were plotting against him, certain we wanted to take his children away from him. His children's behavior mirrored his, all of them becoming angry, insolent, paranoid, and combative. When they kidnapped and enslaved children from neighboring colonies, it was decided to quarantine him. We created an impenetrable energy sphere around his colony, sealing Sensus and his children from the outside world. The quarantine dome will be removed upon his death."

"How long do most brains live?"

"I am three hundred and twenty-one years old and considered to be young."

"Whoa. How old is Sensus?"

"He is slightly older, but suffers from the unknown

illness. We believe he was exposed to toxic waste buried beneath the planet's surface."

"How do we find him?"

"Travel due north until you reach the quarantine dome, a six hundred mile journey. You will find your missing friend somewhere inside the dome, if she is still alive. I will send one of my children to guide you. If you wish to speak to me, simply ask him. He will have no memory of your question, or of our conversation. Sleep in the inn tonight. Rooms will be prepared for you, as well as meals. In the morning your guide will be waiting for you outside."

Sephie said, "Thank so much for helping us, Karolus. Your kindness will not be forgotten."

"Be aware that the world within the quarantine dome is far different from ours. The children of Sensus are to be deeply feared for what they have become, dark and murderous creatures. Do not trust them."

# Chapter 41

# Jarin's Tale

A cacophonous pounding jolted Odo from sleep. He rolled over, eyeing the door. There was only one person he knew who knocked on doors with both fists.

"Sephie! Five more minutes, this bed is so comfy."

"Snap to it, Odo Whitley! Time is money. You're missing breakfast!"

Odo crawled out of bed and pulled his clothes on, combing his hair with his fingers. He swung the door open and stumbled downstairs. Sephie and Cyra were sitting at a table eating.

"Yum, that looks good."

"It is good. Karolus must have scanned our memories."

"It's kind of creepy that he can poke around inside my head."

"Would you rather have a big bowl of crunchy ant pudding?"

A Stirpian wearing a white apron strode briskly over to the table, setting Odo's breakfast down. "Enjoy your meal, sir."

"Thanks, it looks delicious, just like Madam Beffy's Diner."

When breakfast was done they grabbed their packs and headed out the front door, greeted by a young Stirpian wearing hiking gear and a large backpack.

"The innkeeper asked me to guide you on your journey north. I am called Jarin."

"Nice to meet you, Jarin. I'm Odo, and these are my two friends, Sephie and Cyra." Odo realized at that moment how much he liked introducing them as his friends.

"You wish to visit the great quarantine dome?"

"Right, it sounded like it would be interesting. You know, good for sightseeing. Do many people go there?"

"I am the only one from our colony who has seen it. The others have no interest in such things. Shall we go?"

They followed Jarin out of the village, heading north.

It was early afternoon before Odo realized Jarin was not going to stop unless they asked him to.

"Say, Jarin, we're getting kind of hungry, could we stop for lunch?"

Jarin stopped in his tracks and sat down.

"Right, this looks like a good spot."

Sephie sat down next to Jarin. "This is such beautiful country. I love all the wildflowers. I can see why you like hiking here."

"Yes, it is quite lovely."

Jarin's eyes widened when Cyra flicked her wrist and blinked a large picnic basket into existence. She opened it and handed sandwiches to Odo and Sephie.

"Jarin, would you like a sandwich?"

"They will not poison me?"

"No, they're just cheese sandwiches."

"Created by dark magic."

"It's not dark magic, it's science. I compress energy into physical matter using the power of my mind."

Jarin took a very small bite of the sandwich. Then another. "Very good. Perhaps in this particular case it was science, and not dark magic, which created the sandwich. I have a certain interest in science." He gave a nervous glance at the others.

"That's wonderful, Jarin. Have you read much about it?"

Jarin shook his head.

"Such books are forbidden. Everything I know I have learned from studying the world around me."

Sephie smiled. "Then you are a true scientist indeed. It is a remarkable person who makes discoveries on their own. Learning from books is admirable, but there is still so much more to be learned about the world around us."

Jarin look pleased. "This scientifically created sandwich is very good."

The adventurers continued their trek toward the quarantine dome, stopping whenever Jarin would point out curious plants and wildlife. Over a period of three days the landscape transformed from lush pastoral countryside to dense forestland, the magnificent trees towering above them.

Jarin pointed to a nest made of branches and dried blossoms in one of the trees. "Kukululu birds live there. They are brightly colored and have a marvelous song. I have seen them dive into lakes for fish. They pull their wings close to their body, streaking down like a feathered arrow."

"Is there any dangerous wildlife here? You know, things that might try to eat us?"

"Nothing in the forests, only in the old underground–" He slapped his hand over his mouth, mortified by his own words.

Odo was suddenly curious. "Only in the old underground what? What were you going to say?"

"I was mistaken. There are no terrifying monsters."

"Could you give us a hint? We're adventurers, we've seen a lot of scary creatures."

Jarin hesitated, then said, "We are not the first to live in this world."

"Are you talking about the Atroxians?"

"You know the name of those who came before us?"

"Yes, we know of them. What have you seen?"

Jarin's voice was a whisper. "You cannot reveal my secret to the villagers. You will promise me this?"

"We won't tell anyone." Odo neglected to mention that Karolus was listening to every word.

"I discovered one of their old dwelling places. It is vast and dark, hidden deep beneath the ground. That is where the dangerous creatures live. I barely escaped with my life."

"You found an old Atroxian city?"

"It is where those who came before us used to live, full of strange metal structures, the ground so hard my knife could not mark it. I explored the great rooms, finding many curious objects, but was afraid to touch them. The creatures came after me, but I managed to escape by yelling and waving my torch. They fear the light, as all demons do. Twice I have gone back to revisit their dwelling place, but each time was too afraid to enter, too afraid of the demons who live in darkness."

Cyra said, "Will you take us there?"

"You wish to visit such a place?"

"Yes."

Sephie nodded. "I'm being pulled there."

Odo frowned. "The creatures who live there... what exactly do they look like?"

"I never saw them in the light, only as dim shapes darting through the shadows. They were very fast, making a terrible scratching noise when they ran."

Odo's hands were strangely cold and clammy.

Sephie was studying his head, a wide grin on her face.

On the tenth day of their journey the forests had transformed to the familiar rolling green meadows and farmland. They passed within a mile of a village several times larger than Jarin's.

"That is the central village of Wiscar, our neighboring colony. It is a farming colony, much like ours."

"What is your colony called?"

"Ours has always been, and will always be, Karolus. There are many villages in Karolus, ours is a small one near the border."

Sephie's ears perked up when she heard the familiar name. "Jarin, do you have friends in other colonies?"

"I have met many outsiders at the markets where we sell our produce. Each colony brings their wares, such things as furniture, fish, cloth, and iron products. Everyone enjoys the markets. There is always lively music and entertainment."

"Have any of your friends seen this underground city?"

"They would not speak of it even if they had. It is known to some that those who came before us were demons whose breath spewed poison into the air, killing all living things. The demons still dwell in that underground world."

The party of adventurers veered northwest, toward Jarin's ancient Atroxian city. Odo questioned Jarin several times about the creatures who scuttled around in the dark, learning nothing new. He managed to convince himself they were rambunctious little mice.

On the fifteenth day of their trek, Jarin pointed across the rugged rocky terrain to a low rectangular structure.

Odo gazed at the building. "That doesn't look much like a city."

"That is not the city, it is the entrance."
Sephie was getting a very bad feeling.

# Chapter 42

# Fear

Odo studied the once massively reinforced structure.

"That whole side is demolished, like a bomb hit it or something."

Cyra ran her hand across the ravaged outer wall.

"Only a heavy particle pulse beam could have done this. Where is the entrance?"

Jarin stepped into the shadowy interior of the building.

A brilliant sphere of light shot out from Cyra's hand. Jarin froze.

"It's not dark magic, it's science. This is the same light that shines from your sun, gives life to your world. How do we get in?"

"Your scientific light will keep the demons away." He pointed to a circular black slab in the center of the room. "That is the entrance. It was only by chance that I discovered its hidden mechanism."

He pressed his hand against a barely visible dark

gray disk embedded in the slab, stepping back as it moved silently to one side, revealing a wide silver ladder.

A shiver rolled through Odo.

Cyra stepped over to the ladder, peering down into the inky blackness. She drew three symbols and a stream of brilliant glowing orbs shot down the shaft.

"It goes down about two hundred feet."

One by one the adventurers made their way down the long ladder. Sephie was the last to go, murmuring, "The box is empty. I'm two feet above the ground."

Odo hopped off the ladder into a long rectangular room lined with massive armored doors.

"I guess they didn't like visitors."

Jarin pointed to a ragged hole at the far end of the room, a twisted and misshapen door lying on the ground next to it.

"In there."

Odo said, "It looks like something melted it. What could do that?"

Cyra stepped over to the nearest armored door. She drew four symbols, then held out both hands, palms facing outward. A blinding purple light blasted out at the door. Ten seconds later the beam stopped.

She held her hand inches from the door, then touched it. "Not even warm. It must absorb energy, using it to strengthen the defense field."

She turned and headed toward the ragged opening at the rear of the room.

"The door was blasted out from the inside. Something was trying to get out, not in."

"That's good news, right? Whatever was in there is gone?"

"Unless there were a lot of them."

"Oh, right. Don't forget your invisibility disks."

Sephie sent an orb of light through the doorway.

"It's a hallway. Let's go. "

The adventurers trailed behind the glowing orb for several hundred yards, finally reaching a cavernous room.

"Whoa, what are those things?"

Odo was looking at a row of gleaming dark blue cylindrical objects, each over a hundred feet long and thirty feet tall.

"They have windows, but no wheels or tracks. They all have the same silver stripe spiraling around them. They look like submarines."

Jarin pointed to a dark circular indentation on the side of the cylinder. "I tried to enter, but could not."

Cyra said, "They're interstellar ships, probably scout vehicles. It's a little like the ship my parents were…" She did not finish her sentence.

"How do they get up into space? There's no way they can fit through those doors."

"Interstellar ships don't work like that. They blink from one place to another without moving through the space in between. Once they're in dark space they can fly around if they need to, usually if they're exploring a new planet or something. These ones have weapons and defense shields."

"That doesn't seem like something you'd find in a city."

"It's not. This is a fortified Atroxian military base, not a city. I don't know what happened here, but it wasn't good."

"I can't believe it's still here after two thousand years."

"The synthetic materials used to build it aren't affected by the elements. It will be here ten thousand years from now."

"That's amazing."

"It lasted a lot longer than the Atroxians did."

"Let's check out some of the rooms."

"Remember, this is a military base. Don't touch anything, it could be a weapon. One mistake and this fortress could turn into a ball of molten plasma."

"Right, good to know."

Jarin pointed to one of the doors lining the room. "That is the room where the demons live."

Odo grinned. "And the door we're not going to open."

Cyra shook her head. "No, this will be a good lesson for Jarin, a good lesson for all of us. We're going in there and we're going to find out exactly what the demons are."

Odo glanced at Sephie. "Does anyone else think that is an extraordinarily bad idea?"

Jarin raised his hand.

Cyra walked over to the door.

"Everyone stay together. I'm going to put a powerful

energy sphere around us that no living creature can pass through. Whatever is in there will not be able to harm us. I'll blink off the light orbs, open the door, and we'll walk in together. Once we hear them running around I'll send out an orb of light so we can see them."

Jarin's breathing was shallow and fast.

Odo moved next to him. "Nothing to worry about, probably just little mice. We'll be safe inside the energy sphere."

"I will see the demons with my own eyes. I am terrified but... also strangely curious. I have never stood face to face with a demon."

"Here we go." Cyra waved one arm, a rippling violet energy field surrounding them. Odo pressed his hand against it.

"See, nothing can get through it. We're safe."

Jarin nodded. "Safe."

Cyra flicked her wrist and the light orbs vanished, the adventurers enveloped in heavy darkness.

Odo could hear Cyra opening the door. Her voice was a whisper. "Stay together, follow me." They shuffled forward, Sephie's hand on Cyra's shoulder.

"We're in. Now we wait. Don't make any noise."

Odo's heart was pounding. He jumped when he heard something scuttle across the floor. "I hear them!"

"Shhh. Quiet!"

"I feel sick."

The scratching sounds were louder now, coming from all directions.

"This is bad, really bad. There's a lot of them. I

think I might throw up."

"Odo Whitley, if you barf on me I will vaporize you."

"It's just an expression. I wasn't really going to– wait, do you hear that?? They're scratching at the energy sphere, trying to get in."

Cyra whispered, "Is everyone ready to see Jarin's demons?"

Jarin gave a low moan.

Odo's legs were shaking.

A dozen brilliant orbs shot out from Cyra's hands.

All four adventurers screamed.

Jarin's creatures were not rambunctious little mice as Odo had optimistically suggested, but were hideous two foot long insects with shiny blue iridescent shells, twelve legs, and bulbous red eyes on long wiggling stalks. Hundreds of them were jammed up against the energy sphere, their spiky legs and powerful mandibles thrashing and snapping wildly as they tried to claw and bite their way inside the sphere.

In less than five seconds they were gone, scared off by Cyra's brilliant orbs of light.

Cyra snorted. "Those were your demons, Jarin. Big insects. Look around the room. This was the food repository for the base. Somehow the insects got in, probably through an air duct or a tunnel. It's the perfect environment for them, cool, dark, and lots of food."

Odo had managed to regain his composure. "I figured it was something like that. You know, little rambunctious mice or maybe a horde of giant bloodthirsty insects trying to tear me to pieces and eat my brains."

Sephie burst out laughing.

Jarin turned to Cyra. "This was a good lesson indeed. My fears were far worse than the creatures I faced. There were no demons, only hungry insects."

"Big enough to ride like a skateboard."

"What is a skateboard?"

Sephie grabbed Odo's hand. "Come on, Odo Whitley, let's check out the other rooms. Maybe we'll get lucky and find more demons."

# Chapter 43

# **Mum**

The adventurers split up into two groups, setting off to explore the ancient military base. Jarin's fear had transformed to deep curiosity once he discovered his dreaded demons were not demons at all.

Sephie pointed to a door at the end of the cavernous hangar. "Let's see what's in there."

"I wish we could ride in one of those interstellar ships. Wouldn't that be fun? Do you think they're hard to fly?"

"First things first, Odo Whitley. We need to find Addy and the doll, but maybe one day we'll come back again. Cyra could probably fly one."

The two friends strolled past a dozen of the long ships as they made their way to the far side of the hangar.

Sephie approached the door, pressing her hand against it, her head swaying back and forth.

"Odo, I don't want you to worry, but something is going to happen. Something unexpected."

"Maybe it's something good, like finding a big chest of gold coins."

"I don't think so." Sephie pulled the door open and sent in an orb of light.

Odo peered into the room. "It looks like a locker room."

"Interesting. Look at all the uniforms hanging from hooks. See how small they are?"

"The Atroxians were short and green. Maybe this was a locker room for interstellar pilots. There might be cool stuff in the lockers."

Odo stepped over to the long row of dark metallic doors, pulling one open.

"Old clothes, boots." He pulled out a pair of pants, holding them up for Sephie to see. "They look like little kid clothes. I bet they weren't even four feet tall."

"What's that cube on the top shelf?"

Odo grabbed the iridescent cube, studying it.

"It has a button on it."

Before Sephie could warn him, Odo pressed the button. He skittered backwards, crashing into Sephie when the four Atroxians appeared.

Sephie popped up a defensive energy shield around them.

"What are they doing?"

"They're waving at us."

Odo called out to the Atroxians. "What do you want?"

Sephie blinked off the energy sphere, walking over to the waving Atroxians. She passed her hand through one of them. "They're not real, they're projections."

"There's a tall one and three little ones."

"It's a family, a holographic image of a pilot's family."

"Oh, that's kind of sad. They're all gone now." Odo picked up the cube and shut off the projection.

"It is sad, Odo Whitley. I wish the Atroxians had taken better care of their world. I hope the same thing doesn't happen to our world."

"Was that the unexpected thing you were feeling?"

"I don't think so."

"Let's go through those doors." Odo walked over to a pair of black doors at the far end of the locker room, pushing on one of them. "They're locked."

"Press the violet tab on the wall next to them."

Odo hit the tab and the doors whirred open.

"Whoa, how cool is that? The floor is covered with rows of big blinking violet circles. There's nothing else in the room. That's kind of weird. I wonder they're for?"

He stepped into the room.

"Odo, I don't think we should go in. I'm getting a–"

"It's just purple lights." Odo stepped onto one of the blinking violet disks.

"Hey, it stopped blinking when I stepped on it. Maybe it's some kind of–"

Odo rippled and was gone.

Sephie stared at the empty space where he had been.

"That was the unexpected thing, Odo Whitley."

She entered the room. Odo's violet circle was blinking again. Sephie stepped onto it, rippled, and vanished.

Odo found himself standing in a circular enclosure lined with silver consoles, long rows of small blinking lights, and flickering oval screens. His eyes were not on the consoles, however, but on the large round windows. More precisely, on a trillion stars floating in an infinite sea of blackness.

"Not good, this is not good." He ran over to the windows, hopping up onto the console.

"No, no, no! This can't be."

"We're in dark space."

Odo whipped around to see Sephie standing next to a blinking violet disk.

"How could we be in space? It's not possible!"

"And yet here we are, gazing at the stars. There are so many of them. It's really incredible."

"Where are we? What do you think this is? Hey, maybe we're in an interstellar ship."

Sephie was about to answer when they heard the soft melodious voice.

"Please identify yourself. Name first, then rank."

Odo gaped at Sephie. "What is that?"

"Name and rank, please."

"Sephie Crumb, Commander."

"Greetings, Commander Crumb, and welcome aboard Platform 1215. Apologies for not recognizing you. I have been unable to contact the Central Defense Network for one thousand, nine hundred and seventy-seven years. How may I assist you?"

"Who are you, exactly?"

"I am the engineered intelligence for an autonomous high orbit weapons platform linked to the Atroxian Iron Shield Planetary Defense System."

"I knew that, I was simply wondering what I should call you."

"I am commonly referred to as Mum."

"Right, Mum it is. This is Captain Odo Whitley, recently transferred to Iron Shield. Please inform him of your duties."

"Of course, Commander. I am one of three thousand and twenty-nine orbiting Iron Shield platforms protecting Atroxia from alien invasion, fully capable of neutralizing all defensive energy shields and responding with an arsenal of heavy particle fusion beam weaponry."

"Thank you, Mum. That will be all for now."

Odo whispered, "What are we doing here?"

"I'm not sure, Odo Whitley, but I do know this is where we're supposed to be."

"Mum said we're orbiting Atroxia, but all I see are stars."

Sephie called out, "Mum, please turn the platform so the surface of Atroxia is visible."

"Yes, Commander."

The stars around them seemed to rotate.

"Whoa!" Odo gaped as the planet rolled into view.

"It's beautiful, Odo Whitley. Look over there, it's the Atroxian moon."

"It's way bigger than ours. This is amazing, I can't believe I'm seeing this."

"All those stars."

"Look at the surface of Atroxia. It's so green, and there's an ocean way over there, a really big one."

"Odo, look down there, what does that look like to you?"

"That shiny thing? A big dome maybe? The quarantine dome! That has to be it."

Sephie called out to Mum, "Is there any way to magnify the view? We'd like to zoom in on the energy dome directly below us."

"I will magnify the image on your viewing screens."

The sparkling dome filled the windows.

"Mum, please analyze the nature of the dome."

"Yes, Commander. It is an impenetrable high energy defensive sphere. The dome appeared on the surface of the planet approximately two hundred years ago."

"Is there any way to get through it?"

"I can neutralize it for a three minute period if you wish."

"How would you do that?"

"With a MEAPS."

"Please explain to Captain Whitley the function of a MEAPS."

"Of course, Commander. Captain Whitley, a MEAPS is a Massive Energy Absorbing Positronic Shell, usually projected at half light speed. They are used to neutralize an interstellar destroyer's energy shields long enough to vaporize them with a particle fusion beam."

"How big is a MEAPS?"

"They are produced in a wide variety of sizes, dependent on their intended use."

"How about for something like the energy dome below us?"

"An A3 MEAPS would prove quite adequate. They are small enough to be held in the palm of your hand, often used by ground forces to breach such high energy shields."

"Do you have any on board?"

"Of course. Would you care to examine one?"

"We would indeed."

# Chapter 44

# Magic Show

Odo and Sephie returned to the military base using the violet transporter disk, finding Cyra and Jarin standing next to one of the interstellar ships.

Cyra called out, "Where have you been? We couldn't find you anywhere."

Odo pulled a MEAPS from his pack. "We had a little visit with someone called Mum. She gave us two tickets into the quarantine dome."

Sephie told Cyra and Jarin about their excursion to the orbiting weapons platform, and how Mum had given them the MEAPS.

"She said they'll absorb the dome's energy shield for about thirty seconds, plenty of time for us to pass through. We have two of them, one to get in and one to get out."

"We explored more of the base while you were gone. There's a huge weapons arsenal, but nothing we can really use. We're not here to kill Sensus and his children, just to find Addy and the doll."

"Maybe we can stop the invasions."

"If we did that, Fortisia wouldn't need the spectral moat."

"And you could go home."

"So could thousands of other Fortisians, Wikerus Praevian, for one."

The adventurers exited the underground Atroxian base, continuing their journey to the quarantine dome.

"What do you think it will be like inside?"

Odo's eyes brightened. "Hey, what if they thought we were slaves? Jarin could pretend to be one of Sensus' children and say he captured us. They'd take us to wherever the slaves were."

Sephie frowned. "We'd be slaves, Odo Whitley. They'd take our power shields and dusters and time throttles."

"There are hundreds of thousands of Sensus's children in there. Even with everything Advenus gave us, we're hopelessly outnumbered. We'll have our invisibility disks, and you and Cyra will still have all your powers. They won't know you're Fortisians."

Cyra nodded. "It might work. I was thinking about formshifting into a Stirpian, but they would probably see through that, like Advenus did when I was a Plindorian."

"What do you think, Jarin? Would they know you weren't one of them? "

Jarin froze, his unblinking eyes staring straight ahead.

"You have been busy. Very impressive how you

found the MEAPS."

"Karolus?"

"I've been following your exploits with some interest. The underground city was fascinating. I wish I could have seen the planet from the orbiting defense platform. It must have been lovely."

"It was beautiful. Stirpians have been good caretakers of this world."

"Thank you. To answer your question, Sensus' children would instantly detect Jarin's true identity, but not if I alter his memories. I can make him believe he is one of Sensus' children, that he captured you inside the dome. He will remember nothing of his previous life."

"You can restore his memory when he leaves the dome?"

"Of course, I am the holder of all memories. I will wait until you have entered the dome before I begin. Be aware he will show you no kindness, he will not be the Jarin you know."

"Do you know what they do with the slaves?"

"I do not. All communication with Sensus ended long ago."

"Well, all we have to do now is get captured, find the doll, rescue Addy, and escape from the dome. How hard could that be?"

"And we have to put an end to their invasions."

Jarin's eyes blinked back into focus. He turned to Sephie. "I am certain I can conceal my true identity from them."

Sephie was having a hard time imagining Jarin as one

of Sensus' murderous children.

Five days later the adventurers crested a mountainous ridge, Odo spotting the sparkling dome in the distance.

"There it is. It's in a desert. Great, more sand."

Sephie eyed the monolithic dome, a dark feeling rolling through her. She looked at Odo, Cyra, and Jarin. She couldn't bear the thought of losing any of them. She pressed a hand to her homestone. They could leave right now. She and Odo could shift home to a world unaware of Atroxians or Stirpians or the myriad of other civilizations populating the universe. She could be back in school with Odo, passing notes, eating lunch, laughing. They could sit on the roof outside her window and talk for hours. She closed her eyes, listening to her deeper self.

*"Audaces fortuna iuvat."*

These were the words she had laughingly spoken to Odo when he asked her about his ring. *Fortune favors the bold.* That was all she needed to hear.

"Let's not keep Addy waiting." She grabbed her pack, stepping onto the rocky trail.

After a wild scramble down the steep ridge they reached the desert below.

"At least it's not hot like it was on Plindor, and no crazy wind."

They set up camp to get some much needed rest. The journey over the ridge had been arduous, and once they entered the dome there would be little time for sleep. Cyra shaped tents and sleeping bags to ward off the chilly night air.

Odo was awakened in the middle of the night by an eerie light streaming through his tent flaps. He pushed them aside, peering outside.

"Whoa!"

Quickly throwing on his clothes, he crawled out, gazing up at the astonishing source of the light. He heard Sephie's voice behind him.

"Have you ever seen a moon like that, Odo Whitley?"

Odo shook his head. "It's incredible. Magical."

The two friends sat on the sand, watching the titanic moon drift slowly across the desert sky.

"You know how you always say there's no magic, only science?"

"That's true, Odo Whitley. There is only science."

"Have you ever been to a magic show?"

"When I was seven my parents took me to one."

"I was eight when I went. What's the first thing you did when you saw the magician do a trick?"

"I tried to figure out how he did it. It only took a minute, he wasn't a very good magician."

"I did the same thing."

"What are you saying, Odo Whitley?"

"I'm saying the universe is a magic show and we're all trying to figure out how the tricks are done."

Sephie smiled.

Odo looked at her, then up at the glorious moon. It was a moment he would treasure for the rest of his days.

# Chapter 45

# Spies!

"Are you nervous?"

Odo nodded. "A little. Maybe more than a little. I wish we could see inside the dome."

"You have the MEAPS?"

Odo held up the small spherical device. "Got it. It doesn't seem possible this little ball could shut down that gigantic energy dome. It's fifty miles across, five miles high."

"Mum wouldn't dare lie to Commander Sephie Crumb."

Odo laughed.

"Okay, Mum said to twist the top of the sphere as far as it will go, then throw it onto the dome. One minute later the energy wall vanishes for thirty seconds. Once were inside, Jarin will start hollering that he's captured three intruders."

Cyra said, "We should leave the devices Advenus

gave us outside, especially the dusters. It will arouse a lot less suspicion if we're not armed."

"They'd take them from us anyway. Keep your invisibility disks."

"Done. Are we ready?"

"Wait!" Cyra drew a quick symbol in the air and her hair turned jet black. "Okay."

Sephie grinned. "You look kind of cool. Here we go."

Odo twisted the top of the MEAPS, hurling it onto the dome.

Sephie checked her watch. "Twenty seconds."

There was no thundering explosion or blinding blast of energy. The energy dome simply vanished.

"Let's go!" The four adventurers darted inside.

Odo gaped at the towering black structures, turning around just in time to see the dome blink on again.

Jarin stopped, his eyes fixed and staring. He shook his head as though trying to focus, then pointed to Odo, Sephie, and Cyra, shrieking, "Spies!! Intruders! Assistance!!"

Six heavily armed Stirpian soldiers charged around the corner of an enormous black building, aiming their deadly Atroxian dusters at the three friends.

One of the Stirpians held up his hand, motioning for the others to lower their weapons. "Don't kill them until we find out why they're here."

"Should we take them to the Gate?"

"We will do whatever the Supreme Commander orders us to–"

The soldier stopped abruptly, his eyes losing focus.

"What's happening to them?"

"Sensus has taken control of them, just like Karolus did with Jarin."

The Stirpians holstered their dusters.

"I'm hungry, let's get some lunch." They turned and walked away.

"What just happened?"

Cyra shook her head. "I don't think Sensus wants us to be his prisoners."

"Why?"

"I don't know."

Sephie gazed at the sprawling maze of towering black structures surrounding them. "I've never seen buildings like this. They don't have any windows."

"They're not buildings, they're Atroxian interstellar battle cruisers."

Jarin spotted three more Stirpian guards, shouting, "Spies! I have captured three spies! Intruder alert!!"

The guards sauntered past as though Jarin wasn't there.

"Why aren't they listening to me? Spies!!"

Cyra turned to Jarin. "We're not spies. All the other soldiers know that. That's why they're not paying any attention."

"You're not spies? What are you doing here?"

"We're sightseeing. The Supreme Commander invited us here as his personal guests."

Jarin fell to his knees. "I did not know, I was not informed of this. Please forgive my reprehensible behavior. Your words shall bend my will."

"Relax, there's no way you could have known, he only invited us yesterday. Why don't you come with us while we tour the colony? It's an amazing place, isn't it?"

"Yes, I… it does look quite… amazing." Jarin's eyes were on the titanic battle cruisers, clearly baffled by what he was seeing.

Odo whispered to Sephie, "He doesn't know what they are."

"Karolus has never seen an Atroxian battle cruiser, so he couldn't implant memories of them."

"Now we know how they invade other worlds. The interstellar ships don't travel through space, so they don't have to pass through the quarantine dome. Sensus must have uncovered an underground Atroxian military base and brought the ships up to the surface."

Odo leaned back against the huge ship. "How do we find the slaves?"

"We know Sensus doesn't want us taken captive. I think he wants us to explore the dome."

"Why?"

"He wants us to find the object we're looking for, the item Sephie lost. He desperately wants it, but doesn't know what it is. They know it's old, an antique, but that's all. Think about it. Who told us about Girard Station? A Stirpian did. Who told us to look for antiques in Pacalia? A Stirpian. They've been watching us since we visited Wikerus, and they've been trying to help us find whatever it is they're after."

261

"Odo Whitley, you're a brainiac. That has to be it. What we don't know is why the object we're searching for is so important."

"What now?"

"We look for Addy."

The adventurers made their way past row after row of the enormous battle cruisers, finally coming to a hundred foot tall white Morsennium wall.

"We're in a restricted area. Look at the guards, there must be twenty of them watching the gate. Should we use our invisibility disks?"

"I think we'll be fine, Odo Whitley."

Sephie strolled casually over to the guard station.

"They're not even looking at us."

She stepped closer. One of the guards yawned.

"I don't think they can see us."

Odo waved at them. "Hello?"

"They can't hear us either."

The four friends walked past the armored doors into the world of Sensus and his murderous children.

# Chapter 46

# The Plindorian

"Odo's jaw dropped when he saw the spectacular gleaming skyscrapers reaching up thousands of feet, hundreds of transparent flying spheres darting through the air above the city.

"Look at the flying cars! Someone just got out of that one that landed."

"I don't like this, Odo Whitley. Something is wrong."

"There's nothing wrong, it's just a big city. Let's look around. Cyra, is this like a city on Fortisia?"

"We don't have big cities. Fortisia is much more like Jarin's world."

"Those flying spheres look really fun."

"Let's head down that big avenue."

"I can't believe how crowded it is. The sidewalks are jammed with people."

They walked along the wide boulevard, pushing

their way through teeming throngs of Stirpians, dozens of the transparent spheres flashing past overhead.

"Another one of those flying cars landed."

Odo watched three Stirpians climb out, the sphere shooting up into the air seconds later. He glanced over at Sephie, his grin fading when he saw her face.

"What's wrong?"

"Odo, look at the Stirpians and tell me what you see."

Odo stopped, studying the crowds around him.

"They all look scared, anxious."

"And so angry. These are not happy people. We need to be careful."

As if on cue, a Stirpian next to Odo bellowed at another one standing in a doorway. "Stop looking at me!"

"You're the one who's looking!"

"I see your true face, demon! I will kill you!"

The Stirpian in the doorway ducked down, reaching into his coat pocket. He wasn't fast enough. A beam of purple light flashed out from the first Stirpian's duster. The only thing left of the Stirpian crouched in the doorway was a cloud of gray ash drifting through the air.

The Stirpian next to Odo jammed the duster into his pocket, pushing back into the crowd. No one had stopped, not a single head had turned.

Odo was stunned. "He killed him! He killed that guy for no reason. Why isn't anyone doing anything?"

Cyra touched Odo's arm. "Remember what Karolus

said about Sensus? He is paranoid, delusional, and brutally aggressive. He thinks the other brains are trying to steal his children, trying to destroy him, take everything he has. His children's behavior reflect his sickness. They are his bodies, reacting to his twisted thoughts, seeing demons where there are none."

"This is not good. Sensus is only keeping us alive until we find what he's looking for. Once he gets it, he'll kill us."

"That's not going to happen. Don't forget what Sephie and I can do."

"I know, it's just…"

Sephie scanned the crowds, searching for any brain-waves which would reveal the presence of slaves.

"No brainwaves, they're all Stirpians. Where are the slaves?"

"We could ask someone."

Sephie gave Odo a dubious glance. "Excuse me, murderous child of Sensus, could you please tell me where you keep all your slaves?"

"Good point. I guess we just keep looking."

"Let's check inside that building, maybe slaves aren't allowed outside."

"That's definitely the tallest building I've ever seen."

A pair of ornate silver doors slid open as Odo approached the sparkling glass skyscraper, the adventurers stepping into the cavernous foyer. Hundreds of Stirpians were milling about, the floor lined with rows of violet blinking disks.

"Transporter disks like the one that took us to the weapons platform. They must use them instead of elevators."

"That Stirpian just stepped on one and vanished."

"Let's go to the top floor. We'll have a good view of the city, maybe see something."

"Like we did on the ferris wheel?"

Sephie laughed, stopping when she noticed Jarin's somber expression. He had not spoken since they entered the city.

"Jarin, are you okay?"

"You will not tell the Supreme Commander that I called you intruders and spies?"

"Are you still worried about that?" She put her hand on his shoulder. "No one is going to hurt you, Jarin. We are your friends and will look out for you, protect you. You are safe with us."

"Safe?"

"We will not let anyone harm you."

"I will help you find your lost Plindorian friend."

"Thank you, Jarin. Odo Whitley, have you figured out which transporter disk to use?"

Odo was studying the huge grid of transporter disks spread out across the foyer.

"All the disks have symbols on them, probably the floor number. The first row of disks have only one symbol, the disks in the back row have four symbols."

"Bigger numbers for higher floors."

"Right. If Stirpians read from left to right, the top floor should be the back row, last disk on the right."

A sudden outburst of angry shouting erupted from across the room. Two Stirpians were fighting, one of them slamming the other into a wall, knocking him unconscious. Two more joined the fight, punching the first one. He shrieked in pain, pulling out a duster.

"Let's get out of here. I don't want to get vaporized."

The four friends pushed their way through the crowd to the last row of disks.

"That one."

Odo stepped onto the disk and vanished.

When he arrived on the top floor Odo found himself surrounded by hundreds of Stirpians. He pushed his way through the throng of sightseers to the viewing windows.

"It's an observation deck. This is perfect, I can see the whole city."

He gazed through the tall windows to the streets three thousand feet below. "I can't believe how many people live here."

Sephie was trapped in the center of the crowded room, several hundred Stirpians trying to push their way to the windows. Odo spotted her, calling out, "Sephie, over here! Look at this!"

Sephie groaned as she squeezed through the crowd toward Odo. "The box is empty. I'm on the ground floor. Safe on the ground floor."

She inched her way over to Odo, feeling dizzy.

"We're high up... so high up."

"Relax, the windows are really thick and they're not

glass, they're made of something a lot stronger."

Sephie stepped closer to the window.

"What are we looking for?"

"I don't know exactly. Just something."

"Everything looks so small from up here. Look at all the flying spheres."

Cyra and Jarin emerged from the crowd.

"It took us ten minutes to get across the room."

"Cyra, do you have those binocular glasses?"

She pulled them from her pack, handing them to Odo.

"Thanks."

Odo slipped them on and twisted the dial, magnifying his view of the city.

"This is great, I can almost make out people's faces from up here. One of those spheres landed on the building below us. Four guys in shiny suits got out."

An hour later Odo was still studying the city. Sephie and Cyra were sitting on the floor, leaning back against the wall.

"Odo, I don't think we're going to find anything up here."

"Maybe not, but it's really interesting, some sections of the city aren't jammed with skyscrapers and crowds. I found something that looks like a park, it actually has some green grass and a bunch of–" Odo stopped in the middle of his sentence.

"A bunch of what?"

"Sephie, come look at this! Is that what I think it is?"

Sephie jumped up, taking the glasses from Odo.

"Look at the tiny green area in the distance. In the middle of the trees there's a yellow dot."

"It's a Plindorian. There's a Plindorian hiding in the woods."

"Maybe it's Addy."

Sephie shook her head. "I don't think so. It's something else, but I'm not sure what. It shouldn't take us too long to get there, half an hour if we take the side streets."

They pushed their way across the room to a row of transporter disks.

"They all have the same symbol. Must be the ground floor." Odo stepped on one and vanished.

Twenty minutes later the four friends were racing toward the park where they had spotted the Plindorian.

"Take the next left!"

They dashed down a side street, weaving through the crowds.

"Which way?"

"Turn right, past that big floating sphere!"

"It's full of Stirpians, it could be a flying bus. I wonder if we–"

"Time is money, Odo Whitley! Hurry!"

"I can see the park!"

They sprinted toward the trees, skidding to a halt in front of a pale violet glowing wall.

"The park is surrounded by an energy field. How do we get in? "

Cyra pressed her hand against the smooth surface of the energy sphere. She shrugged. "It's a weak field, just strong enough to keep people out. Hold on."

A brilliant blue light surrounded her hand, a small hole appearing in the energy wall. Thirty seconds later it was large enough for them to squeeze through.

"Everyone inside!"

Cyra was the last one in, the hole disappearing when she pulled her hand away.

"Where was the Plindorian?"

"Over there, in that thicket of trees."

Cyra held up one hand. "Wait here. I don't want to scare him." She stepped forward, slipping between the trees.

The Plindorian was lying on the ground. He looked weak, barely turning his head at the sound of Cyra's voice, his eyes wide at the sight of her.

Cyra kneeled down in front of him.

"It's all right, we're here to help you. Are you sick?"

"Thirsty."

Cyra flicked her wrist, shaping a bowl of water.

"Drink slowly, not too fast."

The Plindorian drank it all.

Odo and Sephie stepped into the clearing.

The Plindorian attempted a weak smile. "Thank you. I am Antar. Do you have any food? I haven't eaten in almost two weeks."

Cyra drew a small symbol in the air and a platter of fresh vegetables appeared in front of the Plindorian.

"Just a little at first until your body gets used to it."

"I thought I was going to die."

"How did you get here?"

"The Atroxians captured me on Plindor. There were twelve of us on the ship."

"You escaped?"

"I slipped away when the guards were distracted, following the tunnels up to the surface, sneaking through the Gate."

"Tunnels? You were underground?"

Antar nodded. "They put us in a village with other Plindorians, in a place they call Old World. There are many villages, each filled with creatures from different worlds."

"You weren't slaves?"

"Not slaves, but captives, forced to live in the villages with others like us."

"Why?"

The Plindorian shook his head. "I don't know. There were guards, but they never harmed us. They just watched us, listened to us. I was trying to get back to Plindor and get help, but couldn't pass through the dome."

"Was there a Plindorian named Addy in your village? We're trying to find her."

"There was a young girl named Addy, but she's not there anymore."

"What happened to her?"

"She escaped."

"Up to the surface? Do you know where she is?"

"Not to the surface, she said she was going down into the Forbidden Tunnels, that there was something she needed to do."

"Did she say what?"

"She didn't know for certain, and she never returned."

"Antar, how do we get to the Forbidden Tunnels?"

"Through the Gate, the entrance to Old World. It's three miles north of here, a round silver building."

"You have no idea at all why they keep the captives in the villages?"

"None. They just watched us."

A curious thought popped into Sephie's mind. "Are you a shifter?"

Antar gave a start. "How did you know? I am, but they took my homestone."

Odo reached into his pack, pulling out a chunk of green jade.

"This is from Plindor, from the jade mountain in the desert."

Sephie eyed the valuable stone. "Antar, I'd like you to meet Odo the Treasure Hunter."

Odo snorted. "It's nothing like that at all. I knew it would come in handy. Probably a message from my deeper self."

"Don't you mean it would come in handy if you needed extra spending money?"

"How insulting." Odo grinned, handing the piece of lustrous jade to the Plindorian.

"Bless you. I know the jade mountain well, it is not far from my village. I will send help."

"No, his forces are too powerful. We have to do this alone."

"As you wish. You will be in my prayers. I will tell your story, you will not be forgotten."

"We'll be fine."

Antar gripped the piece of jade tightly, closing his eyes. Three seconds later he was gone.

Odo looked at Sephie. "We'll be fine?"

"Of course we will, Odo Whitley. Translucent Boy and Encephalo Girl always save the day. I can't believe you don't know that. Everyone knows that."

Odo's eyes narrowed.

# Chapter 47

# Yardy

The adventurers spent the night in the park, resting up before continuing their search for Addy. Early the next morning they set off for the Gate.

"Old World must be an underground Atroxian military complex discovered by Sensus. It's probably where he found the interstellar battlecruisers and weapons."

Odo walked alongside Sephie. "He salvaged a lot of other technology besides ships and weapons. The city is amazing, especially those flying sphere things. I wish we had those back home. That would be so fun."

"Even with all their advanced technology the Stirpians are angry and afraid, killing each other for no reason. No amount of technology will change that." Cyra tapped her head. "Happiness comes from here, nowhere else. Only Sensus can bring happiness to his children."

"That's a good point. I'd think I'd be happy with or

without technology. When I was young I was angry all the time about being translucent, angry that no one ever saw me, that I didn't have friends. I was thirteen when I realized being angry at stuff made me feel miserable all the time and it didn't change anything. I decided to look on the bright side of everything, and do stuff I liked."

Cyra's gaze was distant. "When I was little my mom said life was like being dropped into the middle of a big dark forest with a tiny flashlight, and you had to find your way out. I didn't really understand what she meant until I lost them. My dark forest was my mom and dad dying in the crash. I'm still trying to find my way out."

"Mine was being born translucent."

"My dark forest is not knowing where I came from, who my real parents were, and why they left me in the snow. I'm still lost in the forest. I don't know if I'll ever get out."

"But now you know your dad was Fortisian and your mom was from Earth. They wouldn't have left you in the snow unless they had no other choice."

"Unless they didn't want me."

Cyra stopped. "I have a plan. Jarin, you tell the guards you're a soldier being transferred to the Plindorian village in Old World, and while you're distracting them we'll sneak in."

Jarin looked pleased. "I will be happy to help you."

The party of adventurers made their way through the early morning crowds, the sidewalks packed with Stirpians on their way to work. During the three mile walk to the Gate, Odo witnessed six fights and two

275

murders. Sephie saw a Stirpian get thrown out of a flying sphere, falling to his death.

"These Stirpians are lost in a very dark forest, Odo Whitley, and I don't think they have a flashlight."

Cyra pointed to a building a hundred yards in front of them.

"That's it, the round silver building Antar told us about. There are four guards at the entrance. Jarin, you go first and we'll sneak past while you're talking to them."

Sephie and Odo tapped their disks, Cyra blinking up a sphere of invisibility.

"Okay, we have ten minutes, plenty of time to get through. Walk behind Jarin, try not to make any noise."

Four stone faced guards in jet black uniforms eyed Jarin. One of them waved him away.

"No civilians allowed. This is a high security area by proclamation of the Supreme Commander."

"I am a new guard on my way to the Plindorian village in Old World."

The guard gave a disgusted snort.

"Get lost, civilian."

"I am a new guard on my way to the Plindorian village in Old World."

"Where's your uniform? Where's your security ring? What's your sector number? Where are your transfer papers?"

Jarin stared blankly at the guard. "My what?"

Two of the guards pulled silver dusters from their holsters.

"You were warned, civilian."

The scowling guards aimed their dusters at Jarin.

"Any last words?"

Jarin's eyes were wide. "I am a new guard on my way to the Plindorian village in Old World."

Odo leaped forward to grab the guards' dusters, but stopped short when he saw their faces change. Both guards holstered their weapons. Seconds later the armored doors rumbled open.

"Right this way, Commander. Welcome to Old World."

The guards saluted Jarin as he passed through the massive doorway, followed by his three invisible friends.

Odo whispered, "Sensus is controlling them. He wants us to go in, to find the thing we're looking for."

"Look at the size of this tunnel."

"Big enough to get the interstellar ships out."

Odo ran his hand along the smooth gleaming tunnel wall.

"What is this stuff? It looks almost like white glass."

Cyra said, "It's a synthetic called Morsennium, one of the strongest materials known."

Sephie tapped her invisibility disk, blinking back into view.

"Let's explore Old World before we go down into the Forbidden Tunnels."

"I wonder why Addy went down there?"

"Maybe they're full of ghosts handing out ancient Roman coins."

"Gold coins?"

"Of course they'd be gold coins. No self respecting Roman ghost would be caught handing out bronze coins. Everyone knows that."

"Are you trying to sound like my dad?"

"One day your dad will see you like I do."

Odo gave Sephie an odd look.

The adventurers made their way through the long winding tunnel, descending deeper beneath the surface of Atroxia.

"My ears are popping."

"The tunnel is leveling off. We must be getting near Old World."

Odo rounded a wide curve, stopping abruptly.

"No way."

Sephie gaped at the sprawling vista of gray spherical structures stretching out for miles across a flat colorless terrain illuminated by shimmering blue lights from the cavern's roof.

"Are those buildings?"

"It looks like a city."

"All the buildings are round. Let's look inside one."

"The streets are made of Morsennium. This is in-credible."

"The grass is gray."

Sephie pointed to one of the front lawns.

"And there are skeletons."

"What?" Odo peered over a low metal fence. "That is seriously creepy. They look human, except small, with big heads and long arms."

"They must be Atroxians. The biggest one is only four feet long."

"I don't like skeletons."

"Are you afraid they'll jump up and start chasing you, Odo Whitley? With big swords and axes?"

"Angry skeletons always carry swords and axes."

"I don't think these ones are going to get up."

Odo sighed. "I don't either. They've been here for a long time. What do you think happened to them?"

"Let's look inside the house." Sephie swung open the gate and walked up a dark gray path to the front door.

"It's open." She slid the oval door aside and peered in. "It's definitely a home, with furniture and rugs. And a gray couch with two skeletons. They're holding each other."

"I'm not going into a skeleton house."

Cyra stepped inside, studying the skeletons. "They died quickly." She spun around. "Did you hear that?"

"Hear what?"

"That rattling sound. It came from next door." A powerful field of energy popped up around her.

"Watch out for angry skeletons with swords."

Sephie eyed the two skeletons on the couch. "We probably shouldn't joke about them, Odo Whitley."

"I didn't want to think about what really happened here."

Odo heard the rattling sound as they approached the next house. "It's coming from the little building in the backyard. It could be a garden shed."

"Everyone keep back."

Cyra pressed her ear to the door. "Something is moving in there." She slid the door open, jumping out of the way when a shadowy figure moved toward her.

"What is that thing??"

A dark green spindly creature emerged from the sphere, a silver pole in one hand.

"It has a duster!"

"It's a rake, Odo Whitley."

The creature stood six feet tall and was astonishingly thin, its torso and extremities made of smooth gleaming flexible tubing. Perched on its neck was a black translucent sphere the size of a large coconut, a swarm of tiny green lights buzzing around inside it.

"What's in its head? Are those bugs?"

"It's raking the lawn."

Cyra blinked off her energy field, stepping over to the curious creature.

"Greetings, I am Cyra."

The swarm of green lights in the creature's head glowed brightly.

"I am a Model 9000 YardMaster, commonly referred to as a Yardy."

"You maintain the yard? Is that correct?"

"The yard and exterior of the home."

Yardy continued raking.

"Yardy, how long have you been inside the shed?"

"I am uncertain. I automatically power down after one week of inactivity, entering sleep mode. I was awakened by your voices. I have much to do, my home is in a dreadful state of disrepair."

Sephie stepped forward.

"Hello, Yardy. My name is Sephie."

"Good afternoon, Sephie. Lovely weather we've been having. The flowers could use some rain. I love your outfit, it enhances your appearance."

"Um... thanks. I was wondering if you had noticed all the skeletons on the lawns?"

"Of course. They will need to be disposed of."

"Why are they there?"

"They belong to the Atroxians who died."

"Do you know how they died?"

"There was an issue with the Global Air Purification Grid. The system crashed, shutting down all the towers."

"You saw what happened?"

"I was raking the lawn when I heard someone shouting about the GAP Grid, telling everyone to put on their masks. The red cloud came in fast, flowing across the ground like water, only a foot deep at first. Citizens were running everywhere. Within ten minutes the cloud was twenty feet deep. By the time I finished raking the lawn everyone was lying on the ground. I returned to the shed. After one week I entered sleep mode."

"That was almost two thousand years ago, Yardy."

"That would explain the yard's state of disrepair. Once the grounds have been tidied up I'll begin work on the exterior of the house. It needs to be resurfaced."

"Yardy, do you know where the Forbidden Tunnels are? We're trying to find a lost friend."

"The only tunnels I am aware of are the First Tunnels, directly to the east. The military base is to the south, but there are no tunnels there."

"Thank you, Yardy."

Odo couldn't take his eyes off the two skeletons lying on the front steps. One of them was very small.

Yardy went back to his raking. As they walked away Odo could hear him humming a catchy little tune.

# Chapter 48

# The First Tunnels

"Exploring the military base sounds more fun than going into those creepy Forbidden Tunnels."

"Maybe, but that's where Addy is. Yardy called them the First Tunnels."

Cyra said, "The First Stirpian tunneled below the planet's surface when he arrived on Atroxia. The First Tunnels could be the tunnels Sensus made when he burrowed down."

"You're saying Sensus is down in the Forbidden Tunnels?" Odo did not look at all pleased by this revelation. "Does anyone know what he looks like? Is he a giant brain?"

"We should look for Addy." Cyra turned down a narrow street. "This way to the other side of the city."

Odo and Sephie strolled along behind Cyra, scanning the yards for movement.

"There's a Yardy fixing that roof. I don't see any

skeletons though, so that's good."

Sephie pointed to a mound of bones on the sidewalk fifty feet ahead of them.

"Oh, I guess he picked them up already."

Odo tried not to look at the jumbled mass of bones as they walked past.

"I do not like skeletons."

Sephie shrugged. "It's a pile of old cars."

"What do you mean? Those are skeletons, not cars."

"What happens to us when we die, Odo Whitley?"

"I don't like to think about it."

"Do you remember what I said about your deeper self existing outside of space and time?"

"I remember. What do old cars have to do with that?"

"Your body is a car that your deeper self drives around the world. When you die, your deeper self gets out of the car and leaves it behind. Skeletons are just old abandoned cars."

"So where does my deeper self go after it leaves?"

"It doesn't go anywhere. It already exists outside of space and time. It lives where time does not exist."

"That's confusing. Besides, I don't want to live outside of space and time. I like this world."

"I like this world too, Odo Whitley. It's fun having you for my friend."

Odo grinned. "We have a lot of stuff to do before it's time to park our cars, Sephie Crumb."

Sephie took Odo's hand as they walked down the long street.

The adventurers camped twice on their trek across the sprawling underground city, passing numerous piles of skeletons collected by the Yardies. Odo refused to sleep in the ancient Atroxian homes, calling them skeleton houses.

It was Sephie who spotted the irregular dark shape on the far wall of the city.

"That looks a lot like a tunnel entrance."

"How do we know it's the right one?"

"Because it's the only one?"

Cyra ran ahead to the tunnel entrance. She was gazing into its inky blackness when the others caught up to her.

Odo peered into the tunnel. "It doesn't look very safe, no Morsennium walls."

"That's what makes it fun." Cyra grinned, drawing a symbol in the air. Three glowing orbs of light shot into the gloomy tunnel.

Odo stepped in after her, his eyes on the craggy walls.

"It looks like a giant gopher tunnel. Look at those claw marks."

Sephie grinned. "Maybe Emperor Geomyidae dug it."

"What does that mean?"

"It's a Latin joke, Odo Whitley."

"Right. What do you think Sensus looks like?"

"Stop asking that or I'll have Cyra throw you in the noggle box."

"I'm not afraid of Sensus, I was just wondering what

he looks like."

An hour later the tunnel widened, opening to a massive cavern, its roof a sea of tiny glowing lights.

"Whoa, they look like blue stars."

Cyra studied the glowing ceiling. "Bioluminescence. Some kind of insect larvae probably."

"I've read about insects called fungus gnats that live in caves back on Earth. They glow just like these do."

"Walk slowly, don't disturb them. They could be dangerous. Very, very, dangerous." Sephie snickered.

Odo rolled his eyes. "You can't scare me."

Sephie pointed to the far wall. "Two tunnels. Which one do we take?"

"One of them is a lot bigger."

"So we should take that one?"

"Let's try the smaller one first. If we don't find her in that one we can always come back and try the big one."

The adventurers entered the narrow tunnel, walking until they reached a second cavern, this one filled with tall glowing orange plants.

"They look like weird puffy cactuses." Odo stepped over to the closest plant and touched it, skittering back with a yelp.

"It moved! There's something inside it!"

"Quiet. Do you hear that?"

"It sounds like someone snoring."

"The plants are breathing. They must be a hybrid, part plant and part animal."

"Do you think they can walk?"

Sephie grinned. "You mean chase you with big snapping teeth?"

"That's not what I meant at all. I'm not scared of them, I was just curious. I've never seen a plant that breathes like a person. It's weird, not scary."

Cyra touched one of the plants. "They're probably harmless, like mushrooms. Mushrooms take in oxygen and give off carbon dioxide like people do. Lots of those bioluminescent insects on the ceiling."

"Let's take that tunnel over there."

That was the moment Odo spotted the gleaming gold coin on the ground next to one of the breathing plants. He darted over and picked it up, feeling its weight. "Whoa, this is real gold."

He glanced up just in time to see the others disappear into the tunnel. Odo ran after them, stopping when he saw the glint of gold coins piled behind several of the bulbous orange plants.

"Whoa! I'll be seriously rich. This will help pay for my college. I'll grab them, then catch up." He ran past the plants, his eyes on the pile of gold coins.

"Hello, my shiny round friends. How about a little ride in Odo's backpack?"

He grinned, leaning over and grabbing a handful of the gleaming coins, stuffing them into his pack.

The last thing he remembered was a sharp pain on the back of his head.

\* \* \* \*

Odo was dreaming that he and Sephie were on their way to Wikerus Praevian's house to tell him about the breathing plants they'd found on Atroxia. Sephie was laughing, pretending to be one of the plants, saying she was going to chase Odo with big snappy teeth. He was rolling his eyes when something grabbed his shoulder, shaking it violently, bringing his pleasant dream to an abrupt end. When he woke he was staring at a large blue snake creature with two arms, red blinking eyes, and a flickering black tongue.

The snake creature hissed at him. "Who are you? What are you doing down here?"

"Are you going to eat me?"

"What? Why would I eat you?"

"Well, you… um… you know, you're…"

"What are you? You're not Atroxian, you're not Stirpian. Did you escape from a village?"

"No, I'm a human. I come from Earth. We're looking for someone."

"Stand up."

Odo staggered to his feet, his head throbbing. "Did you whack me on the head? You could have just asked me—"

The snake waved one arm and ropes appeared, wrapping themselves around Odo.

"What are you doing?" He wriggled wildly, trying to break free of the ropes.

The snake pressed one of its scaly blue hands against Odo's temple. It felt like ants were crawling around inside his head. "Who is Addy?"

"What? She's who we're looking for. She's a Plin-dorian taken by the Stirpians. We're trying to bring her home."

"Go on."

"She has something we want, something that be-longed to my friend Sephie."

"Who are the others you travel with?"

"They're my friends, Sephie, Cyra, and Jarin."

"Why do you travel with a child of Sensus?"

"Jarin's a child of Karolus, not Sensus. He's helping us find Addy."

The ropes around Odo's arms vanished.

"Follow me, Odo Whitley. Addy's been waiting for you.

# Chapter 49

# Addy's Plan

Odo followed the snake creature through a maze of narrow tunnels, emerging into a low cavern occupied by an eclectic collection of curious creatures. He only recognized two of them, a Volucrian and a Plindorian, the others being new to him. Two looked like marshmallows with yellow chicken legs, three were blue snake creatures like his captor, one looked like butterscotch pudding with four yellow translucent wings, and one looked like a furry snail. The one thing they all had in common was they were staring at Odo.

The marshmallow creature jiggled. "Eew, what is it?"

"It's a human, from Earth."

The Plindorian jumped up. "You're from Earth?"

"Yes, I'm Odo Whitley. Are you Addy?"

"I've been waiting for you." She turned to the blue snake creature who had captured Odo. "Dr. Living-

290

stone, please find Odo's friends and bring them back here. Be nice to them."

"Should I whack them on the head?"

"No, I told you before, that's not being nice. No head whacking. Be friendly, polite, tell them Odo is safe and he found Addy. Try not to scare them."

"It would save a great deal of time if I could whack them all on the head and drag them back here."

"No."

Dr. Livingstone curled his lip, slithering off into the tunnel.

"His name is Dr. Livingstone?"

Addy laughed. "His real name is impossible to pronounce, so I call him Dr. Livingstone, named after a famous explorer on your planet. Everyone here escaped from the villages. I found them when I was exploring the tunnels."

"We talked to your dad. We're trying to find the doll you were playing with when the Stirpians took you."

"This one?"

Odo gave a start when he saw the doll with red and white striped legs floating in front of him.

"That's it!" He grabbed for the doll, his hand passing through it.

"Sorry, it's just a mental projection, not the real doll."

The image vanished.

"Do you know where the real doll is? Your dad is really worried about you."

"I know he is. I wish I could tell him I'm okay."

"He hasn't given up hope that you'll come home."

"We'll all be going home soon enough if everything goes according to plan."

"What do you mean?"

"It's complicated. Let's wait till your friends get here. Are you hungry? I could shape you a meal if you'd like."

"I'm starving. How about a grilled cheese sandwich, fries, a box of Proto's Taste-E Kakes, and a glass of lemonade?"

"How about a nice salad?"

"Fine."

Odo had just finished his lunch when he heard Sephie's voice echoing through the tunnel.

"How hard did you hit him? Are you sure he's okay?"

"A harmless whack on the head, he hardly noticed it. Nothing to be alarmed about, I assure you. Your friend Odo is fine, and he found Addy. Did that sound friendly enough? Should I say something nice about your appearance?"

Odo jumped to his feet when his friends entered the cave. Sephie threw her arms around him. "Are you okay? We were so worried."

"I'm fine. It was just a little knock on the head. I hardly even felt it." He glared at Dr. Livingstone.

Sephie turned to the Plindorian. "You must be Addy."

"I am. Dr. Livingstone and I have been waiting for you."

"Who is Dr. Livingstone?"

Odo eyed the blue snake creature. "The guy who likes to whack heads."

"I won't even ask about his name. Addy, you've been waiting for us? We're here to find my doll and bring you home."

"Odo said you were looking for it. Why is it so important? It was just an old doll my dad gave me."

"What happened to it?"

"I hid it in one of the little gray houses when I arrived. I didn't want the Stirpians to take it."

"It's still there?"

"It should be. I never went back for it."

"We need to find it."

"Sephie, there's something else, something far more important than the doll. We need your help and Cyra's help. We know you're both Fortisians."

"What kind of help?"

Addy smiled. "Ever done any brain surgery?"

"What?"

"Sensus is suffering from a brain disease which has drastically altered his personality, making him paranoid and delusional. I think we can cure him, but there are a few major obstacles in our way. First, he doesn't want to be cured, and second, he's incredibly powerful, capable of altering our thoughts, projecting all manner of illusions into our minds. It will take all of us to create an energy field strong enough to block his mental projections."

"How are you going to heal him? I know about brain

mapping, but nothing about brain surgery."

"I told you I read a lot. Maybe more than a lot, and my dad has taught me well. I've studied brain diseases. I'm quite certain Sensus has an accumulation of amyloid plaques in his brain."

Odo's face brightened. "I just read about that in my neurophysiology book. In a healthy brain, protein fragments from amyloid proteins are broken down and eliminated. In certain brain diseases, they're not broken down, and they accumulate, forming insoluble plaques."

"Which can damage neurons and affect the neuronal synapses."

"Altering their personality."

"So we have to get rid of all the plaques?"

"It's more complicated than that. We also need to remove neurofibrillary tangles. They're like plaques, but damage the microtubules which provide nourishment to the neurons. And we need to repair any damaged brain cells."

"That sounds impossible."

"I think we can do it if we work together. We have to put Sensus into an induced coma. Once he's under, Cyra, Sephie, and I will send our deeper selves into his brain and repair it. It may take a while, depending on what areas are damaged and how severe the damage is."

Cyra said, "Are you talking about the Traveling Eye? Moving our center of consciousness outside our physical body?"

"Exactly. Once your consciousness is inside Sensus

you can shape energy beams to clear away the plaques and tangles."

Sephie looked doubtful. "I've only done the Traveling Eye twice, with a lot of help from Cyra."

"You'll do fine. I'll be with you and show you exactly what to do."

"How do we put him in a coma?"

"That's the tricky part. We have to get close enough to inject him with powerful anesthetics."

"Do you know where he is?"

"Somewhere down in the tunnels. We have to find the original tunnel he made when he burrowed into the planet."

Odo couldn't help himself. "Do you know what he looks like?"

Sephie rolled her eyes. "Noggle box."

# Chapter 50

# Sensus

"Jarin, you stay here with the others. We'll go with Addy and look for Sensus. I don't know how long we'll be, but if something happens and we don't come back, use this MEAPS to escape from the dome."

"I will do as you wish."

"Thanks. Is everyone ready?"

"Ready."

Odo, Sephie, Cyra, and Addy headed down the narrow tunnel to the cavern with the breathing plants.

Odo grimaced as he walked through the forest of orange cactuses. "Plants aren't supposed to snore."

"It's just life, Odo Whitley. Every creature adapts to its environment."

"It's still weird."

Addy pointed to the far wall.

"There's a tunnel hidden behind those two big plants. It's the only one I haven't explored."

Odo slipped between the two cactuses and stepped into the dark tunnel. He sniffed the dank air. "It smells like rotten broccoli. Why would it smell like that?"

A brilliant orb of light flashed out from Addy's tentacle, illuminating the eerie tunnel. "Follow the smell, it might lead us to Sensus."

The adventurers trekked through the tunnel, descending deeper into the planet, the rancid broccoli odor growing stronger.

"Fork in the tunnel."

Odo stepped into the first tunnel, sniffing the air. "No broccoli smell." He tried the other one. "Definitely this one. It smells bad."

The adventurers continued on through the tunnel for almost an hour, the noxious broccoli smell worse than ever. Odo was holding his nose when he stopped abruptly, eyeing a gleaming brass door in the tunnel wall. "That's weird. Why would there be a brass door here?"

He stepped over to it, inching it open, peering inside. His jaw dropped when he saw Lost Lake Amusement Park. Sephie was in the crowd waving to him, a huge smile on her face.

"Odo, hurry up! Let's go on the ferris wheel! Come on! It'll be so much fun."

He slammed the door shut.

"Does anyone else see this brass door?"

"Brass door?"

"I think Sensus is making me see a door in the wall. When I opened it I saw Lost Lake Amusement Park.

You were there waving to me, saying you wanted to go on the ferris wheel with me. I don't think I would have come back."

"He knows we're here. We have to put up our energy shield now."

"How do we do it?"

Addy took Sephie's hand. "Everyone form a circle. We'll create a golden energy sphere around us to block his thought projections. Put all your energy into it. Odo, you're not a shaper yet, but do whatever you can to–"

Addy let out a sudden strange, unnatural laugh. "What am I thinking? This is silly, we don't need a shield, Sensus isn't going to–"

Sephie hollered, "Now!! Do it now!"

The four adventurers were instantly enveloped in a brilliant orb of golden light.

Addy looked confused. "What happened?"

"Sensus got to you. Help us make the shield stronger!"

A blinding light shot out from Addy's tentacles, the golden orb now pulsating and shimmering.

"That should do it. What did Sensus make me do?"

"You said we didn't need an energy shield."

"We're close. Keep the orb at full strength. Don't let it down for a second, and keep inside it no matter what."

"The brass door is gone."

"Good, that means the field is working."

The four friends made their way down the long curving tunnel, the smell of rotten broccoli making Odo nauseous.

"This smells so bad. I'm never eating broccoli again."

"Tiny skeletons on the tunnel floor."

"Are those real? Is he trying to scare us?"

"They're real. I think they're some of his children who didn't make it up to the surface."

"Creepy."

Cyra pointed to a steep drop off in the tunnel ahead of them.

"This is it, we go down there. Be careful. Everyone sit and slide slowly down this section of tunnel. Stay inside the energy sphere."

Ten minutes later they entered a glowing blue cavern, the walls and ceiling covered with immense jagged translucent white protrusions.

"Is that ice?"

"No, it's a crystalline formation, probably to reinforce the cave's structure."

"The smell is so bad. I think I'm going to barf. Which way do we go?"

"We don't go anywhere. He's right in front of us."

"What??"

"He made himself invisible."

"What do we do?"

There was a flash of light and Addy was holding a long wicked looking syringe filled with a dark green fluid.

"We make him not invisible. Move forward slowly, inch by inch. If any part of him gets inside the sphere he'll kill us all."

"Wait, I have an idea!" Odo reached down and picked up a handful of crystal shards. He threw one, watching it fly through the air for about ten feet, then bounce off an unseen object.

"You're brilliant, Odo. Keep tossing the crystals."

The adventurers crept forward until the outer wall of the energy sphere was inches from Sensus.

"Nobody move." Addy raised the deadly looking syringe high above her head. "Nighty night, Sensus."

Her long tentacle flashed down, plunging the eight inch needle into Sensus, injecting the green fluid into him.

A blinding white hot pain screamed through Odo's head when the forty foot long black wriggling mucous covered monstrosity appeared in front of them.

Odo staggered backwards, his eyes locked on the horrific undulating aberration and its thousands of sharp thrashing spiky red legs.

Sephie's hands were pressed against her temples.

"It hurts! What's he doing?"

"That thing is disgusting!"

"Stay inside the sphere! Just a few more seconds!"

The serpentine rows of flailing razor sharp legs were the first to stop moving. Seconds later the creature gave a deep shudder and lay still.

The searing pain vanished from Odo's head. He could scarcely breathe, his stomach turning at the sight of the nightmarish creation.

"What now?"

Addy waved a tentacle and the golden energy sphere around them vanished.

"Sephie and Cyra, you're both familiar with the Traveling Eye. We'll move our centers of awareness outside our physical bodies and travel inside Sensus. He's basically a giant brain covered with thousands of digging legs used for burrowing. Sephie, what do his brainwaves look like?"

Sephie studied the immense slumbering creature.

"There's an irregular section fifteen feet from that end that's dark, no brainwaves."

"That's where we go then."

The three friends formed a circle and closed their eyes.

"All right, you've both done this before. Close your eyes, visualize yourself floating above your body. Look down at yourself, focus on your physical form, make it become sharp and clear and solid, circling slowly around it. When your body seems absolutely real, open your eyes."

When Sephie opened her eyes she was floating ten feet above the cavern floor, looking down at herself. Cyra and Addy were floating next to her, their forms vaporous, barely visible. She could hear their thoughts.

"Good, we're all here. Don't forget, move around using your mind. Imagine where you want to be and you'll be there."

Odo studied the three friends standing in front of him. They were motionless, still holding hands in a circle, their eyes closed.

"Are you guys still here?"

A thought popped into his head.

"I'm floating about ten feet above you, Odo Whitley. We're fine. I don't know how long this will take."

"Are you a ghost?"

"Not a ghost, I just moved my center of awareness outside my physical body. It's a weird feeling, but kind of fun. I can float and travel through walls. We'll be fine."

Odo sat down, leaning back against the cavern wall, his eyes on the hideous mucous covered creation known as Sensus.

# Chapter 51

# Crunchy on the Outside

"Fly inside him. He's like an insect, crunchy on the outside, soft and chewy on the inside."

"Eww! I wish you hadn't said that." Sephie shot forward, passing through the chitinous outer shell into a glowing pink gelatinous mass.

"Sephie, check his brainwaves."

"Good here. It goes dark down that way. Follow me."

Sephie passed through the mass of brain matter until she reached the dark area.

"This whole section has been damaged. What do we do?"

"Shrink your awareness down. Keep shrinking until you can see individual neurons, the brain cells. They look a little bit like spiders."

"Did you have to say spiders?"

"No time to be squeamish. Let's go!"

Sephie imagined herself growing smaller and smaller until the great wrinkly lobes of brain matter had transformed into something surprisingly beautiful. "The neurons look like stars. This is amazing!"

"Smaller! We need to be smaller, the size of a single brain cell."

"They do look like spiders, but they're beautiful. There are trillions of them!"

"Over here, see how these neurons are wrinkly and shriveled? Those are the damaged ones. Look for solid round brown masses and tangles between the neurons, then vaporize them with an energy beam. You two do that while I work on repairing the damaged neurons. That's a bit more tricky."

"The plaques are the round brown things?"

"Yes, vaporize them all."

A blinding beam of light shot out from Sephie's translucent hand, a dozen of the round plaques vanishing. "It works!"

Sephie and Cyra soared through the titanic mass of neurons, blasting the plaques and the neurofibrillary tangles.

"How long till he wakes up?"

"I'm shaping anesthetics as we need them. I'll keep him in a coma until we're done."

It took six hours for Sephie and Cyra to clear away the plaques and tangles, seven hours for Addy to repair the damaged neurons.

"I don't see any plaques. I think we got them all."

"How are his brainwaves?"

"The damaged section is dim, but it's glowing, getting brighter."

"Perfect, the network is up again. It will take him a few hours to come out of the coma, and he'll need time to reroute some of his neural pathways. We should know in a day or so if it worked. He'll probably have some memory loss. Let's head back. Odo must be worried."

Sephie's awareness popped back into her body. She turned to see Odo leaning against the cave wall, his eyes closed.

"Odo, wake up! We're back."

He groaned, giving a loud yawn.

"Sorry, I must have fallen asleep. How long were you gone?"

"Seven hours."

"Whoa, I must have been really tired. How did it go?"

"Addy thinks we got everything and repaired all the damaged neurons."

"What now?"

"We free everyone in the villages and go up to the surface. It will take a day or so for Sensus to come out of the coma and become fully conscious."

"I like the part about getting out of here. Was it creepy in there?"

"Flying around the neurons wasn't creepy at all, it was amazing. You can't believe how complicated and how beautiful the neural networks are."

"Not as beautiful as a big blue sky."

Two hours later the adventurers and the village escapees stepped into Old World.

"I don't see any soldiers."

"Addy, can you take us to the villages?"

"We just head north."

The group made their way across the city, watching for Stirpian guards.

"All the villages are on the north side of the main street."

"Do you know why Sensus took captives from other worlds? We thought he was using them for slaves."

"I think he was studying us, trying to understand how we think, learn our weaknesses."

"Know your enemy?"

"Exactly. If he understands us, it's easier to defeat us. He was completely delusional, believing he was the chosen ruler of the universe."

"He's not the first to think that, and he won't be the last."

"You're right, greed and lust for power exist in every culture, on every world."

Odo stopped, pointing to three uniformed Stirpians sprawled out on the sidewalk ahead of them. "Are they dead?"

Cyra walked over to the soldiers and kneeled down, feeling for a pulse. "They're alive. They should wake up when Sensus comes out of his coma."

The group continued on, Odo spotting the first village, recognizing the praying mantis creatures behind the chain metal fence.

"There's the Volucrian village!"

"The guards are unconscious. Spread out and release everyone. We'll meet back here in an hour. Tell them to head up to the surface."

Sephie turned to Addy. "Do you remember where you hid the doll?"

"It was a little gray building next to the main road, about a quarter mile from here. I tossed it inside while I was walking along the street."

"I'm going to look for it." Sephie darted down the road. It didn't take her long to find a small gray sphere next to the sidewalk. The door was open and she stepped inside, a brilliant orb of light shooting from her hand. A ten minute search revealed an assortment of garden tools, but no doll.

"This is the only shed next to the street. It has to be here." She stopped when she heard the soft melodic humming.

"That's it!" She dashed out of the shed, spotting a Yardy by the back fence planting flowers.

"Excuse me! Did you happen to find a doll in the garden shed? It had a blue coat and red and white striped legs."

"Good afternoon, wonderful weather we're having. A little rain would help the flowers. I love your outfit, it enhances your appearance."

"A doll? In the shed?"

"Not one of ours so I tossed it in the trash. A tidy house is a happy house."

"You threw my doll out?"

The Yardy's head glowed brightly. "I know exactly where it is. Follow me."

The Yardy stepped briskly across the lawn, swinging the gate open.

"Quite appalling, the trash hasn't been picked up for ages. You'll find the doll in the thirteenth bin on the left side. That's where I threw it."

Sephie ran to the bin and flipped open the heavy lid, her heart racing. She gave a shriek when she saw the red and white striped leg peeking out from a pile of leafy debris. She grabbed the doll, pressing it tightly to her chest, a flood of memories pouring through her.

"I couldn't sleep without it. The smell of it, the softness of it was so comforting." Her eyes welled up when the image of a gentle orange haired man appeared in her thoughts. He was telling her to keep the doll safe, no matter what.

"Papa gave it to me."

# Chapter 52

# A City Awakens

Odo and Sephie sat on a bench, the sidewalks around them littered with thousands of sleeping Stirpians.

"How long until they wake up?"

"When Sensus comes out of his coma."

"At least they're not killing each other. That's something."

"I hope those days are over, that Sensus will fully recover and be his old self again. Addy thinks it should only be a few more hours until he regains consciousness."

"You said your papa gave you the doll and told you to keep it safe? Did he say why?"

"That's all I can remember. I could see his face so clearly. I still don't know why the doll is special. It's not even from Fortisia."

"Maybe the doll's only purpose was to bring us here so we could heal Sensus and stop the invasions. You saved millions of lives."

Sephie gazed down at the doll.

"Maybe. I feel like there's something I'm missing though. There's some reason Papa told me to keep it safe."

"Wikerus always says we have to let events play out before we can understand their deeper meaning."

"I keep thinking about the Atroxians. I hope what happened to them doesn't happen to us. I hope we don't poison ourselves, that people aren't too greedy or too lazy to take care of our environment."

"Most people don't think about the future, they only care about what's happening right now."

"They need to start thinking about the future, Odo Whitley. If they don't, we'll wind up like the Atroxians."

"I agree. Hey, remember the Sinarians, those weird floating aliens who turned your hair black? They might have some kind of cool technology to get rid of pollution, clean up our oceans."

"You're a brainiac, Odo Whitley. Now that we know how to get to Girard Station we can get help from other worlds, maybe borrow their technology."

"How is Addy going to get home?"

"Cyra said the Atroxian interstellar ships can create gateways to other worlds. It's the same technology as the transition chambers in Girard Station. The captives step through a spectral doorway back into their world."

"What about Cyra? She can't go back to Fortisia because of that spectral moat thing."

"She's coming back with us. She decided Earth didn't

sound so bad anymore, that she was ready to live in a simpler world, one without so much technology."

"Speaking of technology, we should find one of those Cerebral Feedback Synthesizer food machines. I want a giant cinnamon roll from Madam Beffy's Diner. They heat it up and put butter on it. So good."

Sephie stood up, scanning the nearby buildings.

"You're in luck, that looks like a restaurant over there."

Odo headed toward the glass building, stepping around the sleeping Stirpians.

"Nice and peaceful."

Sephie grinned. "Just a sleepy little country village."

"Look! One of them is waking up!"

"Let's go talk to him."

Odo and Sephie darted down the sidewalk to the yawning Stirpian. He turned when he heard their footsteps.

Sephie waved to him. "Hello, there!"

The Stirpian looked puzzled. "Why is everyone sleeping?"

"Just tired I guess. A lovely day today, don't you think?"

"It is lovely. I feel strangely refreshed, but I'm confused. I don't remember falling asleep. The last thing I remember is... I don't know... I think I was angry at someone, but I don't know who or why. Maybe I was having a bad dream."

"You're feeling better? Not angry?"

"Much better. I'm not angry at all. We should probably help all these people. They're going to be just as confused as I was when they wake up. I have no idea why everyone in the city would fall asleep, unless there was some kind of gas leak or something. That's a little scary."

"I have a feeling everyone will be fine."

The Stirpian's eyes abruptly lost focus, his body rigid and unmoving.

"Are you all right?"

A new voice answered.

"You're the ones who injected me with the anesthetic, put me in a coma. I remember trying to stop you, thinking you were trying to kill me, take my children, destroy everything that I was."

"We were trying to help you, not hurt you. You were sick, your neural networks weren't functioning properly."

"I can see that now. You saved my life and the lives of my children, pulling me from a dark world of rage and confusion. I had forgotten my true self, forgotten who I really was."

"Your children have been invading other worlds for almost two centuries."

"I am aware of this. They are returning to Atroxia as we speak. I have communicated with Karolus, an old friend of mine. The quarantine dome will be coming down soon."

"You won't try to invade Fortisia again?"

"There will be no more invasions. All Atroxian weapons of war, including the interstellar ships, shall be destroyed. Atroxia will be a world at peace again."

Odo grabbed Sephie's arm. "They're waking up!"

The two friends watched as tens of thousands of sleepy Stirpians got to their feet, looking around in confusion.

"What happened? Why were we sleeping?"

"I don't know, but it's the best sleep I've ever had. I feel great."

"So do I. What a beautiful day, too nice to go to work."

"I agree. Today should be a holiday."

"Odo! Sephie!"

They turned to see Cyra, Addy, and Jarin running toward them.

"It worked! Sensus is himself again."

Addy grinned. "Everyone is being so nice."

"It won't take Addy and I long to send the captives home through spectral doorways. I'll use my IMS to plug in the coordinates for each world."

"I can't wait to see my dad."

"Addy, tell him if he hadn't bought my doll from the antique dealer none of this would ever have happened. Who would imagine that him buying a rag doll would save your life and bring an end to the Stirpian invasions?"

Odo nodded. "We should celebrate by going to lunch. There's a restaurant right over there."

"And order giant cinnamon rolls just like the ones at Madam Beffy's Diner?"

"Excellent idea. I like the way you think, Sephie Crumb."

# Chapter 53

# Home Again

A great cheer rose from the city when the quarantine dome vanished. Thousands of Stirpians stepped onto the desert sands for the first time, marveling at the snow capped mountains in the distance.

As promised, Karolus restored Jarin's memories, and after heartfelt goodbyes to the adventurers he headed back to his village.

Addy and Cyra sent the captives home through spectral gateways created by the Atroxian ships, including Puero's two missing Plindorian friends.

"Addy, you promise you'll visit us?"

"I promise. My dad has told me so much about your world. I'll formshift into a human before I arrive. He said Earth people are afraid of anyone who doesn't look exactly like them."

"Sad but true. We can meet you at Girard Station if you'd like. It's an amazing place. Say hi to your dad and thank him again for all his help. Oh, I almost forgot, these belong to him. We hid them outside the dome." Sephie pulled the time throttles, dusters, and energy shields from her pack, giving them to Addy.

"I'll make sure he gets them. He does love his technology. I'll tell him everything you did. I know he would love to see you, if you ever come back to Plindor."

Odo grinned. "Of course we'll be back. I want to go land sailing with those pirates again. That was the most fun ever. Arghh, matie!"

Addy gave everyone hugs, then stepped back, gripping her homestone. "See you soon!" There was a flash of light and she was gone.

"I wish I could be there to see Advenus' face when Addy gets home. He'll be so happy."

Cyra smiled. "I haven't had this much fun in a long time. I think I found my way out of the dark forest, thanks to you two."

"You'll love it back on Earth. You'll have to hide your powers though."

"Humans really are afraid of a lot of things."

"They are. They always think Earth is going to be invaded by scary aliens who will destroy everything and take over the planet."

"Not to be rude, but it doesn't sound like a world anyone would bother invading."

Odo snorted. "We have Proto's Taste-E Kakes and Madam Beffy's Diner."

"Odo Whitley, aliens are not going to invade Earth for giant cinnamon rolls and tasty cakes."

"You never know. We should head home, but I almost don't want to. This is such a beautiful city now that everyone is being nice to each other. And I didn't get to ride in one of those flying spheres."

"We can come back whenever we want."

"I can't wait."

The three friends stepped onto the windswept desert sands for a last look at Atroxia, gazing at the distant mountains.

"School is going to seem really boring."

"We can pass notes in science class. That will be fun."

Sephie and Cyra gripped her homestone.

"Are you ready, Odo Whitley?"

Odo raised one eyebrow. "I was born ready, Sephie Crumb."

"Really? I was born ready? You're going with that?"

Before Odo could think of a hilarious answer Sephie and Cyra were gone.

Seconds later Odo Whitley was on his way home.

\* \* \* \*

The sudden appearance of the three adventurers in the sitting room startled Wikerus Praevian and Mrs. Preke.

Wikerus jumped to his feet. "You're back! What happened? Did you find the doll? Who's your friend?"

Sephie set her pack down. "This is Cyra, she helped

us. You should probably sit down, this is going to take a while. We found the doll, but we also brought an end to the Atroxian invasions, which were actually Stirpian invasions. The Atroxians have been extinct for two thousand years.

"Extinct? Who are the Stirpians? You stopped the invasions? They won't invade Fortisia?"

Odo grinned. "Sephie, your hair just turned orange!"

"The Sinarians said it would change color when I got home."

"You met Sinarians?" Wikerus motioned for the three friends to take a seat on the couch. "Mrs. Preke and I will listen while you talk. From the beginning, tell us everything, leave out nothing."

Two hours later Wikerus was staring wide eyed at Mrs. Preke.

"This is incredible, unbelievable."

Mrs. Preke patted him on the arm. "Your plan worked, Wikerus. I knew it would."

"This wasn't my plan at all. My plan was to get the doll back and secure the spectral moat. Odo and Sephie stopped the invasions. We don't even need the spectral moat now."

Sephie looked puzzled. "How would the doll keep the spectral moat secure?"

Wikerus looked as though he was about to say something, then stopped.

Mrs. Preke raised her eyebrows. "It's time, Wikerus. You need to tell Odo and Sephie everything. Everything."

Wikerus sighed. "You have the doll?"

Sephie pulled it from her backpack, handing it to him. "Did you notice anything odd about it?"

"No, it's just an old doll."

"Maybe Odo can show us why it's special." Wikerus tossed the doll to him. When Odo caught it there was a violent crackling spark and he let out a shriek, dropping the doll.

"Ow!! What was that??"

Sephie looked at Wikerus. "It's a Fortisian home-stone. That's why I didn't feel anything."

Wikerus picked up the doll. "It's more than just a Fortisian homestone, it's the last Fortisian secure homestone allowing passage through the spectral moat. All the others have been destroyed."

He ripped open a seam in the side of the doll, removing a glowing green medallion on a thin blue chain.

"If this homestone had fallen into the hands of the Stirpians, they could have used it to send in fleets of interstellar battlecruisers. It would have been the end of our world. Sephie, this medallion belonged to your father."

"You knew my father? Why didn't you tell me?"

"I knew of him. A Stirpian attack scout ship was chasing him through dark space when he spotted Earth on his IMS, the nearest inhabited planet. He blinked down to the surface, letting his ship crash into the ocean. The Stirpians thought he was dead. Unfortunately, he had no way of contacting Fortisia, no way to call for help. He lived as a human for almost a year before meeting your mother. They fell in love and he decided to stay on Earth. You were born a year later.

"They sent me to find him and recover the last secure homestone, a one way trip for me unless I found it. I did a broad aerial scan, eventually locating his crashed ship at the bottom of the ocean. He was not in it. Six months later I picked up his energy signature in this area.

What I didn't know was the Stirpians were still searching for him. I arrived right after they did. There were three of them. I ran in, but it was too late. I had no choice, I dusted them and tried to save your parents. Your mother was already gone, your father was dying. He told me he had blinked you as far away as he could, that you had the homestone. He died in my arms. He loved you more than you can ever imagine. I promised him I would take care of you when I found you."

Sephie was crying, her hands over her face.

Wikerus waited until she was done, then continued.

"With the death of your parents, the most important task was finding you and the last homestone. It took us six months to locate you, but we had no idea where the homestone was. Your father hadn't said anything about the doll.

"It was sometime after that when my inner voice spoke, telling me a translucent boy named Odo would be the key to finding the homestone, that he and you would save Fortisia."

"How could you know I was going to be born translucent? That only happened because my mom used the perfume."

Wikerus hesitated.

Mrs. Preke pursed her lips. "We have to tell him, Wikerus. You know we have to."

"I have dreaded this moment for such a long time. Odo, I was the one who sent the perfume to your mother. I knew she was pregnant with a boy, I knew the boy's name would be Odo. The perfume had engineered nanobots in it. They altered your genome and made you translucent."

Mrs. Preke's voice was barely audible. "I helped him, Odo. I put the perfume in the mailbox. I know you can never forgive us for what we did, but please understand we did it to save our world, to save Fortisia. It was the most difficult choice I have ever made, and not a day goes by that I don't feel a terrible guilt. I almost cried when I saw you waiting in line for the interview, seeing what we had done. I was the one who ran the newspaper ad, knowing you would see it."

Odo's face was carved from stone. "You gave my mom the perfume, knowing it would make me translucent?"

Mrs. Preke nodded.

Odo stood up and walked out of the room. The front door slammed shut, shaking the house.

Sephie's eyes were on Wikerus.

The only sound was the ticking of the clock on the wall.

# Chapter 54

# Mrs. Preke's Surprise

"Odo, your orange haired friend stopped by this morning. She said she needs to see you. It's almost noon, you should get up."

Odo groaned, rolling over in his bed. "Her name is Sephie, I told you that already. She wants to see me? That's a good one. Get it, she wants to *see* me?"

Petunia sat down on the bed, rubbing Odo's shoulder.

"It was my fault, you know. Your father was right about that, I didn't look up translucent in the dictionary."

"You didn't know, it wasn't your fault."

"I didn't read much when I was growing up. I was more interested in friends and boys and going to movies and dances. I wish I'd read more, gone to college. I would have known what translucent meant."

"You wanted to go to college?"

"I was thinking about it when I met your father. He was so handsome and had so many plans for the future. We married right after high school. He started college and I got a job to support us. It wasn't enough money and he quit in the middle of his second year, taking a job at Silver CrunchCakes. It was supposed to be temporary, but one thing led to another and it turned into a career. It wasn't what he wanted, but it paid the bills. It bothers him that he never finished college. That's why he acts like he knows everything."

"What did he want to do?"

"Start his own business, a hobby shop. You know how much he loves those model trains."

"I didn't know he wanted to start his own business."

"He never talks about it. It makes him feel bad, like he missed out on life."

"Is he embarrassed that I'm translucent?"

"Not embarrassed, but he was hoping... I don't know... hoping you would get to do all the things he never did. He loves you, but he doesn't know how to talk to you about things. His dad never talked to him."

"I'm saving up for college. There's no way I'm not going."

"You should tell him, Odo. He might not say it, but I know he would be proud of you."

"I need to talk to Sephie."

"She seems like a nice girl. Don't get married too early. Wait until after college."

"We're just friends, that's all. She works at Serendipity Salvage."

"I know, but friends can turn into something else in the blink of an eye."

"It's not like that."

"You're growing up, Odo. I'm glad you have a nice friend like Sephie. She's really sweet."

An hour later Odo and Sephie were sitting on the roof outside her window.

"Are you going to quit your job at Serendipity Salvage?"

"I don't know. I can't believe Wikerus and Mrs. Preke did that."

"They feel dreadful about it. I talked to them after you left."

"I don't care how they feel, they ruined my life."

"Odo Whitley, your life isn't ruined, it's hardly even started. And think about it, you've done things no other person on Earth has done. You traveled to other worlds, other dimensions, saved millions of lives, saved my home planet."

"I guess you're sort of right. None of that would have happened if I wasn't translucent."

"*Ex cineribus resurgam.*"

"What does that mean?"

"*Out of the ashes I shall rise.*"

"Oh. I like that. I wouldn't have met you if I wasn't translucent."

"Life is funny that way, Odo Whitley."

"Do you feel better now that you know about your parents, and how you wound up in the snow drift with the doll?"

"I'm sad that I never got to know them, and I love them for saving my life. But, yes, I am glad to know what happened. I'm glad to know they loved me, that they wanted me. It's not a big dark mystery anymore, and I know where my powers came from."

"It sounds like you're out of your dark forest."

"I think I am, Odo Whitley."

"Let's go see Wikerus and Mrs. Preke. I want to talk to them."

"What are you going to say?"

"That it doesn't matter why I'm translucent. It's what I am, for better or worse. I'm not quitting Serendipity Salvage. All the money I make will pay for my college. Plus I have the gold coins I found in the tunnels."

"I'm not quitting either."

Odo and Sephie climbed down the drain pipe and headed toward Asper Street, turning left on Expergo.

Wikerus answered the door after the second knock.

"Good, you're here. Just in time."

"I wanted to tell you–"

"Follow me, Cyra is already here."

Wikerus strode down the hallway, stepping into the sitting room.

Odo yelped when he saw the bulbous headed glowing white Sinarian floating six inches above the sitting room floor.

Cyra was on the couch, a big grin on her face. "What's the matter, Odo, never seen a Sinarian before?"

Odo couldn't take his eyes off the glowing creature. "Why is he here?"

He heard a quiet voice in his head. "We have a gift for you and Sephie."

"Did anyone else hear that?"

"We all did. It's how Sinarians talk. They send out thought clouds."

Odo had no idea what thought clouds were. He turned to the Sinarian, uncertain where to look since he didn't have eyes.

"You may look at my head, if it makes you feel more comfortable."

"You have a gift for us? Why?"

The Sinarian wiggled the end of his long white arm. A small black metallic case appeared, floating in front of Odo.

"Whoa, you can make things float."

"Open it after I am gone. One is for you, one is for Sephie, one is for the oceans of your world. Sinaria thanks you for all you have done. By your kindness to Sensus you have restored a grand balance, your actions affecting many thousands of worlds. Selfless deeds such as this ripple across space and time for eternity. When you are ready, I shall return. There is much to learn, much to do."

The Sinarian was there, and then he was not.

"Whoa."

"Quit gawking and open our present, Odo Whitley."

Odo grabbed the black case and set it on his lap. "I wasn't gawking. What do you think it is?"

"How would I know that, Odo Whitley?" She scooted over next to him, her eyes on the box.

"That was more of a rhetorical question. You know, just sort of wondering out loud what–"

Sephie grabbed the box and flipped it open.

Odo studied the contents. "They gave us rings? And a little vial of blue stuff?"

"He said one was for me, one for you, and one for the oceans."

Odo took one of the rings and slipped it on his finger.

"I don't get it. Why would they give me a ring?"

"Maybe that one is for me."

Sephie took the ring from Odo.

"Ready?"

"Of course I'm ready. Why do you always ask if–"

Sephie slid the ring on and vanished.

Odo jumped back. "Where did she go?"

"I'm right here, Odo. Focus. I'm translucent, just like you."

"You're right, I can see you if I look carefully. Is that how I look to you?"

"All you have to do is really look at me, want to see me. Try your ring on."

"Suppose it turns me into some kind of weird creature?"

"Ring. On."

Odo slipped on the ring.

"I'm solid! This is amazing! I can see my hands... my legs... all of me."

Cyra grinned. "You're handsome, Odo."

"Really?"

Sephie nodded. "All the girls will say how cute you are."

"I'm not sure how I feel about that. I've been translucent for so long, I don't exactly know how to be solid. Everyone will look at me and talk to me, ask me questions and want to know–"

"He said the third gift is for our oceans."

"What does that mean?"

Wikerus picked up the small vial and studied it, holding it up to the light.

"Nanobots. Were you two talking about our oceans?"

"We were saying we hope what happened to Atroxia doesn't happen to Earth, that we wouldn't poison ourselves with all the pollution. That we should clean up our oceans."

"That's it then. Pour these nanobots into the ocean."

"What good would that do? It's just a little vial."

"Nanobots are self replicating. If I were to guess, I'd say they have been engineered to destroy pollutants like oil and plastic and the myriad of other toxic chemicals companies pump into the ocean to save a few dollars."

"Sephie, you and I have a date with the ocean."

Wikerus gave a hesitant smile. "Will you keep working for Serendipity Salvage?"

"Yes, Sephie and I both will."

"Do you think you will ever be able to forgive me and Mrs. Preke?"

"It will take time, but I'm getting there."

"I should tell you that a visit from a Sinarian is almost unheard of. This is the first time I've ever seen one close up. They are extraordinary beings. You have no idea."

Cyra laughed. "And they are also excellent hair stylists. Sephie looked amazing with her black hair."

Odo nodded. "She did look kind of cool."

"I didn't feel any different. It was just me with black hair instead of orange hair."

Cyra stood up, turning to Sephie and Odo. "The Sinarian wants me to use the last homestone to go back to Fortisia, tell them about Sensus and the Stirpians, that they can shut down the spectral moat and join the universe again. He wants me to train for a few more years, work on my powers. The universe needs all the help it can get."

"Will you come back? Will you visit us? You're like my sister now."

"Of course I will, you're my family. Who knows, maybe we'll go on another adventure and save a few worlds."

Sephie turned when she heard a knock on the front door.

"That will be Mrs. Preke. We have a little surprise for you."

"What kind of surprise?"

Wikerus grinned. "If I told you, it wouldn't be a surprise."

Odo ran to the front door and flung it open.

"Hi, Mrs. Preke. You just missed the Sinarian. He gave Sephie and I rings that make her translucent and me solid."

"Yes, I know, Wikerus sent me a thought cloud."

"He can send you thoughts?"

"Of course, he's a Fortisian."

"He said you have a surprise?"

"Just a little one."

Odo followed Mrs. Preke into the sitting room.

"If everyone would please take a seat, Wikerus and I have something to show you. Wikerus, would you care to join me?"

"Of course, Mrs. Preke, I would be happy to."

The friends glanced at each other, eyebrows raised.

"Are you ready, Mrs. Preke?"

"I was born ready, Wikerus."

Sephie burst out laughing. "She stole your line, Odo!"

Before Odo could say anything, Wikerus and Mrs. Preke rippled with a wavering blue light. They were gone for less than a second, then back again.

Mrs. Preke was an enormous yellow octopus. Wikerus Praevian was a handsome orange haired Fortisian.

"No way!!" Odo burst out laughing. "Mrs. Preke is a Plindorian??"

"And Wikerus isn't an old grandpa."

Wikerus smiled. "We all wear masks of one kind or another. Mrs. Preke and I wanted to show you who we truly are."

Sephie jumped up and gave Mrs. Preke a big hug,

whispering, "I know why you chose your name. It's what they used to call octopuses back in the middle ages."

"You are a clever girl, Sephie Crumb."

Odo grinned at Wikerus. "You're not so scary and mysterious this way."

"Precisely why I changed my appearance. It's a sad truth that most people judge you by how you look. They don't see who you really are inside."

Odo nodded, looking down at his ring.

# Chapter 55

# The Plan

They hatched their nefarious plan while sitting on the roof outside Sephie's window, laughing until their sides ached. Sephie would dye her hair black and they would buy stylish new clothes. Odo would wear his Sinarian ring, pretending to be Sephie's secret boyfriend, a handsome and very solid young man.

When they walked down the hall hand in hand, heads would turn. For once they would be the kids everyone was looking at, the kids everyone wanted to be. Odo would be handsome, Sephie would be beautiful.

On the appointed day, Odo rode the bus to school, anxiously turning the ring over and over in his pocket. He waited until everyone had gotten off the bus, then headed for the main entrance. A beautiful black haired Sephie Crumb would be waiting for him inside.

When he swung open the front door he spotted her

leaning against the wall.

"You didn't dye your hair, it's still orange."

"You didn't wear your ring, you're still translucent."

"I changed my mind. People still wouldn't see me, they'd just see my physical body, say I was handsome. The real me would still be translucent."

"That's why I didn't dye my hair and get new clothes. I like being Sephie Crumb. I have orange hair, weird powers, and I don't know the first thing about stylish clothes. That's who I am. Be true to yourself."

"You're also the most amazing person I know."

"We both are. We're superheroes."

"Translucent Boy and Encephalo Girl."

"I'll see you in science class, Odo Whitley. Check your coat pocket."

Sephie turned, heading down the hallway.

Odo reached into his pocket, pulling out a folded note, grinning when he read it.

*It's not your hair, it's what's under it.*

If you enjoyed reading

*The Translucent Boy and
the Girl Who Saw Him*

please leave a short review or rating
on Amazon.com
Reviews are the lifeblood of indie publishers –
we can't survive without them!

If you have any comments or suggestions
or would like to be notified of upcoming book
releases and Free Kindle book day promotions,
please email me at
*OrvilleMouse@gmail.com*

Follow me at:
www.facebook.com/TomHoffmanAuthor/

*Best wishes until we meet again,*

*Tom Hoffman*

## ABOUT THE AUTHOR

Tom Hoffman received a B.S. in psychology
from Georgetown University in 1972
and a B.A. in 1980 from the now-defunct
Oregon College of Art. He has lived in Alaska
with his wife since 1973. They have two
adult children and two adorable
grandchildren. Tom was a graphic designer
and artist for over 35 years.
Redirecting his imagination from art to
writing, he wrote his first novel,
*The Eleventh Ring*, at age 63.

6/22- 1